Alex Kava is the author of the Maggie O'Dell series. A former PR director, Alex dedicated herself to writing full-time in 1996. She lives in Nebraska, USA. Find out more at: www.alexkava.com.

Also by Alex Kava

Ryder Creed series

Breaking Creed

Maggie O'Dell series

A Perfect Evil

Split Second

The Soul Catcher

At the Stroke of Madness

A Necessary Evil

Exposed

Black Friday

Damaged

Hotwire

Fireproof

Stranded

Other fiction

Whitewash

One False Move

Ebook only with Erica Spindler and J.T. Ellison

Storm Season

Slices of Night

Alex

KAVA

Silent Creed

sphere

SPHERE

First published in the United States in 2015 by G.P. Putnam's Sons,
a division of Penguin Random House
First published in Great Britain in 2015 by Sphere
This paperback edition published in 2016 by Sphere

1 3 5 7 9 10 8 6 4 2

All characters and events in this publication, other than those clearly in the public domain, are fictitious and any resemblance to real persons, living or dead, is purely coincidental.

A CIP catalogue record for this book
is available from the British Library.

ISBN 978-0-7515-5583-7

Printed and bound in Great Britain by
Clays Ltd, St Ives plc

Papers used by Sphere are from well-managed forests
and other responsible sources.

MIX
Paper from
responsible sources
FSC® C104740

Sphere
An imprint of
Little, Brown Book Group
Carmelite House
50 Victoria Embankment
London EC4Y 0DZ

An Hachette UK Company
www.hachette.co.uk

www.littlebrown.co.uk

To Deb Carlin and the rest of the pack:
Duncan, Boomer, and Maggie.
You all are my heart and soul.

AND AGAIN TO SCOUT,
THIS WHOLE SERIES IS FOR YOU, BUDDY.

1.

HAYWOOD COUNTY, NORTH CAROLINA

Daniel Tate clenched his teeth and looked away just as the needle pierced a vein in his arm. He'd spent two tours of duty in Iraq and one in Afghanistan. He'd been shot at, dodged IEDs, and escaped a grenade. But needles – damn, he hated needles.

'This will help relax you,' Dr Shaw told him.

When she walked in the door, Tate had been relieved to see a woman. But she had barely introduced herself before she pulled out a stainless steel tray with vials and surgical utensils and, of course, several syringes. Her black hair was pulled back tight, leaving only long bangs that overlapped heavy-framed glasses. She was younger than he expected, with smooth skin that hadn't yet earned wrinkles at the corners of her mouth or eyes. And she was attractive, but instead of looking at her now, Tate let his eyes scan the room. He didn't want to even see the needle, so he stared at the walls.

It was a strange room, empty except for the examination table. The drywall looked spongy, like the foam mats you'd find at the basketball court tacked up under the basket for overenthusiastic athletes to bounce off. Only these mats weren't tacked onto the walls, they *were* the walls – whitewashed and seamless. The term 'padded cell' came to mind.

There wasn't a single thing displayed. Didn't medical exam rooms have diplomas or something on the walls? Not that it mattered. Tate's chance to back out had passed. He knew it as soon as he signed on page seven of that long-ass contract they'd handed him when he first arrived.

He didn't even know where this place was. It had been pouring sheets of rain the entire hour and a half from the airport. That was yesterday, or at least he thought it was. His wristwatch and cell phone were two of the personal items he'd had to surrender. Other than not knowing the time of day, he didn't mind. But

Tate didn't understand why he couldn't wear his own shoes or underwear. The blue scrubs were comfortable, but the paper booties drove him crazy. He felt like he was shuffling, the sound reminding him of the old people in the nursing home where his wife worked.

'After I administer the drug, I'll ask you a series of questions,' Dr Shaw said.

He glanced at her and held back a grimace. She was loading another syringe. Long, slender fingers with bloodred nail polish. A ring on her thumb – that was strange, but young women did that, right? The ring had tiny diamonds dancing around the band. All Tate could think was that this served him right for not reading all seven pages. He'd only cared about the three thousand dollars he had been promised, and he had double-checked that it was in the contract.

He hated that his wife worked an extra shift once a week just to make ends meet. Their oldest daughter had started waiting tables at the coffee shop. Even Danny Junior had a paper route. But Tate hadn't been able to get a job.

Not true. He hadn't been able to *hold* a job since he'd been back.

The doctors called it post-traumatic stress disorder.

But all Tate saw when he looked in the mirror was a perfectly healthy man. Never mind that his brain twisted pieces of information and insomnia kept him pacing the streets of their small town. He needed to start contributing and helping to take care of his family. Even if it meant a few needle pokes.

This time it didn't matter where he looked. As soon as the metal slipped into his vein, he felt the liquid rush into his body. A heat wave crawled up his arm, over his shoulder, and spread throughout his chest. It took his breath away, and he felt his body shudder.

'You may experience a tightness in your chest,' he heard Dr Shaw say. Only now it sounded like she was talking to him from the next room.

He turned his head to look at her, and just that movement made him nauseated. He tried to find her eyes through the blur. The small rose tattoo he had noticed earlier on the side of her neck had grown legs and started to inch along her skin like an insect. Tate blinked hard, trying to focus. Sweat beaded on his forehead and upper lip.

'Nosebleeds are not uncommon,' Dr Shaw continued in her calm, cool manner. 'I'm going to ask you some questions, Daniel.'

Tate, he wanted to tell her everyone called him Tate, but he couldn't take his mind off the bug digging into her neck. His heart galloped in his chest, and it was difficult to breathe.

'Daniel, can you count backward from a hundred for me?'

His mouth had a metallic taste and it took effort to make it move. Teeth and tongue seemed to be in the way of him activating his voice.

'Daniel, can you count backward from a hundred?' she repeated.

Suddenly he heard himself say, 'That would be difficult to do because I don't like rice.'

Even as he said it, he knew it wasn't the correct answer, but already he'd forgotten the question. Nothing mattered except the black insect on her neck. Why couldn't she feel it digging under her skin?

'Dr Shaw.' A voice called from the doorway.

Tate's entire body jerked before he saw the man. His head was shaved and gleamed almost as bright as his long white coat. Tate had to look away. The brightness hurt his eyes. Just as they were starting to focus, the light sent stars and sparks like electrical surges, and he knew he couldn't trust them.

'I'm in the middle of a test,' Dr Shaw told the man.

'It's gotten worse.'

'Can you please wait a few minutes, Richard? I've just started.'

'For God's sake, you didn't give him the serum, did you? It takes seventy-two hours to leave the system. And we need to leave now.'

'Calm down, please.'

Tate couldn't decide if she was talking to him or to the man, because she was staring directly at him.

'They're talking about landslides. We really must evacuate.'

'I've lived through hurricanes, Richard. This is just rain.'

But now she left Tate and joined the man at the door. They didn't bother to keep their voices down. In fact, they seemed to forget about Tate. They didn't even notice that he was panting now and wiping erratically at his eyes, sweat pouring down his face.

'The water is almost over the bridge.' Richard sounded panicked. He was loud and gesturing. 'If we don't leave now, we risk being stranded here.'

Dr Shaw was turned away from Tate and he could

no longer see the insect on her neck. He began checking his own hands and arms.

'We can't just leave behind all of our research material. We're safe here,' Dr Shaw was telling Richard. 'This place is built like a fortress.'

Tate tried to see if there were any bugs on the man. His eyes were finally settling down when he saw a flash of green-and-black fur behind the doctors. It looked like a small monkey running up the hallway.

'Well, I'm leaving. With or without you.'

'That would be a mistake. Let's talk about this.' She glanced over her shoulder, and when she called out to Tate, it sounded like a bellow echoing across the small room. 'I'll be right back, Daniel. Stay right here.'

She joined the man in the hallway and tried to close the door. When it didn't seem to fit the frame, she opened it wide.

'See, that's not a good sign,' Richard told her. 'Doors and windows tend to stick right before. It's bad, I'm telling you. We must leave.'

This time she pulled the door with such force it slammed.

Tate sat listening to the *thump-thump* of his heart. It was beating inside his head, and he put his hands over his chest to make sure his heart hadn't moved. He wasn't sure how much time had passed since the doctors had left. It could have been minutes. It could have been an hour. Then a loud crack jolted him off the table.

It sounded like an artillery shell. Was that possible?

He crawled under the examination table, his body scrambling in twitches and jerks. He listened for more artillery shells. The room started to sway and tilt. Was it the drug? Had it screwed with his equilibrium? His ears popped, and instead of the thumping of his heart, he now heard only a rumble.

He felt it, too. A vibration rattled the doctor's instruments, shaking them off the tray. The floor tiles lifted and rolled beneath him, and Tate grabbed on to the examination table.

That's when he saw the whitewashed walls crack and buckle. They were actually caving in, as if a bulldozer was on the other side shoving them in. Tate felt something coming down from the ceiling. He ducked his head back under the table. He watched, not sure whether to believe his eyes. It was raining dirt and gravel. He could smell the wet earth.

The rumble grew to a roar. Forget the bulldozer,

a freight train was headed down on top of him. He covered his head with his arms and curled into a tight ball.

More crashes. Metal shrieked. Light fixtures exploded.

In the darkness Daniel Tate couldn't see. The floor became a roller coaster. He clawed to hold on to the steel table as the world shattered and roared and collapsed on top of him.

2

FLORIDA PANHANDLE

Ryder Creed had been up for two hours by the time his hired man climbed out of the double-wide trailer. Truth was, Creed didn't sleep much. He'd awakened in the dark and found himself down in the kennel curled up in the middle of his dogs, his head on the belly of his oldest, Rufus.

The kennel was a contemporary warehouse. Creed had a loft apartment above it with all the luxuries and comforts of a retreat. When he designed the place he convinced his business partner, Hannah Washington, that he wanted his living quarters above the kennel so he could keep an eye and ear on the most prized possessions of their business, K9 CrimeScents.

Actually, Creed just liked being near the dogs. Sometimes in the dead of night, when visions and images haunted his sleep, he found comfort being surrounded by them. He and Hannah had rescued each and every dog in one fashion or another. But Creed knew they rescued him in a way he could not explain to anyone. Not even Hannah.

Now he watched Jason Seaver wiping the sleep out of his eyes. As he made his way into the kennel, Creed realized how much Jason looked like a young boy. Almost ten years younger than Creed, Jason had seen his world blow up on him before he reached the age of twenty. The kid was one of Hannah's rescues. She said Jason reminded her of Creed and that was one of the reasons she hired the young man.

Tucked under Jason's arm was his sleepy-eyed black puppy. In less than a month the Labrador pup Jason had named Scout had almost doubled in size. He brought Scout to play with the dog's mom and siblings while he worked. This morning he put the puppy down on the ground before he got to the yard.

'Watch this,' he told Creed as he walked three paces

back, then knelt on the ground facing the pup. 'Come on, Scout. Come give me a kiss.'

The puppy wiggled his entire back end, almost losing his balance in his excitement. He bounced toward Jason and without hesitation stood up on his hind legs, reaching for Jason's face and planting a big slobber right on the lips.

'That'll come in handy when he's searching for cadavers,' Creed said, but he couldn't help smiling.

'I'm thinking chick magnet.'

Jason picked up Scout, and when he came inside the yard the other dogs ran to greet him. They shoved and nudged each other out of the way for Jason's attention. None of them noticed or cared that one of the kid's shirtsleeves hung empty below the elbow. When Creed had first met the young veteran he had been belligerent and moody, self-conscious about the amputated arm to the point of daring anyone and everyone to notice it. That the kid was thinking about picking up women – even with the lousy trick of using his puppy – had to be a good sign.

Now if only Creed could make a decent dog handler out of him.

'We're ready to use the real stuff today,' he told

Jason, and held up a Mason jar with the lid tight over the contents.

'What's inside?'

'Some dirt and a piece of a blanket. Both were underneath a dead body.'

'Cool. How'd you get it?'

'Grace and I helped find the guy. Wasn't a homicide, so the detectives let me have a few things for training.'

'Andy claims you have a whole stockpile.'

Andy was one of the first handlers Creed had trained. At the time she'd known more about dogs than Creed, having spent years as a veterinary technician. This was a second career for her. He knew better than to ask a woman's age but guessed Andy was somewhere in her forties.

'Yeah? Well, don't believe everything Andy tells you. Here, take this.' And he tossed the Mason jar, realizing too late that maybe Jason couldn't do a one-handed catch. But the kid had no problem.

'Take it and hide it good.' Creed pointed to the trail that led into the forest. 'Just before you hide it, remove the lid. There's a cheesecloth stretched across the top. Leave that on.'

'You want me to bury it?'

'Bury it, throw it up in a tree, drop it in the creek, do whatever you want with it. Don't think about it too much. When you finish, come on back.'

The fifty-acre property was surrounded on three sides by forest. The privacy and seclusion it afforded them was one of the reasons Creed chose this place in the northern part of the Florida Panhandle. It also provided endless training ground.

His cell phone started to vibrate as he watched Jason disappear into the woods. He glanced at the screen to see it was Hannah. Less than an hour ago they'd had coffee and Hannah's fresh-baked cinnamon rolls in her kitchen.

'Already miss me?'

'I ought to feed you sugar more often in the morning, you gonna be this sweet.' Then without missing a beat she went on to business. 'Landslide in North Carolina. Some man from the DoD. We got a request for you specifically.'

'Me or Grace?'

Over the summer there had been a lot of media attention, most of it centered on Grace, their amazing Jack Russell terrier. The scrappy little dog had won the hearts of the nation when she helped make several drug busts and stopped one human trafficking incident, resulting in the rescue of five children.

'Actually, you. No specific dog.'

'When did the slide happen? Are we talking rescue or recovery?'

'Late last night into this morning. It's still raining, and from what I understand, there's still potential for more slides. Possible rescues. Definitely recovery.'

'I'll need to leave right away. What is that? A five-hour drive? Can you come finish with Jason?'

'Already putting on my dungarees.'

That made Creed smile. Hannah was the only person he knew who referred to blue jeans as dungarees. She'd hate it if he called her a Southern belle, though her mannerisms sometimes fit. She would say she was corn bread and black-eyed peas and certainly not a lady who lunched.

'But no need to drive,' she continued. 'They're sending a jet. A Gulfstream 550.'

'They're sending what?'

'I know I got it right. I wrote it down. Gulfstream 550. That's one of the pretty ones, isn't it?'

'Wait a minute. I thought you said the request was from the Department of Defense.'

'That's right.'

'What interest do they have in a landslide in North Carolina?' Creed didn't like the sound of this.

'That is not on my list of questions. Maybe they had some training personnel in the area. The gentleman said he knew you. That you two had worked together years ago.'

'I don't know anybody at the DoD. And I haven't worked with a military dog in a long time.'

Creed could hear her flipping pages. She kept impeccable records and always got more information than she actually needed before she confirmed an assignment.

'Here it is,' she finally said. 'Logan. Lieutenant Colonel Peter Logan.'

Afghanistan. Creed felt like acid had slid into his stomach.

Over seven years ago, and yet just the mention of Peter Logan brought back images and memories he had hoped were long buried.

3

PENSACOLA, FLORIDA

Emotion runs down the leash.

It was one of the first things Creed taught dog handlers and something he reminded himself of constantly. As a handler, whatever you were feeling, you needed to tamp it down. Keep it under wraps as much as possible because a dog could sense it immediately.

As Creed walked down the aisle of the Gulfstream, he glanced back to see Bolo practically tiptoeing behind him at the end of his leash. It was exactly the way Creed felt – uneasy in the luxurious interior, like he didn't belong there. And the dog was copying him.

He patted the big dog's head, then ran his hand the

length of his back, over the thin streak of coarse hair that stood up and grew in the reverse direction. The line was a defining characteristic of the Rhodesian ridgeback, and for some reason when Creed petted him there, the dog tended to calm down.

'Hello.' A woman greeted them from the back of the plane, looking up but not interrupting her tasks.

Glasses tinkled. He smelled fresh-brewed coffee. She wore a navy blazer, matching skirt, and black heels. Probably the flight attendant.

'Are you traveling with Mr Creed?'

'I am Mr Creed.'

That stopped her.

He watched her take a step back to get a better look at him. He expected to get right to work as soon as they landed, so he'd worn his usual uniform: blue jeans, hiking boots, a T-shirt, and a long-sleeved oxford left unbuttoned with the tails untucked. His tousled hair crept over the back of his collar and he kept his face unshaved but trimmed with fine lines that made it look groomed instead of like he had just gotten up. But he figured appearance wasn't the only thing that stopped her.

'I'm sorry, it's just that I expected—'

'Someone older?'

Her face flushed the answer before she admitted it. 'Yes, I suppose so.'

And in that moment he could tell she was younger than he initially had thought. In fact, she was much closer to his age, somewhere between twenty-eight and thirty. Maybe she expected her uniform to give her gravitas. So many people did. He worked with a lot of uniforms – official as well as unofficial – and titles. Law enforcement and government loved titles and badges and knowing whose title or badge won jurisdiction. Creed wasn't interested in their pissing contests, and he simply didn't care what others thought of him.

But now, realizing he was her official passenger, not just some casually dressed lackey, she left the galley and the flight preparations to greet him properly.

'I'm Isabel Klein, Mr Logan's assistant.' She held out her hand.

After a firm, brisk handshake she offered her open palm to Bolo to sniff. And because of that small gesture, Creed decided to cut her some slack for her initial mistake. He took a second look at the woman.

She noticed. Caught his eye, and he swore there was

a hint of a blush, but it didn't stay long. She reached out and took the duffel bag from his hand and swung it up into the luggage compartment with little effort. He wouldn't allow her to take anything else and started pulling straps from his shoulder, then shrugging out of the backpack.

'Sit wherever you're comfortable,' she said as she looked around behind him. 'What's his name?'

'Bolo.'

She smiled. 'Like the acronym BOLO?'

'Yep.'

That was exactly where the name had come from – Be On the Look Out. It suited him perfectly. The dog pitched his ears in response to his name and Creed motioned for him to sit while he swung the rest of their equipment up into the overhead bins. He was overly protective of Creed. So much so that Creed had to be careful how and where he used the dog.

Bolo was muscular with great stamina and would be able to handle the long hours as well as the brutal terrain of a landslide. He was one of Creed's multitask dogs and could search for live victims as well as find those not so fortunate.

Ridgebacks originated in Zimbabwe, where they

were used in packs to hunt lions. That's where their nickname 'the African Lion Hound' came from. They could withstand the long heat of the day and the damp, cold nights. Bolo would do well for this assignment, if only Creed could keep the big dog from flattening anyone who might raise a voice to him.

Isabel glanced behind him, looking to the entrance. 'Is someone bringing the other dogs?'

'No other dogs. It's just Bolo and me.'

'Just one dog?'

'One handler, one dog.'

'Mr Logan made it sound like there would be several.'

That was the other thing – people were always looking for there to be more. More dogs, more magic.

Creed pulled his electronic tablet and a paperback from his messenger bag and placed all three items on the seat beside the one he planned to sit in. He directed Bolo to sit next to the leather captain's chair so the dog would be tucked against his legs, at his feet. He wanted him as close as possible for takeoff.

He removed a harness from the bag and slipped it on the dog. It provided a handle instead of just the leash in case the dog got nervous in flight. Bolo hadn't flown before. One of his other dogs, Grace, had her first flight aboard a Coast Guard helicopter a month ago. She'd loved it. Grace would be bored with this luxury ride. Creed directed the air vent to flow across Bolo's back and the dog lay down.

Isabel, however, was still standing beside Creed as though waiting for someone or something more. He stopped himself from taking his seat and turned to look at her.

'Can I get the two of you something? Wine? Scotch? The jet has a well-stocked bar.'

'Couple of bottles of water would be great.'

'Oh, certainly. Of course.'

And finally she turned on her heels and left for the back galley, obviously trained to be accommodating, which probably suited Logan just fine.

He looked around the wood-paneled interior as he sank into the soft leather. All of this seemed a bit extravagant for someone who was a platoon leader in Afghanistan. Logan was probably trying to impress him, but Creed couldn't stop wondering how much this pickup was costing taxpayers.

Hannah had said that Logan was now a lieutenant colonel, but because it made no difference to Creed he hadn't asked what Logan's title was or who in the government he was trying to lead now. He imagined Hannah had included it in the briefing material she'd stuffed in his messenger bag. That's where it would stay. Creed found it was best for him to know only the bare essentials.

If a handler got caught up in details, he could find himself misleading his dog and looking for signals or targets that weren't important. Too many times handlers drove their dogs to find what law enforcement, or the officials who had ordered the search, expected to find. In this case, Creed didn't even want to know how many people were missing. He didn't want his mind focused on statistical rates of survival or calculating how many hours victims could stay alive buried beneath mud and debris.

Facts were fine, but Creed liked to leave room for those few cases that dispelled all rhyme or reason. Maybe it wasn't practical – perhaps some would argue, silly – but he'd never have gotten through the last seven years in this business if he hadn't believed in miracles.

Still, when Isabel brought the water to him, he decided to ask.

'What exactly is Logan's job these days at the DoD?' He tried to make it sound casual, as if they were acquaintances who'd simply lost touch with each other.

She raised her eyebrows, surprised at the question, but without hesitation said, 'He's a deputy director of the Defense Advanced Research Projects Agency.'

He nodded, thanked her as he took the bottles of water, again pretending it was no big deal, and waited for her to go back to her flight duties. At the same time, his mind was trying to grasp what in the world a deputy director of DARPA had to do with a landslide in North Carolina.

Ten minutes after takeoff Isabel was back. Without waiting for an invitation or permission, she sat in the captain's chair across from Creed, careful not to disturb Bolo, who stayed at Creed's feet.

'I was told to answer any of your questions or concerns once we were in the air.'

'So I couldn't back out if I heard something I didn't like?'

She smiled, adjusted herself into the seat, and crossed her legs. She wasn't leaving, even if he had no questions for her.

'I'm not sure how much area is affected,' she said, deciding to give him what information she had prepared whether he wanted it or not. 'The major slide happened around ten-thirty last night. From what I understand, there's been at least two more, smaller debris flows. Are you familiar with landslides?'

'A bit.'

She waited for more. He figured, they hired him, they had to know his résumé. If Isabel didn't know, then she hadn't done her homework.

When he didn't offer anything else, she continued, 'The region that we're concerned about is a research facility on five acres. So we have a much smaller search area. The main structure was a two-story brick building.'

'Where was it in the slide? At the top or bottom?'

'They're telling me it's close to the middle.'

'How many people?'

'I'm not sure. It was after business hours. We're still trying to contact the director. We fear that she and some of the staff may have been inside.'

'Has anyone seen what condition the building is in?'

Her eyes left his, trailed down to Bolo, and glanced out the window before they came back.

'A colleague at the scene said he couldn't find it,' she told him.

'He couldn't reach it?'

'No, he couldn't find it. It's gone, buried under the mud and debris.'

4

WASHINGTON, DC

Senator Ellie Delanor followed her aide as the two of them pushed their way through the protesters and up the steps of the Capitol. Of all things, she found herself thinking the next time she hired an aide she needed to seriously consider brawn over brains. Amelia Gonzalez was brilliant and efficient, but at five feet and maybe a hundred pounds, the woman became little more than a distraction and not even close to the defensive force Ellie needed to lead her through this mass of bodies.

At least today's protesters didn't shove back, but they didn't step aside, either. Ellie watched Gonzalez squeeze her tiny frame in between people without creating a hint of a seam for Ellie to follow in. There was no respect in this city, and less if she was recognized as a senator.

But in fact, she noticed these protesters were downright polite compared to what Ellie was used to. She saw that many of them wore patriotic gear and waved miniature flags. They were older than the typical political demonstrators or activists, and as she glanced around at faces, making eye contact with several and giving them a nod as if in agreement, it struck her how they looked like her constituents back home in Florida. Move them to a conference room at a local Holiday Inn and they could easily pass for members of her re-election campaign.

These were her people – veterans in T-shirts and ball caps, mothers and grandmothers, business owners and civic group leaders. They weren't on the steps of the Capitol to block her entrance. Instead, they were there to remind her of her duties.

It should have been reassuring. It should have invigorated her for the congressional hearings that were slated to start tomorrow. She had fought to be included in them. But it hadn't been these people or even thoughts of defending them or speaking up for them that had motivated her to be on this committee. It had been all about acquiring political clout and arming herself with positive sound bites to win a re-election campaign that had quickly tightened and become messy.

There was a time when her Colombian-born husband – no, ex-husband. She needed to remember that. She couldn't chance mixing that up again. There was a time when George Ramos, with his Hollywood good looks and his charms, had been a guaranteed vote-cincher. But now . . .

Thirteen years of marriage. How could she not have known that he was running drugs? Not just running them! For God's sake, he was the head of a Colombian cartel's southeastern territory in the United States. His upcoming trial could derail her entire career if she wasn't able to change the narrative somehow.

She had done everything she could to publicly show that not only had she done the hard and painful thing of seeing to it that her husband – *damn it, ex-husband!* She had seen to it that her ex-husband – and the father of her two children – had been indicted. There would be no favors, no exceptions, absolutely no help from her during his trial. In fact, she would see to it that he got the harshest sentence possible. As a United States senator, she still had enough influence in her home state to make sure George Ramos paid for his crimes.

But none of that would be possible if she wasn't able to find some positive optics to help her win re-election, and that's what she hoped this congressional hearing would do.

She elbowed her way up the final stretch of steps and made it through the doors without having to make a comment and, more important, without hearing a single derogatory slur hurled at her. A good start to the day. Yes, crazy that no one calling her a drug whore or *puta* was enough to count as a good day.

Ellie's chief of staff joined them in the entrance, taking his usual place, walking alongside her. His greeting was curt. Instead of a customary cup of coffee, he handed her a folded piece of paper without breaking stride.

There were too many people around for her to ask about it, especially after he had taken such pains to hand this message to her without attracting any attention. And because she didn't trust her reaction to not attract attention, she'd need to wait. But she already knew her good start had just been upended.

5

HAYWOOD COUNTY, NORTH CAROLINA

Creed had left behind a sunny, warm day to plunge down into bruise-colored gray that made the afternoon look like night. The pilot managed to land before the lightning kicked up again. Creed asked Isabel Klein how long it had been raining.

'It hasn't stopped.'

Creed had worked the aftermath of three hurricanes, helping to search for survivors as well as those who weren't so lucky. Weather could often be your biggest adversary during a search. Rain and wind affected scent by dispersing it. Temperature added more challenges. Heat helped advance decomposition, but hot and humid weather could wear down a dog and the handler. September in North Carolina should be manageable. He had checked the forecast to see seventies during the day and fifties at night. The rain could change both.

Landslides brought a bunch of other challenges. It might seem counterproductive to want the rain to continue, although a mist would be preferable to this downpour. But as soon as the rain stopped and the dirt and mud began to dry, it would be like hunting for scent through concrete. Last year he'd spent six days in Oso, Washington, after a landslide that claimed forty-three lives.

During the drive to the site, Creed and Bolo sat in the backseat. He'd connected the safety belt through the dog's harness but kept a hand on Bolo's back. The downpour made it impossible for Creed to get a sense of the local terrain. When he glanced at Bolo, the dog's nose was pressed against the opposite window, as if he were trying to do the same thing.

The two of them had worked together in similar weather. The rumble and occasional crash of thunder didn't alarm the dog. Like most of their dogs, Bolo had come to Creed and Hannah as a rescue. He hadn't been a year old, still had his puppy teeth, but they could only guess his pedigree. Hannah was convinced Bolo had to have some Labrador retriever mixed in him. Ridgebacks weren't natural swimmers, but Bolo's webbed toes – similar to those of a Lab – contributed to the dog's love of water. He wouldn't mind the rain, but Creed would need to keep him from bounding into flooded areas. In his mind he was already calculating all the obstacles and risks. That's when he thought about the one that might be the biggest obstacle.

'Is Logan meeting us at the site?'

At first he wasn't sure if she heard him over the battering of the rain on the roof of the vehicle and the accelerated *swish-swish* of the windshield wipers. Then he saw Isabel exchange a look with the driver before she answered. 'No, I think he's stuck in DC until tomorrow.'

Creed pretended it was no big deal. He certainly didn't need Peter Logan there in order to do his job. As a matter of fact, it would probably make his job easier. What didn't sit right with Creed was that the urgency somehow didn't warrant Logan's presence.

'Who's in charge of clearing the area we need to search?' he asked.

Again, the pair exchanged a glance. He wanted to tell them he didn't need to know their classified bullshit. He just needed some basic information. When Isabel took too much time to answer, Creed realized that it might not be a reluctance to share but rather that she didn't know.

As if reading his thoughts, she shrugged and finally said, 'Of this particular area, I guess we are.'

He waited for a laugh that never came. She wasn't joking. And in that short response she had just told him volumes. Isabel Klein had never been involved in a search and rescue of a disaster site, or any other site, for that matter.

Creed stroked Bolo's neck, more in an effort to keep himself calm rather than Bolo. Both of them had worked with amateurs before. Didn't mean he had to like it. Creed wasn't necessarily a rules kind of guy, but protocol in dangerous circumstances helped protect his dogs.

Bolo turned to look over at Creed, eyes searching out his. He knew that look. Bolo was anxious to get to work – actually, to get to play. If only it were all that simple.

6

PENSACOLA, FLORIDA

Hannah Washington couldn't shake the feeling that maybe she should have turned down this assignment despite Creed insisting everything was fine. He sure hadn't looked fine. During the entire forty-five minutes it had taken her to drive him and Bolo to the airfield, Creed had remained tight-lipped and sullen, like some dark cloud had descended over him at just the mention of this Peter Logan. All he'd said was that he'd known the man in Afghanistan and something about a favor.

She glanced in the rearview mirror to see Grace staring at her. The Jack Russell terrier was disappointed that she couldn't go along with Creed and Bolo. Not only was Grace one of their best air-scent dogs, she was a multitask dog. She could sniff out cadavers as well as survivors and had also learned to detect a variety of things from viruses and cancer to cocaine, meth, and heroin.

Grace and Creed had spent most of the summer together working with airport customs and the Coast Guard. They'd even become celebrities. But Creed insisted Grace was too small to work disaster sites. As compensation, Hannah brought her along to run errands with her.

Grace still looked disappointed, staring at Hannah as if that would make her turn around and go get Creed.

'I don't need you judging me,' she told the dog with a glance over her shoulder.

She already regretted sending him. It was Hannah's job to vet the assignments and requests that came their way. Her job to make sure their dogs would be okay and not in undue danger. Same went for the handlers. But she couldn't protect Rye from things she didn't have knowledge about.

They had come a long way as business partners, as

friends, as family, but Hannah always knew there were things that had happened to him in his life before she met him that she might never hear about.

Nothing wrong with that.

Most of the time a person's past belonged right back there, stuffed away in the past. It certainly wasn't hers to judge. She knew too well that there were some things – whether they be mistakes, regrets, or just plain ole memories – that deserved to be kept all to yourself. As soon as you shared them, they were no longer yours.

But she also knew that Ryder Creed had a whole lot of hurt in his past. The dangerous kind that could drive a mind over the edge if left to fester. And although he was getting better about handling it, sometimes it seeped into his everyday life, and when it seeped into her life and that of her two little boys – then it became her business.

Still, he had come a long way from that angry marine she'd met seven years ago. She'd been tending bar at Walter's Canteen on Pensacola Beach. Closing time. She remembered being tired and her feet ached. She just wanted to clean up and get on home when the marine to whom she had served one too many drinks decided to pick a fight. Not just a fight but with three men, bruisers who would have certainly left plenty of damage if Hannah hadn't thrown them out. She'd made the troublemaker stay and clean up the spilled beer and broken glass.

She still remembered the look in his eyes – anger gone and replaced with a bit of alarm and a whole lot of dread. Years later he'd confessed that he'd never had someone get that mad at him in such a quiet, solemn manner. Okay, 'quiet' and 'solemn' were Hannah's words. If she tried to remember, Rye's words were probably closer to 'sermonizing' and 'pissed-off'. Said he'd never had a black woman put him in his place before with a scolding lecture that admonished and shamed him like some evangelical preacher.

Now as she marched down the hallway of Segway House with both hands toting bags of groceries, that idea made her smile – that anyone would even think to compare her to a preacher. She smiled down at Grace as the dog pranced alongside her.

'Hannah, let me help you with those.' A voice came from behind her.

'Frankie Sadowski, what in heaven's name are you doing here? I thought you'd be headed up to DC.'

She waited and let him take one of the bags with his crooked, arthritic fingers. When he grabbed for the other one, she knew better than to argue and surrendered it, too. Despite his gnarled hands and thick silver hair, Frankie Sadowski was tall and lean. If she didn't already know that he was close to seventy years old she would have guessed he was fifteen years younger. Even his weathered face softened with laugh lines used often and blue eyes that seemed to spark with life.

'I'm waiting for Susan to finish her shift. She's going with me. Said she could use a change of scenery. She's been working some long hours at the hospital.'

Hannah knew Frankie's daughter worked at Sacred Heart in the trauma center.

Frankie pointed his chin down at Grace. 'So who's your friend?'

'This is Grace.'

'I hope you aren't expecting her to find any dead bodies here.' He laughed, pleased with the joke, but Hannah just smiled.

'I'm trying to start a program with therapy dogs. Grace is a good sport.'

Hannah glanced at the dog and noticed Grace was

sitting in front of Frankie's feet, but she was staring directly into Hannah's eyes. An intent stare was usually Grace's alert that she had found what she was supposed to be looking for, but Hannah hadn't directed the dog to find anything.

'While I was over waiting on Susan, I spent some time with Gus Seaver,' Frankie said. 'He asked me to stop in and check on his grandson, Jason.'

She knew that Gus and Frankie had served together during the Vietnam War. There was a band of them that had reunited and watched out for each other ever since three of them had gotten sick – too sick to care for themselves.

In the beginning they believed it was mere coincidence that they shared the same debilitating symptoms. Only recently had they learned that their military unit had been exposed to some kind of toxic chemicals. Frankie didn't show any of the symptoms, but he had taken on the crusade. That's why he was headed to DC to testify before a congressional hearing.

Now loaded down with the grocery bags, he waited for several residents to pass, then motioned for Hannah to go ahead of him, always the gentleman. She patted the side of her leg for Grace to follow.

'Actually, I was hoping I'd catch you here,' Frankie said, 'so I could talk to you about him.'

'About Gus?'

'No, Jason.'

She nodded, not wanting to say anything more there in the hallway.

'Let me put a few things in the refrigerator.'

Once inside the kitchen she showed him where to place the bags. She started unpacking them while she checked to make certain no one else was around.

'Jason moved out of Segway House about a month ago,' she told him.

Frankie raised his eyebrows but didn't say anything. Hannah wasn't surprised that Jason had not told his grandfather. Like so many returning wounded, he wouldn't have wanted to be a burden on his family.

Segway House was a halfway home for soldiers who had nowhere else to go after returning from Iraq or Afghanistan. Over the last several years it had morphed into a temporary haven for other lost souls – drug addicts, runaway teenagers, and abused women.

In addition to the housing facility, they also provided mentoring, education programs, and a handful of other services. Hannah was one of the founders and Frankie had been one of the early volunteers.

But Hannah wondered why Jason had not told his grandfather about his new job. That should have been good news to share.

'Is he okay?' Frankie asked.

'He's working for Ryder and me.'

'No kidding?'

'He moved into one of the trailers we have on the property.'

That should have been a relief to Frankie, but Hannah noticed his brow was still furrowed with worry.

'He's living out there all by himself?'

'He's hardly by himself.' But now she understood. At Segway House, Jason had been surrounded by other veterans he'd been able to talk to and get support from. 'He's got Rye and me, the other handlers. We even have a veterinarian out there in our clinic two days a week. Not to mention a kennel full of dogs.'

He nodded but offered only a flicker of a smile.

'He didn't tell Gus,' Frankie said.

Hannah heard his concern and tried to ignore the hint of accusation.

'He likes what he's doing. Seems to be on the right track,' she said, tamping down her growing irritation.

'That what he told you?'

She caught something in his eyes, and now she understood why Jason hadn't told his grandfather. There was a thin line that separated concern and pity. The boy had lost half his arm. It didn't mean he had to lose half his life.

'What exactly is it that has Gus so worried?'

Frankie shrugged and glanced around the kitchen. The tough war veteran, the warrior who had taken on his fellow soldiers' crusade, suddenly looked uncomfortable and at a loss for words.

'I think Gus is worried that Jason might ... you know.'

He hesitated, as though she might help him out and finish the sentence, but instead Hannah stood in front of him with her hands on her hips, getting more impatient.

'I obviously don't know,' she said. Grace was sitting at Frankie's feet again and staring at Hannah.

'Gus is worried the kid might try to off himself.'

7

HAYWOOD COUNTY, NORTH CAROLINA

Creed breathed a sigh of relief when he saw the yellow hard hats of rescue workers and at least one Caterpillar excavator. A staging tent flapped in the wind, secured with concrete blocks. A mobile medical van was parked on the only paved road into the area, nose pointed out and ready to leave.

The thirty miles from the airport had taken them an hour and a half. Even the detours included roads with monster-sized gashes in the pavement, as if a Godzilla-like creature had chomped and stomped a path before them.

Barricades blocked their entrance and a sheriff's

deputy dressed in a rain slicker with plastic stretched over his hat signaled for the SUV to stop. Isabel leaned across the driver with her ID wallet to the window. The deputy motioned for the window to be rolled down for a better look, which drew a sigh of aggravation from Isabel. The rain had eased to a pitter-patter, so Creed could clearly hear her mumble under her breath, 'Don't these people have a clue who we are?'

'Good afternoon,' the driver said as the deputy reached in and took the ID to examine.

He pulled a piece of paper out of his jacket and squinted as if looking for Isabel's name on a list. Creed could see Isabel's jaw go tight, holding back her impatience.

'You're not on the list,' he told her as he handed back her wallet.

'What? That's impossible. We're with the Department of Defense.'

'Sorry, you could be with the White House, and unless you're on this list, I can't let you through.'

The deputy glanced into the backseat, and when he saw Bolo his expression changed. 'Is this the search-and-rescue dog?'

'Yes, and we need—'

'Why didn't you say so?' he interrupted her. 'Big guy with the gray mustache is Oliver Vance. He's the emergency management director for the state of North Carolina. I think he might be under the tent right now. He'll check you in and get you up-to-date. There's some solid ground to your left. Go ahead and park up there.'

As soon as the SUV slid to a stop, Creed gathered his gear and Bolo. He could hear Isabel and her driver still arguing about why she wasn't on the list even as he slogged his way to the staging tent, leaving them behind. Oliver Vance met him before he reached the tent.

'Welcome.' Vance stuck out a gloved hand that was as big as a catcher's mitt. 'I'm Oliver Vance. Everybody around here calls me Ollie.'

'Ryder Creed. And this is Bolo.'

'Bolo?' He chuckled at the name. 'We're sure glad to see you two. Somebody mentioned you were a marine and a dog handler in Afghanistan?'

'That's right.'

'Conditions on the slide field are still unstable, but knowing what you probably dealt with in Afghanistan, you're used to unstable territory.'

Creed remembered what they had said about dog handlers every time he led a unit beyond the wire. 'First out. First to die.' Their job was to accompany the platoon and clear a path through hostile territory, making themselves the first targets – not just first targets of hidden Taliban fighters, but also first to trip over buried IEDs.

'At least here nobody will be shooting at my dog,' he told Vance.

'Bastards,' the man said, shaking his head. 'I was in Desert Storm. Still think we should have taken care of them back then. Saved us a heap of trouble. Hated that son-of-a-bitching place. Some days I feel like I still have sand up my ass.'

That made Creed smile. Vance showed him to a dry bench in the middle of the tent. He petted Bolo while Creed pulled out gear from his duffel. Around them, men called to each other and worked the area.

'How many do you have still missing?' Creed asked.

'Unaccounted is at forty-five.'

'He's here to search an area for Lieutenant Colonel Logan,' Isabel told Oliver Vance as she slogged her way under the tent.

She stood in front of him, a foot shorter, arms

crossed over her chest as if that might give her the needed authority. Before they'd left the Gulfstream she had changed into jeans and added hiking boots that looked brand-new. Her rain slicker looked like she had never worked a disaster site.

'Who's this?' Vance pointed a thumb at her and asked Creed.

Before Creed could respond, Isabel continued, 'Mr Creed was hired by the Department of Defense to search a particular area.'

'Bolo and I can only search what's been cleared to search.' Creed moved between the two, but he stared down Isabel. 'That's why I asked who was in charge. I have to follow protocol.'

'Protocol?'

'Your boss should have told you that.'

'We have instructions—'

'When Logan gets here,' Creed interrupted, 'he can see about changing the protocol. Until then, Bolo and I search wherever Mr Vance tells me he and his people have cleared.'

'We'll see about that.' She pulled out her cell phone and wagged it at him, as if the threat would change his mind.

Creed turned to Vance. 'I need to see a map of the area we're talking about.'

Vance watched Isabel stomp back to the SUV as he pulled a tin of tobacco from a pocket. He opened the lid and offered some to Creed. When Creed shook his head, Vance pinched a wad and tucked it under his lower lip, adding to the lump already there.

'Hard thing to get over,' he said, 'when the one you brought to the dance won't dance with you. She won't likely forget this.'

Creed tamped down his impatience. With the thick cloud coverage and intermittent rain, they'd be losing daylight soon.

'How about that map?'

Vance yanked a laminated one from inside his rain jacket and unfolded it on a makeshift table. With his index finger he outlined the area they had cleared.

'Where do you suspect the slide began?' Creed wanted to know.

'We haven't been able to send up a helicopter for any aerial views. Weather's been a bitch. I'm estimating it started up here.' He pointed to a line just below the top of the mountain.

'And it ends where we're standing?'

'For now. We've felt some additional debris flow off to our right. This rain don't stop, even the area we cleared can't be considered safe. Everything is still unstable. We tried to start in the most populated area. This thing gave way about ten-thirty last night. Some folks were already in bed.

'Houses that used to sit about three acres above slid or toppled down this far.' Again, he ran his finger over the map. 'We have one house still intact. Slid clean off its foundation and rode down until it slammed into another house. But the other houses . . .' He let out a long sigh. 'Hard to even recognize any of the mess. You've done a slide before?'

'Oso.'

Vance nodded. Nothing else needed to be said. Oso, Washington, had been one of the worst.

'Then you know what you get with these things: septic tanks, insulation, propane, a truckload of glass. A wicked brew of toxins that used to be homes.'

'What about survivors?'

'We've pulled fourteen. Two didn't make it. Five were taken by ambulance. Some of the survivors are telling us they have family still in the rubble. But that's just this area. We're hoping you and your dog can help find them.'

Creed pulled the yellow fluorescent vest over Bolo's head and secured it in place. The dog wiggled in anticipation. This particular vest had a strap running along the top from side to side that could be used as a handle if Creed needed to yank the big dog up and out of the muck.

'I didn't realize there was so much gear for the dog,' Vance said from behind them, standing back but watching as Creed attached a tiny waterproof GPS unit inside a mesh pocket in the vest. It would sit just over Bolo's right shoulder.

'Normally I'd rather not have him off leash, but in this case being attached to me will slow him down.'

Then Creed prepared himself. He tucked his pant legs into his hiking boots and ran four-inch waterproof tape around his ankles, sealing the seam. He already had on special socks that would wick the wetness away from his skin. He knew the tape wouldn't necessarily keep his feet dry, but it would discourage snakes and other insects from climbing up his legs.

He strapped on his helmet, a ballistic shell that sat just above his ears. It was similar to the helmets

Vance's crew wore, only Creed's didn't include a communication headset inside. He chose to leave his gloves in his rain jacket pocket. In the other pocket he stuffed a knotted rope toy and zippered it in while Bolo's eyes grew wide and his tail wagged. Most of Creed's dogs were trained with toy rewards. Food was never used. Too many things could go wrong with food rewards. Last, he tugged on a small backpack with other items he or Bolo might need along their search. This particular pack had a one-snap release in case he got caught up in debris and needed to wrestle free.

Ready, he turned back to Vance. Something just occurred to him and he asked, 'How did you know I was coming?'

'What do you mean?'

'Ms Klein wasn't on the admission list but you sounded like you were expecting me. Even knew I was a marine.'

'One of the guys told me early this morning.' He scratched at the thick mass of gray hair under his hard hat.

Creed shrugged it off. It probably didn't matter. Instead he asked, 'What about the DoD's facility?'

'Don't know much about it. It's secluded on federal

property. Classified crap. Nobody around here can even tell me what the facility was for, let alone how many people worked there. I'd say it's about an acre northeast of these homes.'

'You think it was affected?'

'Oh yeah. That's probably gone. But that late at night, I'm hoping there wasn't anyone in there. We don't even have it on our unaccounted-for list because nobody'll give us any information.'

'My biggest challenge is the scent area for my dog,' Creed told him. 'He'll be confined to this area, but the scent could stretch all along the slide or at least as far as it's been dragged. Where Bolo ends up alerting could be a part of the field, but it might not be exactly where the victim is.'

'No matter how far off he is, I've got to think he'll still be saving us time.'

'There is one other thing,' Creed said. 'From what you've described, this slide was powerful.'

'And fast. Never seen one like this before. We get our share in these parts but rarely one like this.'

'I have to warn you. There's a good chance the houses aren't the only things that have been ripped apart.'

8

WASHINGTON, DC

Senator Ellie Delanor stared at the stack of files on her desk. In the corner of her office were a half-dozen boxes with more. Senator Quincy, who was heading the congressional hearing, had sent them over just that morning.

Her chief of staff stood in the doorway. The note he had handed her was supposed to prepare her for this.

'Was there some mistake?' she asked Carter.

She knew the answer but still hoped he could explain the delay as a simple mix-up. She didn't want to believe that her colleague – the four-term senior senator from Illinois who had allowed her to be on the committee – would sabotage her before the hearings even began. But considering what she had put up with in the past, she shouldn't even be surprised. The Senate was still a good ole boys' club. She'd been warned. She already knew she would be the token woman for the camera crews at the hearings. Wasn't this just another way of reminding her of her place?

'They said that the DoD only just released them,' Carter told her, pointing to the boxes. The stack on her desk had been delivered yesterday morning.

She met his eyes, looking for any hint of whether he believed it. Sad, but these days she found herself relying on a twenty-eight-year-old glorified clerk as her bullshit monitor. That's what happens when you discover your ex-husband has lied for most of your thirteen years of marriage. You don't know who to believe.

'I skimmed through a few files,' he continued. 'Blocks of blacked-out copy. Pages of it in some instances.'

'So what are you saying?'

'We never would have found much even if we'd received them two months ago instead of today.'

From the labels adhered to the outside of the boxes she knew the copies were from documents dated between 1951 and 1975. It was amazing to think how records were kept before computers. Hundreds of thousands of documents, sorted page by page. There was no easy way to access information from these bulging boxes of stack upon stack. It would take months to physically look through them, let alone read them.

And what good would it do? The DoD, the very agency that was being investigated, was the same agency that determined what was too sensitive, too classified, and needed to be blocked out.

Or was that exactly what the DoD wanted them to believe? She wondered if her and Carter's responses were what the DoD hoped for – that they would take one look and think that all of the important information was still classified. And maybe they wouldn't bother to look at all.

Carter's cell phone bleated its annoying ringtone. He pulled it out and glanced at the screen.

'It's Senator Quincy's office,' he told her, even as he tapped the faceplate to take the call, not waiting for her permission. 'This is Carter.'

He listened, nodding as though the person on the other end of the line could see him. Ellie watched him, realizing the kid had become a player – poker face, eyes steady, face expressionless, body casual and free of any fidgeting or ticks. When had he gotten so good at this that even she couldn't read him? He had been such a sweet, innocent kid when she hired him, all bright-eyed and ready to adore her.

'Senator Quincy's called an emergency meeting,' he said, interrupting her thoughts so suddenly she didn't notice that he had ended his call.

'About the files?'

'Something about Dr Hess not being able to testify tomorrow.'

'What?'

Colonel Abraham Hess was one of her witnesses. A brilliant biologist and medical doctor, he had earned an indisputable reputation in his fifty-five years in the army. A friend of her father's, Ellie had known Hess since she was a child.

'There was a landslide in North Carolina.'

'He doesn't have any family in North Carolina.'

Carter shrugged, already gathering his messenger bag and waiting for her.

'Something about a research facility,' he told her.

But all she heard was that her star contribution to

these hearings was bailing on her, and she couldn't let that happen. She grabbed a file folder, pen, and leather portfolio, always conscious of looking unburdened and in control. At the door she stopped and turned to Carter, who was ready to follow her. She pulled out a sheet of paper and jotted down several names and phone numbers, then handed it to him.

'Before you join me in the meeting, make a few calls for me. By this afternoon I want a subpoena delivered to Colonel Hess.'

'A subpoena?' He said it like he'd never heard the word before.

'Yes, Carter. It's a congressional hearing. I can do that. He's my witness and he will be there tomorrow.'

She didn't wait for him to ask any more questions. Truth was, she had no idea if it was possible to do what she was asking. But she was tired of people bailing on her, tired of having boxes of files dropped off to be read in less than twenty-four hours, tired of being treated like a skirt who should simply be happy to sit and be pretty. If Colonel Hess thought he could take advantage of their family friendship to screw her over, he was sadly mistaken. Senator Ellie Delanor was finished being screwed over.

9

HAYWOOD COUNTY, NORTH CAROLINA

'Wasteland' was the first word that came to Creed's mind. The gentle slope at the foothills of the slide was once a forest. Now the only indication that trees had ever stood there were the twisted roots that jutted out of the earth.

Creed took careful steps, instructing Bolo to do the same. The toughest part of training a dog for disaster work sometimes included asking the dog to act against his instinct. No running. No jumping. The impact could destabilize the debris and cause the ground the dog was jumping onto to give out beneath him. Thankfully no floodwaters raced across this area, but

Creed knew they would likely encounter some and he'd need to keep his water-loving dog from bounding through it.

He expected the mud to suck at his boots and make walking cumbersome. In seconds the soles of his shoes were caked and heavy, rendering the treads worthless. He slid easily, challenging his balance. The ground was saturated and slick. To make matters worse, Creed could see that the floor of the slope was now made up of slick, green logs, stripped of bark, stuck in the mud, side by side, a long stretch of them for as far as Creed could see.

At first he wondered if a lumber company had lost a heap of their product. On closer inspection he realized they weren't forested logs but tree trunks – upended by the force of the slide – scraped clean of their branches and most of their bark. So this was where the forest – the missing trees – had gone.

Twenty feet in front of him, Bolo was already sniffing and scratching at the ground. He walked in circles over the same spot, his tail straight out. His breathing was already rapid, nose twitching, ears pitched forward. Creed watched as Bolo's tail slowly curled. Then the dog looked over his shoulder, looking for Creed.

When Bolo saw he had Creed's attention, he scratched once more, then sat down.

This was how the big dog alerted. But was it possible he already had found something? The debris field had to be overwhelmed with scent.

Creed approached slowly, trying not to slip. When he took too long, Bolo stood and turned to watch him. He scratched the surface again, as if saying, *It's here. What's taking you so long?*

This time when Bolo sat, he stared at the zippered pocket of Creed's rain jacket where he'd seen his rope toy disappear to earlier. But Creed couldn't reward the dog for a possible false alert.

There was a break in the logs where Bolo sat – no logs for at least a ten-foot stretch. Instead of tree trunks, it looked like a sheet of metal partially buried in mud. It could be part of a building. Maybe a piece of roof. Creed pulled on his gloves and swept one of his hands over the surface. He dug away clots of mud, looking for a seam or an edge. In other places the metal was buried under almost a foot of dirt and chunks of asphalt. Suddenly he jerked back in surprise when he realized what he was looking at.

It was the undercarriage of a vehicle.

He hadn't been able to recognize it at first because the tires and wheels had been sliced away. He could smell gasoline but it was faint, and from the fracture lines in the metal he guessed the gas tank had been ruptured, the contents leaked and spewed over the hillside as the vehicle tumbled.

'We have an overturned vehicle here,' Creed called out to Vance and his crew, who had respected Creed's wishes and stayed back while he and Bolo worked.

'Damn it! How'd we miss that?' Vance said.

'I wouldn't have recognized it either if Bolo hadn't alerted.'

Vance looked from the vehicle to the dog as though the significance had only just occurred to him. That the dog may have sniffed out victims. He turned back to his men and yelled, 'Hurry it up. Get the excavator. We've got a vehicle down here.'

To Creed, he said in almost a whisper, 'So the dog is telling you that someone is still down there?'

'I told you about scent being spread across the entire slide. I can't make any promises.' Creed glanced at Bolo patiently sitting and waiting for his reward. 'He seems convinced, though.'

'Someone's alive?'

'Bolo's a multitask dog.'

Vance stared at Creed, then finally asked, 'So what the hell does that mean? I thought he was a search-and-rescue dog.'

'He is. He tracks human scent, but that includes decomp.'

Vance stared again and Creed waited to see the realization come across his face. That's when he muttered, 'Crap! That's what I was afraid of.'

Just then Bolo stood again. His ears twitched and pitched forward. He lowered his nose to the ground and cocked his head. But he wasn't sniffing. He was hearing something.

Vance started to speak and Creed put up his hand to stop him. He tried to listen.

Nothing. He couldn't hear a thing.

He watched Bolo while Vance waved his arms at his crew to stay back. The big dog was no longer scratching for more scent. He cocked his head from side to side, listening to something below that only he could hear.

Was the earth giving way again? Some dogs could sense landslides before they started. Creed scanned the surroundings, rotating his head only and keeping his feet planted while he examined the wall of dirt behind them.

'You think—' Vance started.

Creed cut him off again with a finger to his lips. Now Vance's eyes darted around, too, but he followed Creed's lead and kept stock-still.

That's when Creed heard a muffled dog bark.

He glanced up. Vance had heard it, too.

'Your dog found a dog?'

Creed shook his head. 'He knows not to alert to animals.'

Vance's bushy eyebrows drew together. Again Creed waited. This time when Vance realized what that meant, he yelled out to his men, 'Get that equipment over here. Now!'

10

Once Creed's dogs alerted he pulled them aside, making way for the experts to do their job, whether it was a forensic team or, in this case, a rescue crew. He tried never to blur the line of where his job ended and their job began. It was important that his dogs knew, too.

As Creed led Bolo away, he tossed him his rope toy, careful to pitch it for a catch that didn't require the big dog to jump. Strings of saliva flew from his mouth as he caught it. Bolo had been drooling because of the wait, even with the distraction of the muffled dog barks.

Creed hated delaying rewards, but false alerts were

always a concern. Whether the people in the vehicle were dead or alive, Bolo had found them despite hundreds of pounds of mangled metal and layers of mud. He deserved his reward. Creed would let him prance around with it for a while before they started back to the staging area.

He guided Bolo to a sloped area above the rescue where the ground felt solid. Closer to the wall he could smell the musty earth. In the debris underfoot he noticed a mixture of broken bricks and splintered branches. Pieces of glass sparkled in the gray muck. Already he was concerned about Bolo's paws.

Vance directed a mini Bobcat excavator instead of the larger Caterpillar Creed had seen close to the staging area. He could hear Vance telling his men to be careful as he waved to the machine operator. Creed guessed they'd try to use the tooth bucket to dig around the vehicle or attach and lift. Either process could trigger another slide.

Creed called to Bolo, his palm up, and the dog surrendered his toy without hesitation. He'd barely stuffed it in his pocket when Bolo's nose started working. Before Creed could stop him the dog moved along the wall of dirt, nose in the air, whiskers twitching, tail straight out. No doubt this entire area was slathered with scent, running with the mud and debris as it rolled and slid down the slope. Creed would need to pull him off. They could start there again later. That's exactly what he was thinking when he heard the crack.

At first Creed thought the sound might have been an echo from the Bobcat's bucket, metal scraping the metal of the vehicle. But even as he glanced back he knew it had come from above.

'Bolo, go!' He yelled at the top of his lungs, but the dog hesitated, sensing danger. His nose was still working. Instinct overrode the unfamiliar command.

Precious seconds were lost as Creed's feet slid. He stopped himself, not wanting his movement to contribute to destabilizing the surroundings. At least not until his dog was out of there. It didn't matter. Dirt began to rain down. He yanked the rope toy out of his pocket. He'd have to depend on Bolo's other instinct.

Toy crazy! Thank God!

Now he had the dog's attention. Creed tossed the twisted rope, the heavy knots at both ends sending it flying. He flung it as hard and as far as he could, a lateral throw, making the dog run diagonally and not in front of where the slide would likely go.

Even that simple toss threatened to upend him. Creed caught his balance and tried to make his feet gain traction as he heard the rumble grow. He felt the vibration. Out of the corner of his eye he saw the slab behind him start to fracture. Chunks fell away, crumbling all around him. A full-out sprint was impossible. Now that he wanted to move – needed to move – his boots became skates, sliding one second, the next jamming toes against rocks and almost sending him sprawling.

He felt pressure against his back. Debris smacked his helmet. There was nothing to grab on to. The impact knocked him off his feet and onto his back. Creed was used to swimming in the Gulf. An excellent swimmer, he knew to take in air with the breaking of the waves and he knew when to hold his breath. But there was no break. A gush of rapids swept him under. Only this wasn't water. The thick sludge overtook him, wrapped around him, sending him careening so fast it was an effort to control his arms and legs.

He ducked his head and pulled his body into a tight ball. Chin to his chest. Knees curled up. Arms criss-crossed with hands fisted, holding on to the front of his jacket. Nose buried in the crook of his arm.

Rolling, tumbling, speeding too fast. The pull of gravity turned him into just another piece of debris, battering him against the rest. Splintered branches poked him in the sides. Rocks slammed into his helmet. Sharp objects shredded his clothes and scraped his skin.

The force yanked at him, attempting to peel his limbs away even as it continued to send him spiraling downhill. Yet he stayed curled and tucked as best he could, holding on. He no longer knew which way was up. There was no sky, only a heavy, thick blur of speckled gray that swallowed all light. He waited for the slide to slow down. Waited for it to stop. Waited to hit the bottom.

Then suddenly it stopped. He stopped.

11

There was no sound. The world had come to a screeching halt and so had he. Everything quieted, unplugged and muffled. Everything except for the throbbing of his heartbeat.

Creed opened his eyes to blackness with patches of gray. He strained to loosen his fingers and dig away grime from his face, from his eyes. He blinked. Tried to focus. Still saw only blackness with patches of gray. Maybe like walking into an unlit room, he needed to wait for his eyes to adjust. He told himself to be patient.

The smell of musty earth already filled his lungs. A sharp stabbing pain kept his breaths shallow and careful when he wanted to gulp air. What little air there was was dense and thick with moisture, making it difficult to breathe. He could taste wet dirt, gravel, and grit on his tongue and between his teeth and cheek. He wanted to spit but stopped himself. Instead, he dug his finger into his mouth, sweeping then pinching and pulling out what didn't belong. With effort he tried to free his arm. He wrenched it and twisted his wrist to loosen the stranglehold around him.

His legs were pinned. His arms were trapped against his chest. He tried to dig in his elbows and push himself up. His backpack remained in place and he heard crunching. All he was doing was smashing the contents of his backpack against the mud, squeezing out what little air existed around him. Weight pressed against him in all directions.

Was the mud already hardening? How many minutes? How many seconds before the shell surrounding him became as hard as concrete?

His eyes should have had enough time to adjust, yet they still showed him nothing more than the dark, gray space inches in front of him. He couldn't let himself panic. There had to be a way to dig out.

He drew measured breaths. Anxiety made you

breathe more rapidly and he needed to stay calm. He could do this, but only if he remained calm. The palms of his hands were close to his face. He could see the shadows of his fingers when he wiggled them. Again, he swiped dirt and sludge away from his face. In the space in front of him, he clawed to create an air pocket. Crumbles fell away.

He stopped.

He poked again and watched more pieces fall. They were falling away from him. He needed to be certain. Clawed some more, and again the dirt didn't hit him in the face.

Gravity never lied.

The realization made his heartbeat start to gallop. Panic gnawed its way into his gut. Not only was he buried alive, he was lying facedown. Any attempt to dig his way out just went from difficult to impossible.

12

Creed slammed the back of his helmet against the weight that threatened to crush him. Small pieces flaked down on his neck. He had rocked mere inches, and each time the space he smashed open quickly filled with debris from above. He reared up and arched his back, sickened by how solid the mass on top of him had already begun to feel. He was encased in a coffin of mud and it was hardening like cement by the second.

He had managed to work his hands free. Protected under his body, this space didn't fill in immediately. But he wasn't creating more air for himself, only a few more inches of movement.

Seconds slipped away. He had no idea how much time had passed. But he was acutely aware of how little air he had. Already he could feel the difference, hot and suffocating like being under a damp wool blanket. And because there was no place for his exhalations to escape, he knew he was contaminating what air was left, saturating it with carbon dioxide. The mixture would eventually start to impair his mental capacity.

Just the thought sent his fingers digging, clawing, searching for an air pocket. Surely there must be more air trapped between the pieces of debris, caught somewhere in the folds. He tried twisting his body again. Bucked against the backpack. Smashed his helmet from side to side.

Suddenly he stopped.

There was crunching above him. And panting. He could hear a dog panting.

Bolo! Had he gotten away in time?

Creed strained to listen. He cocked his head, and that's when he felt the drips on his hand. The panting wasn't a dog's. The panting was his own.

Drips of saliva from his mouth.

How could that be when his throat felt raw and cotton-dry? Swallowing was an effort. He was breathing hard now, sucking in air, and still he was breathless. He tried to calm the panting. He was breathing too fast, too deep. He'd use up his meager supply in no time.

He felt the surge of panic. He had stomped it down several times. Soon it would be something he could not control.

Creed lay flat, palms against the dirt ledge he had created beneath himself. Then he pushed until his wrists and elbows screamed for him to stop. He pushed until his back ached, until the muscles in his neck felt like they would explode, until the pain in his chest sliced too deep. He fought to breathe, clawing away swatches of debris, only to hear and see the space refill. All thought and reason had given in to basic instinct.

When he finally stopped it wasn't because his muscles failed him. It was the hum that started to fill his ears, relentless but almost soothing like a lullaby.

He felt light-headed, and suddenly exhaustion dissolved into an unusual calm. He felt himself slipping into water, letting go of his body. Giving in and allowing the water to carry him.

He closed his eyes, and soon he was floating.

13

WASHINGTON, DC

Ellie sat quietly at the corner of the long conference table. She had listened to Senator John Quincy's long explanation about the documents provided by the DoD. All the momentum she had gathered during her brisk walk down the halls to come to this meeting had evaporated as soon as she came in the door. Senator Quincy derailed her quite easily by inviting her, in front of the rest of the committee, to come sit at the corner of his end of the table. It so disarmed her that she had barely heard him say how 'pretty' she looked today.

This congressional hearing was not the first one on

this particular subject. Senator Quincy reminded them of that. Congress had taken a look at these two classified government projects from the 1960s and 1970s. Project 112 and Project SHAD were a series of tests conducted by the Department of Defense. The purpose, which Senator Quincy read from a document, 'was to identify US warships' and US troops' vulnerabilities to attacks with chemical or biological warfare agents and to develop procedures to respond to such attacks while maintaining a war-fighting capability'.

'Basically,' Quincy continued, 'the DoD claimed they were trying to find out how chemical and biological agents behaved in different environments. How they affected our military personnel and how long it would take to respond effectively. They sprayed ships and dispersed aerosols in controlled areas that were supposed to simulate enemy attacks. Not until 2002 did the DoD admit that actual biological and chemical agents were used in these simulated attacks. Nasty stuff like VX nerve gas, Sarin nerve gas, and E. coli were used on our soldiers and sailors without their knowledge or their consent.'

Yes, Ellie thought, it sounded like a travesty, but she was raised in a colonel's household and constantly heard her father talk about the sacrifices of the few to protect the greater good of a whole society. Military personnel didn't necessarily sign up to be exposed to IEDs or machete-rampaging Taliban, but it happened as part of war. These soldiers and sailors were part of a project to protect the free world against an enemy who would use such weapons.

In her mind, Ellie had already decided that Project 112 and Project SHAD were not the evil and sinister works of her government, like Senator Quincy hoped to prove. But at the same time, she did believe the government owed these veterans some kind of compensation if they had become ill from their exposure. She hated that the DoD would rather bury them in worthless blacked-out, photocopied documents from half a century ago than provide the last of these men the health benefits they deserved. But in order to do that, men like her father and Colonel Hess – men who were hailed as heroes – would need to admit that they had done something wrong.

Instead of getting caught up in that nonsense, since Ellie knew she had no control over the outcome, she committed herself to what she could control. She kept glancing at the door, waiting and hoping that

Carter had been successful in ordering a subpoena for Colonel Hess. After all, she was *not* a novice at using her political credentials. That was one thing she'd learned very quickly in this city. You embraced and used your power and authority or you'd be crushed by those who weren't afraid to.

Now she needed Carter to come in and tell her it was a done deal before Quincy brought up the subject of Hess not being able to appear before the committee on the opening day of the hearing.

Quincy, however, droned on about how important this hearing was, telling them that the failure of those congressional attempts in the past made their task more urgent. A bill in 2008 would have provided those veterans who were a part of Project 112 and Project SHAD with health benefits. That bill had failed. Some of those veterans hadn't given up, even though their congressmen had. They were hoping to push for another bill that would finally acknowledge them.

Ellie knew too well that the 2008 bill failure probably had very little to do with its merits, though she hadn't been in the Senate at that time. In fact, when she first took office she dove in with plenty of good intentions, sponsoring and crusading for worthy causes only to watch the results of her efforts become political fodder, nothing more than bargaining chips. It mattered more what a bill was attached to than what it contained.

To make anything happen, she'd learned, she needed to play the game, keeping score with favors – 'I'll vote for this if you vote for that.' Somewhere along the way she'd lost her passion for the causes she'd believed in so dearly. She couldn't remember when it became more about her own survival than her purpose for being there in the first place. Even now she still watched the door, waiting for her assistant.

Come on, Carter, she found herself chanting in her head. She had seen glimpses of what this man-child was capable of doing. If she was going to create a monster, could it at least be a monster that benefited her? So intent was her concentration that when the stooped elderly man wearing his dress blues shuffled into the room she didn't recognize him. He was accompanied by a younger man, a very handsome man, also in dress blues.

Senator Quincy stopped his rambling, shoved his thick body away from the table, and stood to greet the men. 'Colonel Hess, Colonel Platt, thank you both for joining us.'

Ellie felt the heat rush to her face. The man who had entered the room looked nothing like the brilliant biologist she knew. Granted, it had been years, perhaps a decade, since she had last seen him in person.

She stood as Quincy guided the two colonels to the empty chairs at the other corner of the table, just opposite Ellie. The old doctor's eyes lit up when he saw her, and she was pleased with the recognition. After all, she was the one who had called him and asked him to be one of the experts to testify. She wanted the others to realize that. Maybe they would see that she had some connections of her own. She wasn't just the junior senator from Florida – the one who was fighting for her life to remain the junior senator from Florida.

He took her hand first, ignoring several others who had offered theirs. His grip was firm, even if he added his second hand over the top of hers in that handshake men seemed to think was necessary when addressing a woman. Still, she was beaming.

And then he said to her, 'Look at you. Your father would be so proud, little Ellie Delanor.'

14

HAYWOOD COUNTY, NORTH CAROLINA

It was too damned hot to breathe.

A hundred degrees at ten in the morning. That was Afghanistan.

Creed knew it would only get hotter. He already felt the weight of his gear, seventy-five pounds riding on his back. He couldn't think about that right now. It didn't matter how uncomfortable he felt, he was there to clear a path through hostile territory. The marine platoon he was assigned to certainly didn't care. To them he was a perpetual outsider. Creed and his dog were there to do a job and then move on to the next platoon.

Only now he couldn't see Rufus. The dog knew not to go too far out of his sight. Eighteen months old and he still had that easy lope of a Labrador puppy. But everything else about the dog projected strength and discipline. He got right down to business and worked hard for the same goal.

Always the same goal – *find toy.*

So intent he'd ignore his own discomforts. Creed considered the blistering heat and wondered if he should start an IV on Rufus before dehydration started.

He couldn't see the dog but he knew he was there. He felt his presence even when he couldn't quite see him. Still, Creed watched and listened. He felt his own senses heighten. Unlike Rufus, he couldn't smell the ammonium nitrate of buried IEDs, but he could hear the breeze rustling through the nearby cornfields. His eyes could pick out a humped area of loose dirt. Sometimes even see the wire sticking up.

In camp you'd hear a blast in the distance and you knew a wandering goat or an unsuspecting villager had tripped another IED. You acknowledged it, shrugged at anyone who might have heard it, too, then you went on with your routine. But every time they went beyond the wire, things changed. Creed knew he and his dog were easy targets.

'First out, first to die.'

And in Afghanistan the Taliban targeted dogs. The bastards knew the emotional attachment. They knew what taking out the dog would do, not just to the handler, but to the whole platoon.

Creed thought it was a bit ironic, since each platoon regarded them as outsiders. Marine dog handlers came in for a short period of time and usually moved on. They rarely got a chance to become a part of the tight-knit family the others had created. Creed was used to being treated with some level of suspicion. With each unit he knew they were wondering if he and his dog would get them through safely or if he'd get them all killed.

But Creed and Rufus had been with Logan and his men for almost a month. *Too long.* Creed had seen things he wasn't meant to see, and Logan knew it.

He glanced back to see if Logan was following, carefully stepping in Creed's footsteps like Creed had taught him, looking for the shaving cream they used to mark the safe spots. But now he couldn't see Logan. The huge mud wall blocked his view.

Where the hell was Logan?

He stopped and looked around.

Something was wrong.

There wasn't anyone in sight. He needed to find Rufus. And he needed to find him quickly.

He rubbed his eyes, and when he opened them the mud wall was inches from his face. His fingers were muddy. The sun had disappeared into a dark sky. He blinked. Swiped at his eyes again. He couldn't seem to catch his breath. His chest hurt. His body ached. His limbs were pinned down.

Buried.

Only the realization didn't bring panic. A calmness wrapped around him. All he wanted to do was close his eyes. He invited the dream back. Wanted to return to the sun even if it took him back to Afghanistan. It was better to breathe that godforsaken country's eternal dust than not be able to breathe at all.

Creed's fingers went still. He felt his body relax as his mind surrendered. The soothing hum crackled, almost like static interfering with his brain waves. It was followed by an annoying scrape and crunch. He wanted to sleep. A scratching sound followed, insistent and growing louder.

Something poked his shoulder. Just when he thought he had imagined it, he felt a second hit. And this time it came with a rush of air.

Fresh air!

He gasped and sucked it in. Tilted his head and twisted his neck, pointing his mouth and nose toward the draft over his shoulder as best he could. The object poked through a third time and knocked him in the back.

Creed's eyes tried to adjust to see through the blur. With recognition came relief, sweeping over him along with another influx of air. That's when Bolo's big front paw tapped him again.

15

As soon as he was out of the hole, someone shoved an oxygen mask on his face. Creed fought to pull it off. He wanted to smell the fresh air, not something out of a can. The medic tried to put it on again and Creed pushed it away.

'Let him be,' he heard someone say.

He gulped in air and ignored the stab of pain in his chest. He yanked off his helmet and instantly felt the cool breeze against his sweat-drenched hair.

'Bolo.'

He struggled to look around. Hands came down on his shoulders to keep him still and he shoved at them, too.

'Hell, let him see his dog. If it wasn't for the dog, we wouldn't have found him.'

Creed glanced up to look at the speaker, but his vision was still fuzzy. He thought he recognized the man's voice but he couldn't remember his name. Then Creed felt another shove at his shoulder. Before he could bat it away, he felt the lick on his cheek. Ignoring the aches, he reached up and wrapped his arm around the big dog's neck, pulling him close. Bolo licked his mud-stained face.

The man squatted in front of Creed and waited for his eyes to focus on him.

'Can you tell me who I am?'

Bushy gray eyebrows stuck out from under the brim of a yellow hard hat. An equally bushy gray mustache hung over the man's mouth.

Creed blinked hard a couple of times and he let his fingers caress Bolo's head, running them over the dog's ears then neck. Other than mud, he couldn't feel any wounds or cuts on the dog.

The man looked disappointed and his eyes started searching for the medic.

'Vance,' Creed said.

The man's eyes returned to Creed's.

'But you like to be called Ollie.'

'Son of a bitch!' Then over his shoulder he yelled, 'I think he's okay.' To Creed he said, 'We're still gonna take you down to our triage center. They're letting us use the high school gymnasium. Medic thinks you have some busted ribs. They'll fix you up and find you a nice soft cot where you can get some rest.'

'What about Bolo?'

'He'll go with you.'

'Is he okay?'

'As far as I can tell. I gotta tell you, though, that dog was possessed. We were looking for you up higher, where the edge gave out and the slide began. He kept insisting you were all the way down here. You traveled a good long ways, my friend.'

'What about the other dog?'

Vance scrunched up his face in question.

'The vehicle underground.'

And now the man hung his head and his eyes went down as well. When they returned, Creed knew the results.

'Driver and two passengers were dead. They were pretty bloodied up. I don't think they survived the impact. So at least they weren't down there suffering.'

Vance stood up and waved for the medics to come back over.

'What about the dog?'

'I think she'll be okay.'

'She's a scrappy thing,' the medic said, keeping his distance from Creed as if to make sure it was safe to approach him.

'She was cushioned between the seat back and one of the passengers. Probably protected her from serious injury,' Vance said.

'She didn't try to bite anyone,' the medic told him. 'She's back in the ambulance. We've got her subdued on pain meds. You and Bolo mind riding along with her?'

'Not at all.'

Creed let the medic help him to his feet. It took more effort than he expected and Vance came on the other side to assist. His legs felt like spaghetti. He couldn't get his knees to hold. His head started swirling and suddenly he was struggling to catch his breath again. This time when the medic offered the oxygen mask, Creed didn't fight him.

'Let's sit you back down,' the medic told him, easing him back to the ground. Then into his shoulder radio he said, 'Bring up that stretcher.'

'Hey, Ollie, we've got something here,' one of Vance's men yelled to him, even though he was close by, less than twenty feet away. 'Smells bad.'

Creed watched them pull and tug at something buried under the mud, digging around the edges. They were being careful. It didn't take long to realize it was a body. He saw the urgency slip away from their shoulders and hands when they realized the victim was dead.

'Looks like there's more than one.'

But even this revelation didn't bring with it a sense of urgency.

Vance helped lift a body out from the hole. They turned it to lie faceup.

'Holy crap!'

Creed craned his neck to see but the men were standing too close around the body, staring down at it.

'What's wrong?' he finally asked the medic who returned to Creed's side. 'They're dead, right?'

'Oh yeah, they're dead all right. But not from the landslide. One has a bullet hole in the middle of his forehead.'

16

Daniel Tate shoved hard and another piece of concrete gave way. Finally he felt rain pouring down on him. He tilted back his head and opened his mouth, so thirsty he wanted to yell in relief. But he stopped himself. He had no idea how close the enemy might be.

All night long he'd heard rumbles and muffled explosions. The debris beneath him shook and the walls vibrated as though the whole place could give way again.

His fingers were raw and bleeding from digging. He had scraped out a cozy but teetering cave. Now that he could see sky – though cloudy and dark – he could see his surroundings.

The examination room had crumbled. Branches pierced through the walls. Frayed electrical wires dangled along trails of insulation from what used to be the ceiling. The door that Dr Shaw had slammed shut and locked had been ripped away. Tate could see the dark hallway beyond the splintered doorway. Pieces of glass and broken equipment littered the floor.

What interested Tate most was the hole he had finally opened up above. It looked large enough for him to escape through. And yet he hesitated. He crouched in a dark corner atop a tattered pile of what used to be the examination table he had clung to and hidden under. It had probably saved his life.

Now he tried listening for the sounds beyond the hole that was just a foot over his head. He managed enough courage to push himself up and peek out. His eyes flew to the treetops and he scanned the branches. Before the earthquake, explosion – whatever the hell had happened – he had seen tiny green monkeys scurrying up the hallway outside his room. He looked for them now. Surely they were harmless, but what did he know about monkeys?

He crawled out onto jagged rocks slick with mud. Only then did he notice that his feet were swollen and covered with tiny cuts. It must have been the glass on the floor. His arms were cut, too, the shirtsleeves shredded. He had only been concerned about his hands as he dug his way out.

In the open air he felt light-headed. Blood dripped from his nostrils and he wiped his nose with an arm stained with dried blood. He heard a noise behind him and spun around so quickly he slipped in the mud. He came down hard on his knees. So hard he felt it in his jaw.

His eyes searched for the cause of the noise. There! Behind a tree not fifty feet away he saw someone duck into the bushes. Tate kept completely still. Lowered his body closer to the mud, keeping to the ground where he'd be hidden by the debris. He never let his eyes leave the spot where he swore he had seen a face.

They were still here. And they were still after him. He knew it wouldn't be safe up here. His heartbeat kicked against his ribs. He could barely hear over the sound of it pounding in his ears. This close to the ground he could smell something awful, like sewer gas. Still, he slithered his way through the mud and over the sharp edges of metal and rock poking up out of the ground. His eyes stayed glued, watching the bushes and the tree that he'd seen the face disappear behind.

He found the hole and slipped back down into the space he had spent hours digging his way out of. But this time he started looking for provisions he'd need: water, light, and most important – a weapon.

17

WASHINGTON, DC

Benjamin Platt knew better than to offer assistance to the man walking beside him, despite his slow and laborious effort. The two men saw each other almost every week either at meetings or during their weekly lunch together. Colonel Abraham Hess had been Platt's mentor for almost twenty years. He was the backbone of DARPA, a valued consultant at USAMRIID. Never once would Platt think to use the word 'old' to describe Hess, yet today he thought he glimpsed a tired and worn-out fatigue in the man's step.

He knew that Hess was concerned about the

DARPA facility affected by the landslide in North Carolina. But Platt sensed there was something more than just concern. By the time they reached Hess's office, Platt could hear the older man's raspy breathing. Perspiration beaded on his upper lip and forehead. Platt watched him as they took their seats, careful not to let Hess know that he saw him using both hands to steady himself as he dropped into the club chair. His office was massive and included a huge desk and floor-to-ceiling bookcases. There was also a sitting area with a small kitchenette in the corner.

'Should we have some coffee?' Hess asked.

Platt knew the offer meant that Hess wanted his guest to make and serve it. He didn't mind. He was on his feet before he answered with 'That sounds good. I'll make us a pot.'

'Little Ellie Delanor,' Hess said, shaking his head and smiling. 'She turned out to be a beautiful woman. She was all knobby-kneed and skinny as a girl. She has her father's eyes. Reminded me how much I miss him.'

'I never had the pleasure of meeting Colonel Delanor.'

'He was one of the best men I ever knew. I'm glad to see his daughter is on our side.'

Platt knew 'our side' simply meant a public official willing to stay out of the way of their jobs to research and develop what was necessary to keep the military and US citizens safe. He wasn't sure what made Hess think Ellie Delanor was on their side. As soon as they had left the conference room, Hess was handed a subpoena by a young staff member whom Platt recognized as one of Senator Delanor's.

He said nothing, however, as he scooped and measured coffee grounds from the economy-sized, discounted can. The man could more than afford one of the fresh-ground designer brands and still chose this one. Platt saw it as a telltale sign that the genius behind so many innovative and technologically advanced ideas still liked to keep some things just the way he'd always had them.

'I need to ask a favor of you, Benjamin,' Hess told him as Platt handed him a ceramic cup that rattled against the saucer as soon as the two were in Hess's brown-spotted hands.

'I already told you, Abe, I don't mind testifying. The committee should hear about all the groundbreaking research USAMRIID is working on. All of us could be affected by the results of this hearing.'

'And I appreciate your help, but that's not what I was going to ask.'

Hess pursed his lips to take a sip as he held up his finger, a familiar gesture that Platt knew meant to hold on a minute and he would explain.

'I'm concerned about the facility down in North Carolina. If there's an investigation, it could be messy, especially now, during these hearings. I wonder if you might know someone, perhaps at the FBI, who might be able to go down there. Someone who would be discreet.' Then he waved his hand and said, 'You know, someone on our side.'

Again that term, only this time it brought Platt to the edge of his chair. 'How badly was the facility affected?'

Hess shrugged as if it weren't a big deal, but his eyes flitted back and forth across Platt's face without settling.

'It's too early to know. I haven't been able to talk to Dr Shaw yet. I've asked Peter Logan to find out what's going on. He promised to send down a few of his people.' He glanced at his wristwatch and shook his head in disappointment. 'I expected to hear from him by now with an update.'

Platt knew Peter Logan. He was a soldier, not a scientist, and Platt had never quite understood why Hess had taken him under his wing – so to speak – even making him a deputy director. But that was what Hess did with many young men, including Platt. He saw potential where others did not, and as a result fostered an amazing loyalty. There were men who would literally take a bullet for Colonel Hess. Platt wondered if Logan was one of them.

Logan and Platt were about the same age. Both had served in Afghanistan and Iraq, though Platt served as a medical doctor and surgeon and Logan as a platoon leader. He wasn't sure why he didn't like the man.

'Why the FBI?' Platt finally asked when Hess didn't offer anything else.

'They will, most likely, be the ones asking questions if something has gone wrong. I'd like to know we at least have someone who will be—' He stopped, as if to select his words carefully. 'Someone who will be on our side.'

There was that phrase again, as though they were schoolchildren choosing up sides for a game of flag football.

'What exactly was at this particular facility?' Platt asked.

Another shrug from Hess, and Platt noticed how slumped his shoulders had become.

'I'm not sure at this time. You know we purposely allow our facilities and directors much leeway for their research.'

Platt did know that. There were dozens, perhaps more than a hundred, research facilities across the country like the one in North Carolina. Giving them a generous amount of independence was an attempt to relieve them of the many constraints the politicians tried to saddle them with. Platt understood all too well from his own experience at USAMRIID how much politicians could get in the way. Everyone wanted a cure for Ebola but few wanted to know the deliberate and tedious process it took to develop a serum or vaccine. Until recently they couldn't even experiment on human cases.

'I do know Dr Shaw, who's the director of this facility,' Hess told him. 'She's a brilliant woman. Very impressive. I doubt there's a virus she wouldn't be able to replicate.'

Platt felt a knot tighten in his stomach with the sudden realization.

'Hold on, Abe. Are you saying there could be Level 3 or Level 4 samples at this facility?'

'You can't find cures without having the samples.' When he saw Platt's concern, he continued, 'They take every precaution to keep them safe. Our laboratory lockboxes are made to withstand a terrorist explosion.'

'But can they withstand the destructive forces of a landslide?'

The phone began to ring on Hess's desk, interrupting them. Before Platt could offer to get it for him, Hess struggled to his feet, shuffling as quickly as he could to pick up the receiver.

'This is Colonel Hess.'

Platt watched the colonel's face as he listened to the caller. The downturned mouth, the taut jaw, the perpetual lines in his forehead remained unchanged. The perfect poker player except for his eyes, which again darted from side to side, giving away his worry.

He was quiet for almost a minute before he said, 'I'll get back to you with instructions.' And then he hung up.

He stayed behind the desk, leaning against it as if needing an anchor. This time when he looked up at Platt, he couldn't hide the anxiety.

'One of the scientists was found.'

Platt waited to see relief that never came.

Then Hess added, 'He's dead.'

'He died in the landslide?'

'No. Probably before. It appears that he was shot in the head.'

18

HAYWOOD COUNTY, NORTH CAROLINA

Creed kept his palms flat against the tiled wall and let the warm stream of water course over his battered body. Beside him, Bolo was doing the same, standing still, head down, and enjoying the spray.

After he examined Creed, the medic, named Kevin, had taken him away from the noisy gymnasium that was being staged to accommodate the rescue crews. He had led Creed and Bolo down a long hallway to a small locker room with a private shower and bath. Creed guessed it was normally used by the high school's coaching staff.

He couldn't shake the pressure from inside his

head. His ears were ringing and if he moved too quickly he got dizzy enough to see stars. Kevin had barely left them when Creed had caved to his knees, emptying his stomach in the toilet. Bolo kept close the whole time, nudging Creed and allowing him to use the big dog's back to help him get to his feet. Even now the dog kept so close his side touched Creed's leg. Every once in a while he noticed Bolo looking up at him.

As soon as Creed felt he had his balance back, he knelt down again, only this time he ran his hands over Bolo. He let the water help him clean and examine the dog's back, his legs, his neck and chest. Gradually Creed felt the dog relax his muscles, and he didn't tense when his owner palpated his sides and belly.

Suddenly another wave of nausea washed over Creed and he stopped. Leaned his forehead against Bolo's side and felt the dog's muscles go rigid. Creed waited, head pounding, ears ringing. There was nothing more in his stomach to churn but acid. Bolo stood still, also waiting. Then the dog twisted his neck to look back at Creed. He didn't move his body away, letting Creed continue to lean on him.

'I'm okay, buddy,' Creed told the dog, but he still didn't move. Right now the slightest motion threatened to drop him. And Bolo seemed to know this.

He remembered the medic showing him his helmet. The back had cracked like an eggshell.

'You're gonna feel like a truck hit you then backed up and ran over you,' Kevin had said to him.

He told Creed they could transport him to the nearest hospital to get X-rays, that he was almost certain Creed had a few broken ribs. Creed had refused the transport, but agreed to have Kevin wrap and treat him after he scraped the mud off.

He wasn't sure how much time had gone by. How long had he been on his knees, eyes closed, forehead nestled against Bolo? He hadn't heard the door open. Hadn't sensed anyone else's presence.

'Mr Creed?'

He heard Kevin's voice but still didn't move.

'You doing okay?'

The man was older than Creed, shorter but lean and muscular. Callused hands suggested he had another job – perhaps part-time – or a hobby that required other skills. He had been careful when he examined Creed earlier, experienced in knowing how much pressure he could get away with. But now he stood across the room, waiting for permission.

'Wishing the room would stop tilting.'

'Sure I can't talk you into that ride to the med center in Clyde?'

As if he needed to prove it to himself as much as to Kevin, Creed pushed himself to his feet, holding on to Bolo with one hand and the wall with the other. He needed to catch his breath while he shut off the water and grabbed a towel.

'I'll be okay. Just need some rest.'

He bent to dry off Bolo and bit his lip when the pain in his chest took him off guard.

'You have anyone who can keep an eye on you tonight?'

'This guy right here.'

Kevin didn't look pleased. He was digging in his medical duffel, pulling out bandages, ready to work on Creed's body again.

'How's the dog doing? The one we dug up?' Creed asked, remembering he wasn't the only patient in the ambulance back from the slide site.

'About as good as you. Battered but stubborn.'

'She gonna be okay?'

'I think so. She actually didn't refuse to be taken to the animal hospital.'

'What'll happen to her?' He remembered Vance saying that all the other passengers in the car they had pulled up out of the mud were already dead. Her entire family, gone.

'If there's no other family or friends to take her, she'll probably go to a shelter.'

'Can you do me a favor? If there's no one else, would you make sure I get her?'

'Seriously?' Kevin looked up at him. 'The rescue of that dog almost got you killed. You sure you want it?'

'It wasn't her fault.' Finished with Bolo, he grabbed another towel for himself. 'Can you do that for me?'

The guy shook his head like he still couldn't believe Creed wanted the dog. He filled his hands with scissors and ACE bandage, but when he looked up again, Creed could see the hint of a smile when he said, 'Sure, I can do that for you.'

19

NEWBURGH HEIGHTS, VIRGINIA

Maggie O'Dell grabbed the ringing cell phone off her nightstand. Eyes too bleary to see the caller ID. Instinct from too many late-night calls made her simply answer.

'This is O'Dell.'

'I woke you.'

The surprise in Benjamin Platt's voice was warranted. O'Dell rarely slept more than a few hours a night, and even those were interrupted by nightmares. Some of which Ben had experienced firsthand. If she'd had her way earlier tonight, he would have been there beside her.

Theirs was an odd relationship. Friends wanting to be more, but neither willing to give in and admit it. Too many ghosts. Too many expectations. Too much discipline. Or both just simply cowards.

'I must have fallen asleep for a change,' she laughed. Eyes focused now, she glanced at the glowing faceplate of the digital alarm clock. It was 1:36 AM. 'Let me guess. You haven't been to bed yet?'

He had stopped over earlier on his way home. Her Tudor-style house in a suburban, private neighborhood wasn't anywhere close to Fort Detrick and definitely not on his way home from the District.

His excuse – or what he had said – was that he wanted to find out about her friend Gwen Patterson, who was recovering from a mastectomy. But he also wanted – maybe needed – to talk about the upcoming highly publicized and overly politicized congressional hearing.

She let him talk while they enjoyed a couple of beers on her patio, watching O'Dell's dogs play in her backyard. They laughed at Harvey biting at lightning bugs. The sun had set before Ben arrived. While they sat in the dark enjoying a pleasant buzz from the alcohol, O'Dell wanted to ask him to stay the night. The last month had been a tough one. Something about cancer and the thought of possibly losing her closest and oldest friend had left her with a hollow feeling.

But she didn't ask.

What was worse – he didn't suggest it, although all evening she sensed there was something he wanted to ask her.

And once again, they continued to play the worn-out game. Perhaps they were nobly protecting each other or selfishly protecting themselves. O'Dell didn't even know anymore.

Now, hearing his voice on the phone, she simply wished he was there with her.

'About tonight,' Ben said.

O'Dell pulled herself up and leaned against the headboard. So maybe he was feeling the same way she was.

'This hearing has been weighing on my mind more than I realized,' he continued. 'I don't mean to drag you into this.'

'You were only venting.'

'Actually, not just venting. I need your help, but I was waiting to hear back from Director Kunze.'

Raymond Kunze was the assistant director of the

Behavioral Science Unit at Quantico, and he was O'Dell's boss.

Now she was confused … and maybe a bit disappointed.

Before she could ask, he began to explain.

'There was a landslide in western North Carolina. One of DARPA's research facilities was affected. Yesterday a rescue crew found the body of one of the scientists. He'd been shot in the head.'

'And the other scientists?'

'We haven't heard from any of them. The first slide – the major one – happened about ten-thirty at night. Should have been minimal staff. Most of them live in the vicinity, so their homes may have been affected, as well. It's too early to know. Everything's still a mess. There were other bodies but no one's certain who they are. They may be from the facility or they could be others in the community who were caught in the slide. It's been difficult getting much coherent information.'

'So how is it you've already identified this scientist?'

He was quiet for too long.

O'Dell ran her fingers through tangled hair, pushing it out of her eyes. She leaned over and snapped on a lamp. Harvey looked up at her from the foot of the bed, then plopped his head back down. She didn't see Jake. The shepherd had taken on her bad night habits and was probably patrolling the downstairs.

When Ben still hadn't responded, she asked, 'What does this have to do with you?'

Ben was a medical doctor, an army colonel, and director of USAMRIID (United States Army Medical Research Institute of Infectious Diseases) at Fort Detrick. DARPA reported to an entirely different chain of command. And yet he was using 'we' as if this facility was one of his responsibilities.

'We're working with DARPA on several projects. Sometimes they can do things we can't. Many of their remote facilities, like this North Carolina one, work off the grid with little regulation or oversight. Vaccines, protective military gear – there's a wide variety of projects.'

'And this facility, what project was it working on?'

'Unfortunately that's classified.'

At first she thought he might be joking. He had a dry, sarcastic sense of humor, but the longer he hesitated, yet again, the more she realized he was serious.

'Let me get this straight,' and now she couldn't hide the irritation. 'I think you're getting ready to ask me to go check out why a scientist working for DARPA ended up murdered in the middle of a landslide, but you're not going to share with me what he was working on? Even though it may have been what got him killed?'

'I know it sounds odd, but I actually don't know yet. Details of each operation are on a need-to-know basis. Right now the concern is how this scientist ended up dead. And if there's still possibly a threat to the others who may have been at the facility.'

'Is there a chance it was a suicide?'

'I honestly don't know. Possibly. Again, details are murky. But you see the challenge. Until we find out what happened, it would be premature to release any information that could be harmful to the success of the operation.'

He sounded like a bureaucrat. Of course, as the director of a government agency and an army officer, he *was* a bureaucrat. But she still hated when he sounded like one. As an FBI agent for over a decade, she was officially a government official, too, but O'Dell usually found herself bucking the system. In her own defense, she did what she believed was the right thing. Unfortunately, others in the bureau didn't necessarily agree with her on what was right, especially if it wasn't politically correct. Unlike Ben, she didn't always play by the rules. And consequently, she had a reputation for going rogue. Which made her wonder why in the world he'd want her to go down and check on this.

'Everything has been happening pretty quickly. Peter Logan, a deputy director of DARPA, is trying to find out what happened to the facility, but the FBI will be in charge of the murder investigation. Because of the sensitivity of that facility's research, Colonel Abraham Hess asked if I could recommend someone we could trust to be discreet, and of course I thought about you.'

Ah, so there was her answer. It was her expertise he needed as much as her discretion.

He paused and she wondered if he was waiting for her to feel grateful or flattered. It was O'Dell's experience that when government agencies needed to keep secrets, it usually amounted to covering their own asses. But Ben had helped her several times, actually saved her life once. He didn't ask for favors. This had to be something terribly important to him.

'Of course, I'll do whatever I can.'

He surprised her when he said, 'You don't have to do this just because it's me asking, Maggie. You can say no.'

And this time his tone was gentle and filled with concern – the Ben she knew and respected and maybe even loved.

'I'll leave in the morning after I check in with Gwen.'

'It should only take a few days,' he told her. 'Logan already has some people down there. His assistant, Isabel Klein, is there, and he hired a K9 unit. The dog handler is someone Logan knew in Afghanistan. I believe he said his name is Ryder Creed.'

She had worked with Creed twice before. The last time only about a month ago. And suddenly O'Dell was glad they were on the phone so Ben couldn't see her reaction. Because she could feel herself respond involuntarily.

How was it possible that just the mention of Ryder Creed's name could send an annoying but pleasant rush through her body?

DAY 2

20

HAYWOOD COUNTY, NORTH CAROLINA

Dust blurred Creed's vision. He could taste it, clots of it stuck in his throat, trying to suffocate him. Somewhere on the other side of the mud wall he could hear Peter Logan telling his men to stand down until the dogman cleared the way. But when Logan appeared from around the corner, none of his men accompanied him. Instead, he was walking with a small boy.

Creed recognized the kid. His name was Jabar, but the men in the platoon called him Jabber because for an Afghan kid he talked a lot and fast, no matter which language he used. From what Creed had observed, Jabar spoke at least three, including English.

He guessed the boy was nine or ten going on twenty. The men thought it was funny that Jabar acted so grown-up, even bumming cigarettes off the men and smoking alongside them. The first time Creed met him, Jabar took one look at Rufus and backed away. It wasn't as if he was frightened but that he thought the dog was bad luck. He warned Creed that the other children in his village would throw rocks at dogs and if Creed didn't want the animal to be hurt he should not take him beyond the camp.

Jabar came and went as he pleased. The men barely noticed him, and if they did, they teased him. But even after a few weeks Jabar still kept his distance from Rufus. Creed had put it off as superstition, until that last day, when he discovered the real reason.

He was back there again, seeing it as if he were standing off to the side, watching and knowing what happened next but not able to change the outcome. So many warning signs. Why hadn't he seen them?

Jabar's bright white athletic shoes should have been a tip-off. A size too big and laced up around his long skinny legs. But the kid was always showing up with crap like that. Most likely the shoes came from Logan.

The two exchanged contraband on a regular basis. It was one of the things Logan expected Creed not to notice, or if he did, to look the other way. Especially since Creed had made it clear that he wasn't interested in 'free' designer sunglasses or athletic shoes or diver's watches. And he declined the experimental cough drops and cough syrup. He knew there was other experimental stuff Logan distributed to his men. That was the real reason for the gifts. Where or how Logan got any of those things, Creed didn't know and didn't want to know. He and Rufus would move on to the next platoon in another week or so.

Jabar showed up that day wearing a baggy jacket, a sleek zip-up windbreaker in addition to the white athletic shoes. The sleeves were rolled up to the kid's elbows, bulging with too much fabric and making his stick arms look even more fragile. Likewise, the rest of the jacket bulged, but in ways that indicated there was more than only Jabar's slight frame hidden underneath.

At first Creed thought certainly Logan must know that Jabar wasn't exclusively his little con artist. The kid was a hustler who could swindle and trick even someone like Logan.

But on that day Jabar jabbered faster and louder than usual. He had the swagger and belligerence of someone twice his age and three times his size. Creed heard him yelling at Logan, climbing on rocks and jumping down with his arms out, making the baggy sleeves look like wings.

Logan seemed annoyed but not alarmed. He cursed at the boy, then laughed at him, but it wasn't in jest. Instead it sounded too much like mockery, too much like he was daring the boy.

Rufus started whining at Creed's side, straining at the end of the leash. Nose in the air, neck hair bristling, tail curled, ears pricked forward. The dog was alerting.

That's when Jabar saw Rufus. Creed didn't notice that the boy's hands were balled up. The first rock he threw hit Creed in his temple. The next landed with a sickening *thud* against Rufus's shoulder. Jabar yelled at them, digging into his pockets, plucking out and throwing rocks, his arms swinging in exaggerated wild loops. Even Logan took a hit.

'What the hell are you doing?'

'He's loaded,' Creed yelled, pulling Rufus back along with him.

He saw the boy dig into the folds of the windbreaker. Saw the cord. Knew he'd never make it behind the boulder ten paces away. He snatched up Rufus, all eighty squirming pounds of him, and he dived for shelter as he heard the explosion. It blasted him off his feet.

Dirt and rocks crumbled, raining down. Burning pieces of metal shredded his back. The last thing he heard was Rufus's whimper before everything went black.

Creed felt the wet tongue licking his cheek. His eyelids were heavy. When he tried to open them it was as if sandpaper scraped against the lenses. Blurred figures danced in the dim light above him. A dog nose hovered, then the licking started again. Creed reached up and caught the small head between his hands, massaging the ears and containing the licks.

When his vision finally focused he was surprised to see not Rufus but Grace, his Jack Russell terrier.

'What are you doing here?' Creed asked the dog as his eyes darted around the large area, a towering ceiling with steel beams and massive light fixtures on low. The bed beneath him screeched under his movement and he remembered the small cot in the corner of the school gymnasium.

North Carolina. Not Afghanistan.

Landslide. No explosions.

Bolo butted his big head up against Creed's side. Grace scampered along the other. Just as he was trying to put the pieces together in his fuzzy mind someone said from behind him, 'It's about time you woke up.'

He twisted his neck to see Jason Seaver, his hired dog trainer. But he had left him back at his facility in the Florida Panhandle.

'What the hell are you doing here?'

21

WASHINGTON, DC

Maggie O'Dell stepped off the elevator and immediately felt the knot in her stomach tighten. She wasn't looking forward to telling her friend that she needed to leave her side for an out-of-town assignment. Last night, when she was leaving Gwen, O'Dell caught a glimpse of something in her friend's eyes.

Gwen would deny that it was fear. She had tried to put up a strong front even this summer after the realization had sunk in that she had breast cancer. For too many months she had sought second and third opinions, as if searching for someone – anyone – who might tell her something different from the inevitable truth. O'Dell had watched the brilliant psychiatrist, who for decades had counseled generals and politicians for a living, retreat into a state of denial when faced with her own frightening battle.

Gwen was fifteen years older than O'Dell. They had become friends while O'Dell was a forensic fellow at Quantico and Gwen an independent consultant on criminal behavior. Their early days had been spent poring over files and crime scene photos, looking for signature details and motives, sometimes doing so while sharing cold pizza and warm beer into late-night hours. Not exactly the bonding experiences of ordinary friendships.

Almost ten years later it still surprised O'Dell how a sophisticated and mature woman like Gwen had put up with a wet-behind-the-ears newbie like her. Truth was, she still looked up to Gwen as a mentor. She counted on her strength and counsel. Gwen was the only person in her life whom O'Dell cared about unconditionally. Gwen had always been there when she needed her, and a few times when O'Dell didn't even realize she needed her. Now it was her turn to repay Gwen, if only she knew how. And if only Gwen would let her.

For the last week O'Dell had spent as much time as possible with Gwen, taking vacation time from her job. During Gwen's hospital stay O'Dell had sat by her side, giving up her post only when she knew Gwen's significant other, R. J. Tully, would be there. And even then, she stayed perhaps longer than necessary, almost as if making certain that Tully was okay, too.

O'Dell had partnered with R. J. Tully on dozens of FBI cases before he and Gwen fell in love. To O'Dell they seemed an unlikely couple. Gwen was pearls, oysters Rockefeller, and evenings at the Kennedy Center. She was a gourmet cook and kept her kitchen, her home, and her office meticulous. Tully, on the other hand, couldn't seem to go a day without getting a stain on his tie or his shirt cuff. He was tall and lanky and loved to eat but wasn't picky. Their last road trip, O'Dell had watched him devour – and delightedly so – a honey bun with a month-old expiration date from a rest stop vending machine. But despite all that, O'Dell trusted him with her back. More important, she trusted him with her best friend.

Last night before she left she had asked if there was anything she could do for Gwen. Her friend thanked her, but O'Dell knew Gwen wouldn't ask for help, just like she wouldn't admit how frightened she was. She looked completely uncomfortable and so very vulnerable in the ill-fitting button-down shirt – an item far removed from her fashion style, but necessary to accommodate the drain tubes. Then she shook her head and said that she was glad to be home. But before she looked away O'Dell caught something in Gwen's eyes that didn't look remotely like relief. Just like she wouldn't ask for help, Gwen would never admit that she was frightened. But O'Dell had seen a flicker of fear, maybe panic. Something that whispered, *Please don't leave me.*

And O'Dell had no idea what to do about it.

Maggie O'Dell had grown up too soon, taking care of herself from the time she was twelve. She had to, after her father's death and her mother's downward spiral from beloved wife and mother to suicidal alcoholic. The independence and emotional detachment, perhaps even the lack of trust that she had learned as a child, came in handy in her profession as an FBI agent specializing in criminal behavior.

However, those same traits that helped her to excel at her job were a hindrance in her personal life. A busted marriage only added to her distrust and to the barricade she built inside herself. It took such effort to let anyone in, and with few exceptions she no longer even made the effort. In these last several months, and in particular the last two days, it had struck her like a dagger to her heart. She couldn't imagine what her life would be like without her best friend. She could not lose Gwen Patterson.

Now, walking down the hallway clutching the vase of flowers, she felt a sense of how small and inadequate the gesture was. How little difference it made. How totally helpless she felt. She didn't have a clue as to what she was supposed to do.

She used her key and let herself into Gwen's condo, announcing her presence as soon as she stepped in. As she made her way to Gwen's bedroom, she suddenly felt guilty that she was more comfortable dealing with killers and dead people than she was taking care of someone she loved. She hated that when Ben asked her to go to North Carolina she didn't mind cutting short her vacation time. What was worse – she was almost relieved.

O'Dell was surprised to find Gwen asleep and alone. On tiptoe, she placed the vase of flowers on the window ledge alongside the others. She had racked her brain trying to find some other display of her feelings, only to come up empty.

'Calla lilies,' Gwen said from behind her.

'I didn't mean to wake you.'

Gwen waved a hand at her, gesturing that it made no difference, then pointed at the chair next to her bed, inviting O'Dell to come sit beside her. But even as she obeyed, O'Dell couldn't help noticing how drained and pale her friend's face was. She still hadn't gotten used to seeing Gwen with her golden red hair chopped short in preparation for what was to come.

'How did you know calla lilies are my favorite?'

It was the first smile O'Dell had seen in days.

'Sometimes I remember stuff.'

'You mean stuff other than details about killers and dead bodies.'

O'Dell's turn to smile, pleased to hear the familiar ribbing.

'There's something I need to ask you,' O'Dell said as she sat down.

'It's okay. I already know.'

'What are you talking about?'

'Kunze called me.'

'He called you?'

'He wanted to know how I was doing.'

'Are we talking about the same Raymond Kunze?'

Gwen smiled again. She had worked with the man on a case last spring, acting as a consultant. O'Dell suspected Kunze ended up very fond of Gwen. Most men were. It was after working together on a case that Tully had fallen for her. But that Kunze would actually call to see if it was okay to pull one of his agents away from Gwen's bedside – that was beyond anything O'Dell would have expected.

'He promised that you wouldn't be away for too long. A few days at most. Something terribly classified. Bodies unearthed after a landslide? Obviously not victims of the landslide, I gathered.'

'No. One of them has a gunshot wound. They believe it happened before all of the slides began.'

'All of the slides? There's more than one? Are they still happening?'

A slip of the tongue. O'Dell needed to backtrack. She didn't want Gwen to worry. But she knew there had been more slides and smaller ones were expected. Conditions hadn't changed. It was still raining. Part of the area where one of the bodies had been discovered was already flooded.

Instead of telling her friend any of this, O'Dell said, 'Hey, I've handled worse. It can't be as bad as a hurricane, right? Or chasing a serial killer through graveyard tunnels?'

O'Dell meant to make light of this assignment, but her friend didn't smile. Instead Gwen added, 'Your last out-of-town assignment landed you in a pit of scorpions.'

She couldn't argue that fact. Some nights O'Dell awoke from her regularly scheduled nightmares swatting at her arms and batting at her hair. It would take a special compartment in her mind for her to forget how it felt to have them scurrying across her body, stinging her over and over again.

'I'll be okay,' she told Gwen, this time serious, all joking set aside.

Then she caught and held her friend's eyes, and she could see that Gwen was thinking the same thing – how quickly, once again, they had reversed roles. But going down for a few days to deal with a couple of dead bodies wasn't anything close to her friend's battle. It certainly wasn't a life-or-death matter, or at least that's what O'Dell thought at that moment.

'Are you doing this only because Ben asked?' Gwen wanted to know.

'He's done a lot for me without asking for anything in return.'

'When you care deeply about someone you don't expect anything in return.'

O'Dell knew Gwen wasn't Ben's biggest fan. She thought he was playing mind games with O'Dell. By telling her that he couldn't be in a relationship with any woman who didn't want children, Gwen said he was only testing her, pushing her to make a decision.

O'Dell didn't want to hear it. Instead she tried to change the subject and found herself suddenly saying, 'Speaking of scorpions, Ryder Creed's there working the North Carolina site with one of his dogs.'

'Really?' And now her friend was smiling again. O'Dell had confessed to Gwen about her attraction to the man the last time she had worked with him. 'Well, now that makes things interesting.'

22

HAYWOOD COUNTY, NORTH CAROLINA

Creed watched Jason shovel in ham and eggs like a man who hadn't eaten for a week. He didn't even put the fork down to pick up a biscuit or the glass of water. Creed couldn't help thinking the kid was already learning some one-handed bad habits. At the same time he sort of admired his survival skills.

The community had set up the high school gymnasium with cots for the rescue workers. The school cafeteria was right next door. Volunteers prepared meals, trying to accommodate the different shifts, and even providing sack lunches.

Creed and Jason took up a corner table out of the

way, where they could also feed Grace and Bolo. He glanced down at the dogs and noticed that both of them ate slower and with more manners than Jason. Creed grabbed the last biscuit from the plastic basket and Jason noticed, stopping long enough to look sheepish about having devoured three to Creed's one.

'I drove most of the night,' Jason said by way of explanation. 'Nothing open after midnight.'

'Usually Hannah packs me a little something.'

'Oh yeah, she made me a couple of sandwiches and a thermos of coffee.'

Creed raised an eyebrow, but now Jason was preoccupied with slathering butter on his last biscuit.

Both men were in their twenties – Creed at the end and Jason at the beginning – but Creed realized the gap between them was a cavern when it came to many things, including appetite.

'She was pretty worried about you,' Jason said.

'Hannah worries too much.'

'She didn't even want me waiting for Dr Parker. Otherwise we could have rode together.'

'Dr Avelyn's coming?'

'I guess she got a call from some organization she belongs to.'

'VDRA,' Creed said. 'Veterinarian Disaster Response Assistance. That's good. That means she'll help set up the decontamination process for the work dogs, too.'

'Yeah, I saw about a half-dozen dogs and trainers getting in this morning.'

Creed had convinced Hannah a few years back that they needed to have a veterinarian on-site at their facility. Avelyn Parker had her own practice with two other vets in Milton, Florida. When Creed built a clinic on his property, he convinced her to spend at least two afternoons a week there, paying her a generous monthly retainer that covered emergencies, too.

It made more sense having a vet come to them instead of crating and driving dogs continuously for even the basic services. But Dr Avelyn had been adamant about being a volunteer member of an organization and needing to be ready to go at a moment's notice. VDRA was one of several organizations that sent veterinarians to disaster sites like this one. They set up protocol for decontamination and were ready to treat any working dogs that got injured while on duty. They were also ready to treat animals harmed by the disaster – like the dog Vance's crew had found buried in the car.

Thinking about that poor scared dog, Creed said to Jason, 'Hannah shouldn't have sent Grace with you.' He glanced down at her, and she was staring up at him from the mention of her name. He patted her, keeping his voice conversational and trying to leave out his concern. 'She's too small for this kind of terrain.'

'I don't think Hannah expects her to work. She said she's been missing you.'

That's exactly what Hannah had told Creed when they talked just an hour ago. Although from the tone of her voice he suspected that Hannah thought he needed Grace to lift his spirits more than Grace needed him. Either way, Creed couldn't deny that her presence always made him feel better. He had a special connection with each of his dogs, but Grace – whom Hannah called 'Amazing Grace' – seemed to bring out things in Creed that even he didn't know existed.

'I don't like this man, this Peter Logan,' Hannah had said to him earlier, after explaining that Logan had called last night insisting K9 CrimeScents was obligated to send backup. He had demanded this only seconds after he told her that Creed had been buried under a landslide.

Creed knew she was giving him a way out. She would handle the business end and the consequences if he wanted to cancel the job assignment. But if Logan thought he had a debt that needed to be repaid, he wouldn't allow a cancellation.

One of the cafeteria ladies came by with a carafe of coffee, refilling their cups without asking.

'Get you boys anything else?'

'We're good, thank you,' Creed said, shooting Jason a warning when he saw the kid look at the empty basket of biscuits. 'This was all delicious,' he told the woman, sending the crinkles in her face into a smile.

'How 'bout the dogs? I'm sure we've got a couple ham bones back in the kitchen.'

'That's very kind of you, but I've got to keep them on a special diet.'

'Oh sure, I never even thought of that. We heard about you getting caught in that last slide up there.'

She pointed at the cuts on his face. The medics told him the one above his eye probably needed stitches, but they butterflied it instead. Said it was too close to his eye and neither of them wanted to be poking a needle there.

'We sure appreciate you all being here. You need

anything, just holler. I'm Agnes. I'm here for the long haul.'

He nodded his thanks as she went on to the next table.

Creed had spent almost an hour in the boys' locker room shower trying to restore his body while he ignored all the bruises and cuts. He still felt like he had mud in his ears and gravel scratching his eyes. His chest hurt. They suspected he had a broken rib or two. The medic had wrapped him up after his shower and Creed swore the bandage felt like it was crushing his lungs. But he'd had broken ribs before and knew better than to remove the wrap.

He shifted in his chair and realized he must have winced from the pain, because now Jason was watching him. Finally finished eating, Jason sipped his coffee. Sipping, not gulping. Maybe there was hope for this kid after all.

'So what was it like?' Jason asked.

'Breaking my ribs?'

'No, being buried alive.'

23

Creed guessed that he hadn't thought about it like that. Not yet anyway. Buried alive seemed so ... final.

He reached for his ceramic mug, wrapping his fingers around it instead of using the handle. It smelled good and strong, just the way he liked it. He took a sip, taking his time to answer, and when he glanced across the table at Jason, he saw that the kid was waiting, willing to give him a chance to consider it.

'After I quit trying to fight it, it was actually kinda peaceful.'

'Kinda like going to sleep?'

'No dreams, though. More like hallucinations.'

They were both quiet for a while, then Jason asked, 'You suppose that's what dying's like?'

'Maybe. You didn't feel it with your arm?'

Creed knew that Jason must have been close to dying, having lived through an IED explosion that had literally blown off the bottom part of his arm.

Jason shook his head. 'I guess I went into shock. Everything sort of happened in slow motion. I didn't know my arm was gone until I woke up later in the hospital.'

That was the way it had been for Creed, too. One minute Jabar was grabbing for the cord on his suicide vest and the next thing Creed knew, he was waking up in a hospital reaching for Rufus. Yelling for him, then trying to climb out of bed to go look for his dog. But Rufus hadn't been harmed. Creed's body had protected the dog. Protected him so well that he was considered well enough to be reassigned to another handler and get back to work. Because that's what the military did back then. Dogs were classified as equipment, given numbers that were branded into their ears. Rufus was N103 and he was fit for duty.

Creed knew all this too well. He had been ready to sign up for another tour of duty just so he and Rufus could stay together. And a stupid kid that Peter Logan had allowed to come and go in and out of their camp had blown everything apart.

'You suppose when you plan it that it's that peaceful?' Jason asked, interrupting Creed's thoughts. 'You know, just like going to sleep?'

Creed had lost track of what they were talking about. 'Plan what?'

'Death.'

'You mean like suicide?'

'I've got five buddies that I served with – maybe more. I haven't stayed in touch with some. All we went through. We risked our lives every single day over there. We couldn't wait to get back home. But they get back and then decided to eat their guns or swallow a shitload of pills. One guy managed to hang himself.'

Creed watched Jason over the rim of his coffee mug. He didn't need to ask. He figured the kid had thought about it himself. Hannah had met Jason at Segway House, a place that took in returning soldiers who didn't have anywhere else to go or couldn't afford to return to their previous lives for one reason or another. He didn't know Jason's circumstances. He never asked. Figured he didn't need to know. They hired him to do a job. Offered him a chance to learn how to train dogs. Even provided a double-wide trailer on their property for his housing. If the kid was looking for therapy he should have stayed at Segway House or, at the very least, talked to Hannah and not him.

Instead of telling Jason this, Creed told him, 'My dad committed suicide.'

Jason stared at him. It wasn't exactly what the kid had expected of this conversation, but he didn't seem thrown by it at all. Finally he nodded and said, 'Because of your sister?'

This time Creed was surprised.

'How do you know about my sister? Did Hannah tell you?'

Jason shook his head. 'She didn't need to tell me. All you have to do is Google your name.'

Creed's sister, Brodie, had disappeared when she was eleven and Creed was fourteen. His dad was driving them back home, a daylong road trip from their grandmother's house. His mom had stayed to take care of his grandmother, who had been sick. They stopped at a busy rest area because Brodie needed to use the restroom. Creed's last image of his sister was of her skipping in the rain, the puddles lit up with orange and red neon from the reflections of eighteen-wheelers' running lights and the dozens of brake lights.

'How'd he do it?'

Appeared the kid had very little manners.

Creed glanced down and saw that both Grace and Bolo had lain down at his feet. Grace, however, was watching him. Of all his dogs, she seemed the most sensitive to his moods. She looked anxious. He dropped his right hand and she nudged it.

Finally Jason realized his mistake. 'Sorry. Just seems like if people talked about it more they might not actually do it.'

'Are you thinking about doing it?'

Another rescue crew came into the cafeteria, adding noise and distraction, but Jason kept his eyes on Creed's and Creed could see the answer.

'You accepted a puppy from me,' Creed told him. He leaned down and scratched Grace behind the ears. 'I understood you'd be around to take care of him.'

'A dog?' Jason half snorted, half chuckled, like he didn't think Creed was serious.

'There's been a time or two that these dogs were the only reason I stuck around.'

Jason got quiet and eyed him suspiciously, as if still waiting for a punch line.

'You don't owe Hannah a thing, and you certainly don't owe me, but you have an obligation to Scout. Yeah, a dog.' He sat up and leaned his elbows on the table, hands wrapped around his mug again. 'You take a dog in, you earn his trust, his unconditional love. If you think there's a chance that you might not be sticking around, then you need to give him back to me.'

'Seriously?'

Creed held his eyes, saw that what he was presenting was actually a decision for Jason to make, despite his attempt to make light of it now.

'Yeah, I'm serious. Most of my dogs have already been abandoned in some way. You need to remember when I found that puppy he was stuffed into a burlap bag with his siblings, ready to be tossed into the river. If you're planning on offing yourself and abandoning that dog again, you might as well give him back now.'

Jason's eyes flitted away, suddenly interested in the rescue members shedding gear and clanking trays and silverware. He looked at Creed again and there was still too much curiosity when he asked, 'Did you see your dad do it?'

Creed wondered if the kid had heard a word he'd said because he certainly didn't seem to take any of it seriously.

'No,' he told Jason, 'but I was the one who found him.'

Creed saw Oliver Vance across the room. When he spotted Creed he waved at him. He had shed his gear and, though still a giant of a man, he looked half normal. He made his way toward them.

Creed put his mug on the table with an exaggerated tap and told Jason, 'Time to work.'

'How are you doing?' Vance asked, pulling up one of the metal folding chairs. He swung his leg over it like he was saddling a horse, sitting on it backward so he could lean his arms on the back.

'I feel like I rolled down a mountain,' Creed told him.

The big man laughed, loud and hard.

'Actually, the mountain rolled on top of you.'

'Oliver Vance, this is one of my trainers, Jason Seaver.'

'Call me Ollie,' he said, holding out his hand to shake Jason's, and when he realized Jason's right hand wasn't there, Vance didn't flinch. He simply switched and offered his left one.

Then he looked at Creed, not wasting time and getting down to business. 'I heard that your Mr Logan wants you back up there to recover those bodies we found. Last night we pulled two more people alive out of the rubble of what used to be their home. They're pretty beat-up but there's a good chance they'll make it.'

'That's great,' Jason said.

Vance's eyes stayed on Creed's. 'Just got word that an eighty-two-year-old woman across the bridge over in the Hillcrest development's been missing since the first night. They got some flooding over there but houses are intact. None of the properties were affected by the slide. She has dementia. They think she might have walked off, looking for her daughter. They live together and the daughter got caught up in the downpours. Got home late. Found the front door left open. Family's been searching the woods. No sign of her. That's two nights she's been out in the dark, alone, confused, lost. Temperature's supposed to drop tonight so we can add cold to that list.'

'If she's still alive,' Creed said.

'That's true. I've got a few hours before I have to get back to work. I thought I'd run over there.' Vance glanced around the cafeteria. A group was leaving and waved at him. He waved back. 'All I know is there's a chance one of your dogs might be able to find her. Save her life if she is still alive. Those bodies Logan wants you to find . . . Hey, I know he's paying you and you gotta do the job.'

Vance looked around again, and Creed wasn't sure if he was expecting Logan to walk in the door at any minute. Then his eyes came back and locked on Creed's as he said, 'All I'm saying is that those dead guys aren't going anywhere. Maybe they can wait a little while longer.'

24

WASHINGTON, DC

Frankie Sadowski hated waiting. Butterflies had invaded his stomach. The palms of his hands perspired as he clutched the rim of his hat. His daughter, Susan, sat quietly by his side. They were told to stay outside the hearing room and asked not to wander far from the corridor. He tried to keep his mind focused on why he was there in the first place. The reason he had agreed to do this.

It all started with the reunion. They'd grown into old men who complained about their various health issues as though their surgeries were badges of honor. Frankie smiled at that. Once upon a time this same group bragged about their children, their promotions, even their golf handicaps. But this reunion was a litany of ailments. It wasn't long before the eight men realized each of them had gone through or suffered from too many of the same things: pulmonary infections, chronic respiratory problems, and pulmonary fibrosis. Duke Hutchins had had five heart bypass surgeries. Calvin Clark was getting ready for his fourth.

At first they had laughed. By the end of the evening they were elbowing each other in smaller groups, whispering their suspicions. Was it possible that their time in the service had had anything to do with so many illnesses?

Frankie shared their concerns with Susan, who was a nurse. Immediately she said it was a strange coincidence. She started doing research. Frankie had never even heard of SHAD until she explained that it was an acronym for Shipboard Hazard and Defense. The tests were part of Project 112 and were conducted secretly from 1962 until around 1974. She told him about veterans getting sick.

The government, of course, had denied any such tests until 2002. Since then Congress had held hearings, ordered study after study, tried to enact legislation – but all of it had simply put off doing anything about the servicemen who had been exposed. And consequently, it allowed the VA to deny those servicemen any benefits or compensation.

Frankie figured they would just keep putting it off until all of them were dead. He wasn't sure how anyone had managed to bring it back to life. Another congressional hearing. Another possibility of getting some help for his friends.

Frankie's buddies had christened him their crusader. Slapped him on his back and wished him well. They even took up a collection among themselves to pay for Frankie's flight to DC. He felt bad about that. None of them had extra money sitting around. He hadn't asked for their money or their trust. He simply wanted answers, and he wanted his friends to finally get the medical benefits they deserved.

Frankie started coughing and Susan offered him a bottle of water. He took it and sipped. The cough had gotten worse. He hadn't told Susan about the blood he'd hacked up the other day. At Segway House he was afraid Hannah would notice that her little dog named Grace could obviously smell his cancer. Hannah had barely finished telling him that the dog was capable of doing just that when Frankie noticed Grace staring at him, long and hard.

Now all Frankie cared about was that if he could help Gus and the others, then this would be worth it. He thought about Gus being worried about his grandson. The kid had come home from Afghanistan without one hand. What they'd been through might have caused them some health issues, but at least all his buddies were in one piece. He couldn't imagine going through life with only one hand.

Maybe they were silly to be fixated on a stupid government test that had been kept secret for sixty years. Even Gus had said that if they were able to keep secret who killed Kennedy for this long, how did they ever expect to bust open Project 112?

Frankie shook his head thinking about Gus. He knew his friend didn't have much time left, either. Frankie knew Gus was dying, too. But he knew this not because Gus had told him. He wasn't sure Gus even knew. Nor did he know it because of his daughter, who was a nurse at the care facility that Gus went to. If she did know, she'd never divulge that information to her father.

No, Frankie knew that Gus was dying because

that's what the man from the government had told him. The man who had visited him a week ago and suggested what Frankie should and shouldn't say during his testimony.

Frankie and his friends knew the government might try to discourage them from testifying. They had battled with their VA for years now. And they knew there were others like them who had been fighting this fight for many more years. All of them had been denied benefits, first because the government denied Project 112 and Project SHAD even existed, then because the government's studies claimed those projects did not hurt any military personnel. Of course, their own studies would not show any evidence despite private studies showing the opposite.

So Frankie wasn't surprised to have someone visit him and try to guide his testimony. He didn't care. It was too late to worry about himself. But he didn't want the others to worry, so Frankie hadn't told Gus about the man. He hadn't told Susan, either. In fact, he hadn't told a single soul.

25

Senator Ellie Delanor tried not to be distracted by the reporters and cameras. They were sprawled below in the tight area between the row of senators on the dais and the table where witnesses would testify. Some of them looked ridiculous squatting or sitting on the floor, bracing their foot-long lenses. She hid her delight in their discomfort. It was nice to have them focused on someone else for a change.

'To fully understand Project 112,' Dr Hess was telling the committee, as if he were a professor in control of a classroom instead of an expert who had been subpoenaed to be there, 'you must understand the nature of the world at that time. There was a deep, almost visceral, distrust after World War Two. Russia had been an ally out of necessity only. But the Russians were happy to split the spoils of war. For the most part we imported German scientists and their minds. The Russians got the laboratories and they literally disassembled them piece by piece and transferred them to places inside their borders. We had no idea what may have been left in those labs.'

He reached for his glass of water, slowly taking a sip as if he wanted the committee to sip on that last bit of information. When Senator John Quincy started to say something, Dr Hess held up his index finger and stopped the senator cold.

Ellie couldn't help being fascinated by the colonel's air of authority. At first glance he looked like a stodgy old man, his shoulders sagging as if from the weight of all the medals that decorated his dress blues. His full head of hair had gone thin; the feathery wisps barely covered the brown spots on his scalp that matched the ones on the back of his hands. But there was something about him – the piercing blue eyes, the confident gestures – that demanded respect.

'We knew the Russians were way ahead of us in the chemical and biological warfare department. The Cold

War was something no one had ever experienced. Two countries literally had the ability to wipe each other off the face of the earth and take everyone else with them. We were all looking for alternatives to nuclear weapons. President Kennedy ordered his secretary of defense, Robert McNamara—'

'With all due respect, Colonel Hess,' Senator Quincy interrupted, and this time managed to ignore the scowl he received, 'I don't believe we brought you here today for a history lesson.'

There were a few nervous smiles and nods as the cameras turned. Even the reporters seemed to be waiting for some kind of confrontation.

'How old were you, Mr Quincy, in 1962?'

'I'm not sure how that's relevant. I certainly wasn't old enough to enlist, if that's your point.'

'I'm guessing you were in elementary school, perhaps?'

'Actually, if you must know, I was five years old. Not quite in school yet.'

'Ah, I see. That explains things.' Hess was now nodding and smiling, and Senator Quincy suddenly looked uncomfortable, as though he'd missed out on a joke. 'You never experienced the school drills of the

1960s, where children were instructed at the blaring sound of an alarm to climb underneath their desks in preparation for an attack. You probably don't remember the evening news showing soldiers slogging through the jungle or the daily casualty report from Vietnam. You have no idea, Mr Quincy, what kind of fear and panic existed at that time because you were simply a child. But let me tell you as someone who was there, someone who helped prepare us for a new generation of threat – we were in the race of our lives.'

Ellie, along with the other senators, kept quiet. She wasn't born until a decade later. Project 112 – from the little homework she had done – existed between 1962 and 1974. As far as she was concerned, these hearings seemed more for show than anything else. Veterans who were unknowingly a part of Project 112 had been attempting to get VA medical benefits and disability since 2002, when the Department of Defense finally acknowledged this project even existed.

There had already been hearings that produced studies that later went nowhere. A legislative bill passed the House in 2008, only to die in the Senate.

Maybe that's why she hadn't bothered to read beyond those facts. She already knew this hearing would most likely be only for show, too. And that's why she had signed up. Why she had fought to be included. She needed to look like she was fighting for veteran voters without really engaging in any controversy that could alienate her from the powers that be within Congress. It was a safe political bet for an embattled incumbent who needed to look like she was working hard for her constituents.

'These tests that a handful of veterans are complaining about nearly forty to fifty years later were not conducted with the intention of hurting them. These tests were to determine the vulnerability of US warships to attacks with chemical and biological agents that we understood could wipe out more than just our troops if used by a willing enemy. These weapons could wipe out entire cities. So excuse me, Senator Quincy, if I insist that knowing a bit about history is important in this matter.'

Without raising his voice Hess had managed to deliver a scolding that silenced the room. Except for the clicks of the cameras. Hess milked it, waiting patiently with a stone-cold stare that made Quincy squirm and shift in his chair. Ellie watched him give a slight tug on his collar, as if it were choking him to release the four words he finally said: 'By all means, continue.'

26

HAYWOOD COUNTY, NORTH CAROLINA

Daniel Tate had discovered an entire tunnel system. Fractured walls and splintered furniture made it a challenge, as did the many cables and electrical wires tangled in clumps or strung from one side to another. Ceiling tiles dangled, and in some spots he could see all the way up to the clouds. He climbed over burst pipes that spewed disgusting sewer mixtures.

This was nothing.

He'd been through much worse – a bombed village outside of Baghdad. He remembered the soles of his boots melting from walking on the charred remains. As long as he lived he'd never forget the smell of burnt flesh.

Earlier, searching through a caved-in storage room, Tate had hit the jackpot. He found night vision goggles, something that looked like a Kevlar vest but was lighter, and a helmet with two different lighting options. With a flick of a switch he could change from LED to infrared. The helmet and the goggles allowed him to see whatever he wanted without filling his hands with a flashlight. And he needed his hands to pull and shove and push as he made his way through the tunnel system.

Despite all the gadgets, he had yet to find a pair of shoes. He had found bottles of alcohol and cleaned his bruised and bloodied feet by pouring stinging amounts of the liquid over them. Then he carefully wrapped them with ACE bandages. If he couldn't walk – and if necessary, run – it wouldn't matter what weapons he had.

Now if only he could shut down the prickly feeling that stabbed at his skin like a thousand tiny needles. His nose kept bleeding even after he had stuffed wads of tissue up his nostrils. And his heart raced in his chest so fast and so hard it felt as if it would crack his ribs open at any moment.

Enough time had gone by that Tate suspected these

things were probably side effects of the drug that Dr Shaw had given him. He tried to tell himself that they would wear off.

He heard a noise and stood stock-still. Cocked his head and listened to see if he could identify it. By now he knew the sound of pipes belching or walls cracking. There was something different about this sound. He didn't have to wait long. He heard it again.

It came from somewhere in the tunnel ahead of him. A rhythmic *clack-clack*, then the crunch of glass.

Footsteps!

27

'They stopped after they pulled out the first body and realized it could be a crime scene because of the gunshot wound,' the National Guardsman explained. He looked back over his shoulder as he led O'Dell and the medical examiner through the mud. 'We've had someone securing the area since last night. The only problem is that some of it's underwater now.'

His long legs made it an effort for him to slow his pace to keep close to theirs. He maneuvered around the debris sticking out of the ground. The slight incline didn't seem to affect him. O'Dell, however, found herself slipping just when she thought she had her balance. And still, she put out her arm to help the older woman beside her.

She guessed that the woman's slight limp made her look frailer than she actually was. She swatted away at O'Dell's offer and continued marching in big rubber boots that swallowed her feet all the way up to her knees.

When O'Dell first met Dr Gunther she found herself thinking they had reached the bottom of their barrel – so to speak – and that all the more capable law enforcement officials must already have been overwhelmed in rescue efforts. The dead – or at least the dead not associated with the landslide – would have to settle for whoever was left.

Ben had made it sound like this was a top secret mission. Yet from the moment O'Dell arrived, she couldn't help thinking the government had pieced together a slapdash team. She was told that Peter Logan was held up in DC and that his assistant, Isabel Klein, was supposed to meet her. But instead, a young National Guardsman named Ross showed up in her place.

Dr Gunther looked as if she herself had been through the landslide. Her long gray hair was tied back and tucked into a headscarf, but strands waved across her face. One end of her scarf wrapped tightly around her neck and into the collar of her baggy jacket, as if she were prepared for deathly cold temperatures. The rain had stopped for the moment, leaving a gray sky masked behind a thick cloud of fog. The breeze brought a damp chill, but nothing that warranted Dr Gunther's wardrobe.

The top of the woman's head came to O'Dell's chin, and the oversized clothing made her thin frame look even smaller. And though she didn't use a cane or a walking stick, she moved with a pronounced limp. Even when it slowed them down she made no excuse or explanation for the handicap.

'And where is that first body being kept?' the medical examiner asked.

That surprised O'Dell. She had presumed Dr Gunther had already been involved.

'It's my understanding a temporary morgue has been set up a couple blocks from the high school.'

'A couple blocks from the high school?' The woman's brow furrowed as she tried to retrieve what must have been familiar territory. 'You don't mean Ralph's Meat Locker, do you?'

The guardsman's ears flushed with his answer before he said, 'I wouldn't know, ma'am. I haven't been involved in that aspect of the recovery.'

By now they were at the top of the incline and O'Dell could see three guardsmen setting up equipment. They already had two tents, one most likely being used to shelter the remains. O'Dell could hear rushing water. Not more than a couple of feet away a muddy stream raced over rocks and debris.

Guardsman Ross pointed at the water and said, 'The last slide broke that free. Someplace underneath is where they left at least one body buried.'

'Is this where the research facility was located?' O'Dell asked, knowing that one of the bodies had already been identified as one of the scientists.

'It's my understanding that the facility was located about a half mile up.' He pointed in the direction, but there was nothing that looked remotely like a brick building – only debris and mud.

'We're still trying to find it,' Ross added when he noticed O'Dell still searching. 'Landslides can dismantle buildings and relocate objects – vehicles, furniture, bodies – miles from where they originated. That body we think is under the water might not even be there anymore. We're waiting on the K9 unit to relocate it. Hopefully it didn't get washed farther downhill.'

'I thought the K9 unit was already here?' O'Dell asked, expecting to see Ryder Creed and trying not to sound disappointed.

'Actually, he and his dog found the bodies yesterday. Then all hell broke loose. It's my understanding he was buried under that last slide. If it wasn't for his dog, they might not have found him in time.'

'Is he okay?'

'Must be.' He checked his cell phone. 'Sounds like they're sending him back up here.'

28

Creed had to take several detours to get to the Hillcrest area. Vance had warned him that some roads and bridges might be ripped up a bit. That proved to be an understatement. Thick layers of fog replaced the rain, making it difficult to see chunks of the road missing until he was practically on top of them. But still, he was glad to be back in the driver's seat of his own Jeep Grand Cherokee. Even more glad to have Grace sitting in the back watching the road through the space between the front seats, where she could also see and catch her owner's eye every now and then. The girl was excited to be getting back to work.

He had packed what he needed for himself as well

as for Grace. Though Jason had insisted that Hannah hadn't meant for Grace to work the disaster area, she had still loaded a duffel bag with all of the dog's gear, including two extra pink squeaky elephant toys that Grace loved as her reward.

Vance had promised they'd do this quietly. He'd have his back if Logan had a problem with it. Creed had to admit he was surprised Logan still hadn't shown up in Haywood County. So it seemed possible that they might be able to offer this family some help with little attention. Possible until Creed saw a local TV van and camera crew waiting at the curb in front of the two-story house that belonged to the missing woman and her daughter.

He parked around the corner, making sure that the neighbor's house blocked them from view. He wanted to put Grace's vest on and slide on his own gear before drawing any attention.

Hannah always told him that publicity was a good thing. Over the summer she had even convinced him that it could help to locate his sister, Brodie. That's if Brodie was still alive. Creed couldn't hide the fact that the small possibility of that being true was one of the things that helped him get out of bed each day. But he and Grace had had their fill of publicity over the past months.

Okay, he'd had his fill. Grace was already prancing and wagging in the direction of the TV van. He ignored the camera crew even as they came at him. He ignored the female anchor, too, as she shoved a microphone in his face.

'What exactly will you and your dog be doing to help find Mrs Hamlet?'

When he didn't answer and kept walking she continued a barrage of questions.

'She's been gone for almost forty hours. Is this a cadaver dog? Does that mean you think she might be dead?'

He saw Vance in a group on the front lawn. When he noticed Creed and Grace he hurried up the sidewalk.

'Your dog seems so small,' the anchor said, still walking in front of him. Creed was trying to be polite and not shove her or the cameraman out of his way. 'Will you be bringing in other dogs?'

'Folks, please let the man and his dog through so they can get to work.' Vance stepped between Creed and the woman, opening his long arms to create a path, but more important, blocking the TV crew.

He led Creed up over the mud-slick lawn. Debris was scattered where the receding floodwaters had left the heavier items, like rocks and branches, pieces of siding, and a few shingles. Already Creed kept an eye on what Grace might step on. Grace was straining at her leash to greet the group that waited and stared at them.

Before Vance even introduced them, Creed had picked out the grieving daughter. The entire group looked exhausted. Clothes wet and mud-stained. Shoulders sagging. But the daughter, Charlene, was in the center. Her short blond hair was windblown, damp strands stuck to her forehead. Her eyes were bloodshot with swollen bags underneath. She was biting at a fingernail as Vance introduced them, and then she absently presented Creed with the same hand to shake.

'We've looked everywhere,' she told Creed. 'My fear is,' and she stopped as tears began to choke her words. A man standing behind her moved up and squeezed her shoulders. 'This is my brother, Lonnie.'

But the man didn't offer Creed his hand. Instead he eyed him and Grace suspiciously, keeping his hands on Charlene, more protective than comforting.

'I keep imagining that she's hurt,' Charlene continued. 'That she's stuck under some branches. She's just a little bitty thing. Barely a hundred pounds.' She dragged a sleeve over her runny nose. The fingernail found its way between her teeth again.

'I need to ask a few questions,' Creed told her, waiting for her eyes to quit flickering to Grace, then to her friends and her brother. They darted back to the woods that started at the edge of the cul-de-sac.

'Miss Hamlet?'

Finally she looked at him and offered a hint of a smile as she said, 'Call me Charlene.'

'Charlene, how advanced is your mother's dementia? Are we talking Alzheimer's?'

'Early stages. She gets confused very easily. Can't remember things. She doesn't recognize anyone except me.' She looked down at her finger. It was bleeding now. 'Some days I'm not sure she even recognizes me or if she's just pretending to.'

'What does she do when she's confused?'

Charlene had to think about this and her nose scrunched up as she did. 'Sometimes she sits down. Other times she paces, almost like she's looking for the correct answer.'

'Does she ever go outside the house alone?'

'No, never.' She shook her head to ward off more tears. 'She was probably worried about me. I tried calling, but sometimes she doesn't remember what the phone is.' She looked back at her brother as if she needed to convince him. 'Sometimes she doesn't know where the ringing is coming from. You know how hard of hearing she is.' Her eyes trailed back to the woods. 'I don't know if she can even hear us calling for her.'

Grace sat patiently at Creed's feet. He glanced down to find her looking at Charlene Hamlet, tilting her head from side to side, ears pitched forward, listening as though she were taking in all the information, too. She would definitely be focused on the woman's emotional state.

He'd already explained to Vance that Grace was an air-scent dog. She found dead people by the particular smells of decomposition that every human being gives off after death. She was also trained in rescue, just like Bolo. Live humans emitted particles of scent, millions that go airborne and are carried by the wind or get caught on items in the environment.

Most lost or trapped people ended up in remote

areas where there were no other people, so it didn't matter whether Grace could distinguish one person's individual scent from another. She was trained to simply find human scent. But in this case there had been dozens of people roaming through the woods already looking for Mrs Hamlet. They would have left human scent everywhere. And unlike trailing dogs or tracking dogs, Grace had never been trained specifically to take in an individual's scent off a personal item and then go find that same person.

However, she was trained for scent discrimination. That's how she had become a celebrity over the summer when she was able to track down illegal drugs hidden in anything from jars of peanut butter to a drug mule's stomach. And recently Creed had been working with her to recognize the scents of different illnesses, including viruses and cancer.

Still, he warned Vance that he wasn't sure she'd be able to do what they were asking here. In order to specifically find Mrs Hamlet, Grace would need to know definitively what the woman smelled like, independent of everyone else around her, and then understand that she needed to go find that scent despite the downpours, fog, and wind that could have taken Mrs Hamlet's scent far away from where the woman ended up.

When he glanced back at Charlene she was staring at him. So was the rest of the group, waiting, expecting, hoping.

'Is your mother right- or left-handed?'

'What the hell does that have to do with anything?' Lonnie asked.

Charlene looked back and forth between the two men.

'When a person's lost' – Creed kept his tone calm – 'they tend to move in the same direction of whichever hand is dominant. Right-handed people usually go to the right. Left-handed to the left.'

'Even if they don't know their right from their left?' Lonnie questioned him, and Creed could tell the man had already decided this was a waste of time.

'It's an involuntary reaction, so memory or thought doesn't necessarily affect it. Because they're always going in the same direction, sometimes they end up going in circles.'

'She's right-handed,' Charlene said.

Everyone continued to stare at Creed, periodically looking down at Grace or glancing at Lonnie. Creed was used to it. People were either skeptical, like Lonnie, or they expected to see a magic act and were waiting for it to begin.

'I'll need to take Grace inside your house. Is there a chair or perhaps even your mother's bed that hasn't been disturbed since she was last in it?'

'Sure thing.'

Charlene started to walk toward the house, but Creed reached out and stopped her.

'I'm sorry, but you won't be able to go with us.'

'What the hell?' Lonnie asked again, and this time he stepped in front of his sister, as if challenging Creed.

Now Creed could feel the others' suspicions, too. Even Vance shot him a look.

He tried to explain to Charlene. 'I'm afraid if you come with us, it'll confuse her. You live in the house, too. Your scent is all over the place. I need Grace to be focused on your mother's scent only.'

'Right,' Lonnie said. 'How do we know to trust this guy?'

'Lonnie!' Charlene's cheeks flushed. 'Mr Creed is here because I asked Mr Vance to bring him here.' To Creed she said, 'I am so sorry.'

'I can't promise this is going to work,' Creed told her. 'But Grace has made some amazing finds.'

Charlene looked down at the Jack Russell as if seeing her for the first time. She squatted down and offered Grace her hand, then petted her.

When she stood back up she said, 'The recliner in the living room is Mother's. The quilt that she uses to cover her legs is still bunched up in the seat. Upstairs, her bedroom is the first on the right.'

He nodded, then called to Grace. The entire distance to the front door he could feel their eyes on him. Grace pranced beside him, happy to find a couple of puddles to splash through.

Creed's head began to throb and his chest ached, reminding him of his tumble not even twenty-four hours earlier. He hated when families were on-site. Fifty percent of the time he would disappoint them. He hoped this wasn't one of those times.

29

'This is a totally inappropriate process for recovering a body,' Dr Gunther scolded the four guardsmen who stood towering over her, heads bowed though they had no control over those details.

O'Dell was impressed and mildly amused that this small woman – the word 'elfish' came to mind – could reduce these lean, tough soldiers with the command of her voice and her presence, despite her lack of physical stature.

'Even if Mr Creed's dog alerts to the exact spot,' Dr Gunther continued, 'how are Agent O'Dell and I supposed to retrieve the remains? Surely we're not expected to wade into those floodwaters and fish them out?'

O'Dell was thinking the same thing and could only imagine the force of the water knocking both of them off their feet. Although she had helped recover bodies from stranger places. This landscape reminded her of a past crime scene with dissected bodies stuffed into fifty-five-gallon drums, then buried in a rock quarry.

There were no manuals that dictated recovery instructions for many of the scenes she had helped process, so Dr Gunther's complaint about 'inappropriate' seemed a bit silly to O'Dell. But she also knew that coroners and medical examiners were oftentimes precise and detail-minded, with more experience in the laboratory than in the field.

'We were instructed to secure and assist,' Ross defended his team.

'Of course you were.' The woman's irritation bit through her stoic demeanor.

She glanced up at O'Dell. 'Well, Mr Logan's boss told me that *you* are in charge of this recovery operation. How would you suggest we proceed?'

O'Dell looked out over the rushing water. In several areas it had carved deep crevices in the mud. Downhill it widened and she could see debris riding on the surface. Branches tangled with electrical wire passed by.

Uphill it was impossible to determine where the stream began. The fog was too thick. But one thing she knew for sure – it didn't look like it would be slowing down to a trickle anytime soon. As if to emphasize that fact she heard a low rumble of thunder in the distance. She could feel Dr Gunther staring at her. The guardsmen waited patiently for her reply and instruction.

'We'll wait for Mr Creed and his dog. If they can give us a smaller area to search, we'll still need to stop the water or divert it.' She sought out Ross's attention. 'There must be some sort of equipment you have available that can send the water in a bit of a detour?'

He held up his cell phone and said, 'I can check.'

'Yes, do that, please.' Then to Dr Gunther, O'Dell pointed at the tent and said, 'Let's take a look at the remains that are not underwater.'

The older woman nodded and started a slow limp in that direction. Ross finished his text and followed. O'Dell fell into step alongside him this time.

'You've seen these remains?'

'Yes, ma'am.'

'Her title is agent,' Dr Gunther corrected him without turning to look back.

Ross looked to O'Dell and she simply ignored the

comment and continued, 'What equipment do we have to recover this body?'

'I was told to bring shovels and trowels. We have tarps and several body bags.'

O'Dell heard Dr Gunther making a *tsk-tsk* sound while she shook her head. Obviously she was not pleased. Again, Ross noticed and his eyes darted back to O'Dell, looking for instruction or absolution. She wasn't quite sure which.

O'Dell ignored the woman's reaction a second time and simply trudged through the mud. She had brought her own backpack with items she'd anticipated needing, including a digital camera, rubber gloves, and evidence bags. She imagined Dr Gunther's satchel held whatever she expected she'd need.

All four sides of the tent were screened in. Ross unzipped the door and held the flap open for the two women. The floor was uneven ground – or rather tamped-down mud – but other than removing the bigger pieces of debris, O'Dell imagined the rescue crew had left the scene the way they'd found it. The guardsmen had pitched the tent as carefully as possible so as not to disturb what was covered by a tarp in the center of the area.

Dirty water pooled between creases in the black plastic. Underneath, O'Dell could see additional pools. The body and tarp had been left in the rain until the tent could be set up.

O'Dell shrugged out of her backpack, found her digital camera, and took a few shots of the scene before they disturbed it. Then she nodded for Ross to remove the tarp.

He lifted the corner, slow and easy, folding it over to let the water run off and away. The pile of dirt underneath looked unremarkable, pocked with rock and gravel. The hole was only a foot in diameter. Even with the screened walls it was difficult to see because of the thick fog and cloud cover. Dr Gunther pulled a flashlight from her satchel and turned it on. As Ross uncovered the hole, she shot a stream of light into the shallow depths.

She stopped at the blue-gray skin washed clean by the rain before the rescue crew had covered it. At first glance O'Dell didn't recognize that it was part of a face until the light flicked over the chin, lips, and then an eye looking straight up at them.

'Oh, my good Lord,' the woman said, taking a step back so quickly she almost stumbled.

O'Dell reached out to help steady her, but Dr Gunther waved her off again. This time she looked embarrassed about her reaction. O'Dell watched her take a deep breath, then step forward. She moved in closer, pointing the beam of light back down the hole. And before she could control it, O'Dell saw her wince.

At that moment all O'Dell could think was that this was not going to be quite as simple as Benjamin Platt had made it sound.

30

Creed led Grace directly to the old woman's chair. Made her sit in front of it. He wanted her to focus on him instead of all the different sounds and smells inside the house.

He gave her a few minutes to glance around. An ear twitched toward the ticking of the grandfather clock. Her head jerked when an appliance's motor kicked on in the kitchen. Finally she settled down, shifting her weight and looking up at him.

He took the quilt gently from the recliner and held it in front of her nose, offering it to her for inspection. She sniffed at it and he let her put her nose inside the folds. There was a faint medicinal smell and Creed had no clue if that would help or hinder. Individualized scent was always tricky.

Like he had told Vance earlier, although Grace had proven herself in finding a variety of scents Creed had asked her to search out, she wasn't trained as a trailing or tracking dog. Those dogs – usually bloodhounds – were trained to sniff a particular item or article of clothing that belonged to a specific person, take in the tiny particles of human tissue or skin cells cast off by that person, and then go search for that specific scent. Yes, Grace could rescue lost people, but she did that differently.

Grace was able to rescue the lost by picking up traces of human scent that drifted in the air. The same scent that all humans give off. Throw in some extras like universal body odors from fear, anxiety, and perspiration. Maybe even blood. Grace didn't look for any specific person. She simply searched for human scent.

One of the reasons this worked was because people tended to get trapped or lost in remote areas. So if Grace picked up human scent in the woods, she searched for the cone of air, an area with the most concentrated scent. She zeroed in on where it was the strongest, and usually the person was nearby.

In this case, the forest around Mrs Hamlet's house was already filled with human scent from those who had been trying to find her.

'Grace,' Creed said, and waited for her eyes. He held up the quilt and very slowly said, 'Hamlet.'

He put the quilt aside, then waved for her to come smell the chair. She stood on her hind legs, sniffing. He patted the seat and allowed her to jump onto the recliner.

'Grace.' He waited for her to look up at him from her new perch. He tapped the arm of the chair and said, 'Hamlet.'

Her nose went to work on the fabric from the creases to the tufted buttons on the back where he could see a treasured strand of hair had snagged. When she was finished she jumped back down to the floor and sat down.

As a test he unsnapped the leash from her vest. He pointed at the door on the other side of the room, the entrance they had come in. The same door that Mrs Hamlet would have left through.

'Go find Hamlet, Grace.'

She took off across the room but skidded to a halt on the polished wood floor. She turned around, nose in the air, and headed back toward him. She stopped at the coffee table, her nose twitching. Then she sat down and looked up to find his eyes. It was her alert. Her way of telling him that she had found what he had asked for.

Then he noticed the TV remote and a wad of used tissues on the tabletop. They probably belonged to Mrs Hamlet. But it wasn't what he was looking for. He couldn't reward her even though these items most definitely had the same scent on them. He didn't want her to find Mrs Hamlet's things. He needed her to find the old woman.

Creed held back a sigh of frustration. The throbbing at his temple had changed to a continuous dull beat. Maybe this would never work.

31

Creed snapped the leash back in place. Last month at the Atlanta airport Grace had alerted to cocaine stashed in plastic bags and stuffed into jars of peanut butter. He knew she could do this if he could figure out a way to tell her what it was he wanted her to find. He decided to start at the last place they knew Mrs Hamlet had been.

He led her through the door onto the front steps. Because of the debris in the yard he hated to take her off the leash again. He dug into his daypack and pulled out a retractable lead that would give her twice the roaming distance. Grace was watching him closely. She knew he also kept her pink elephant in that same pack.

'Grace, find Hamlet.'

She looked back at the door, as if to say that Hamlet was inside. Creed didn't flinch. When he wouldn't indulge her with even a glance back, she started sniffing the air again. He knew he was asking a lot. Mrs Hamlet's scent had been washed away by downpours and blown around since she stepped out two nights ago.

Grace tugged at the end of the leash. Creed felt his adrenaline kick in when she took a turn to the right, a hard right. Mrs Hamlet was right-handed. This was a good start.

He saw the group on the lawn start to move toward him and put up his hand to stop them.

Grace strained hard now. She was pulling in air at a rapid rate. But she was keeping close to the side of the house. He kept his eyes on her paws, watching for glass or pieces of metal. She was following a narrow gully that the overflowing gutters had created between the foundation of the house and the beginning of the lawn.

At the corner of the house Grace took another hard right. She picked up her pace, skittering in the mud. There was more debris in the backyard than the front and Creed tried to slow her down.

The woods began about fifty feet from the back of the house. Fragrant bushes lined the yard, creating a natural barrier. In the fog it was difficult to see anything beyond them. The thick bushes had also acted as a stopgap for the floodwater that had come through earlier, gathering pieces of debris left behind. He worried that the grass held equal amounts of foreign objects that could pierce Grace's pads. His boots crunched glass and a knot tightened in his stomach.

Grace stopped suddenly, interested in something stuck in the bushes. She looked back at him and sat down.

Another alert.

He took a closer look and saw a couple more wadded tissues pierced on the prickly bush. To anyone else they'd simply look like garbage, but Grace insisted they were 'Hamlet'.

Creed glanced back toward the front of the house. Vance hadn't allowed anyone to follow. He remembered the daughter had found the front door open. The search party had spent hours going up and down the neighborhood and, from what Vance had told him, they had ventured into the forest that started across the street and at the end of the cul-de-sac. They had tried to track the footsteps of an elderly woman who had come out her front door on a dark and stormy night, thinking that she had gone looking for her daughter who hadn't come home.

They had done their best to guess the mind of someone old and confused with dementia. Had they looked in the backyard, they would have seen what Creed saw now – nothing.

'Good girl, Grace,' he told her in an even tone and not the excited, high-pitched one he used when she found what they were looking for. Still, her eyes left his to glance at the backpack where she knew her pink elephant was waiting.

'Grace,' he said, and her eyes came back to his. 'Find Hamlet.'

She stood up and sniffed at the tissues. Glanced up at him.

They could have blown there from anywhere, even if they had belonged to Mrs Hamlet. Just when Creed thought they were at a dead end, Grace's nose started twitching. And once again she tugged and strained, pulling him toward the thick barrier of bushes. She turned right and led him along the row. At the end she took another right and headed back toward the house.

Before she got there she stopped in her tracks.

Her tail stood straight out. No motion. Ears perched forward. Nose up, twitching and sniffing rapidly. She turned right again but didn't go far. She circled and stopped. But she wasn't finished.

This time she took off and raced for the back line of bushes. She pulled Creed through a narrow gap where the branches didn't touch her but scraped and scratched at his jeans and snagged his shirt, ripping it before he could set himself free. On this side the grass ended and mud greeted his boots, sending him sliding. He kept his balance even as the forest floor sloped down. Grace didn't slow a bit.

In seconds the canopy above cut their light. The fog seemed to come alive, moving between the trees like smoke in the wind. Dampness settled around them. Branches dripped. The smell of earth and pine was overwhelming. Yet Grace's nose continued to work the air.

Creed glanced back up to get a sense of how far they had come, and he could no longer see the bushes that separated the Hamlet backyard from the forest. He knew that Grace was still leading him toward the right but it was subtle now. None of the sharp turns like in the backyard. He was starting to get concerned about how deep they were going. His head hurt. The cut above his eye throbbed a new rhythm of pain. Already he felt that his sense of direction was slipping away.

He wanted to reel Grace in. Take a break. Get both of them some water. Before he had a chance to do any of that, Grace skittered to a halt. She sat down and looked up at him, her eyes finding his.

Creed's pulse was racing, his breath uneven. His eyes darted around the area. The fog was thick along the floor of the forest. He squinted but all he could see were trees, downed branches, a pile of rubbish, leaves and pine needles, thigh-high shrubs, and vines growing from trunk to trunk. He scanned higher, looking for more tissues stuck in branches, pieces of fabric, anything that could have once been Mrs Hamlet's.

He glanced back down at Grace and she was staring at him hard. False alerts weren't uncommon. It happened. But not with Grace. He saw her eyes slip to his daypack. She was ready for her reward, getting impatient.

Creed took another look around, this time turning slowly and trying to take in the surroundings in small clips. The throbbing over his eye was causing it to twitch. Maybe it and the fog were making him miss something. He could feel Grace watching him.

Then suddenly she stood back up and casually strolled over to the pile of rubbish. It looked like someone's garbage dump with twigs and vines growing over it. There were pieces of cardboard, an old sofa cushion, cans and bottles, a tangle of rope and wet newspapers, along with other unrecognizable musty throwaways.

The tang was a mixture of smells, one of which could be human decomposition. Was Mrs Hamlet's body buried under this pile of garbage?

That's when something stirred beneath that mess.

Creed jerked back a step, but Grace's tail started wagging. She stuck her nose into the pile and a hand nudged its way out, reaching to touch Grace.

Creed dropped to his knees and started grabbing at pieces, pulling and tugging. Grace licked at the dirty fingers. Before he finished uncovering her, the old woman shifted from lying on her side. She was filthy – mud streaked her face. Strands of garbage dangled from her hair. Her clothes looked like part of the rubbish and so did her small body of bones.

She sat up on her own without Creed's help. He didn't want to alarm her by touching her, so he tried to use his eyes to look for cuts and blood. He scanned her arms and legs to check if he could see any bones protruding.

'Mrs Hamlet, are you okay?'

It seemed like a silly question to ask a woman who had been under a pile of rubbish for two nights.

Her eyes were bright and anxious and didn't leave Grace as she petted the dog with muddy, blue-veined hands. She stroked her from head to tail over and over.

'Aren't you the prettiest thing,' she cooed, and Grace continued to wag, even forgetting about her pink elephant for the moment.

Then suddenly the old woman looked up at Creed as if she'd only just noticed him. 'What in the world took you so long?'

32

Daniel Tate lay on his belly and watched from inside a bent metal air duct. He was proud of how quietly he had moved in the dark, the night vision goggles providing him views that the intruder didn't have beyond the stream from the handheld strobe light. Only one time did the metal creak beneath his weight, and he worried that it might crash down. The spaceman below didn't seem concerned, glancing up only briefly before going back to his mission.

Tate's first thought when he saw the oversized white suit was of a spaceman, because it covered the trespasser completely from the hood and glass shield all the way to the black rubber boots and gloves. But he knew it was a hazmat suit.

If he pushed back the paranoia and anxiety that pounded in his chest, Tate could almost convince himself that the spaceman wasn't there to destroy him. Instead, he seemed more interested in the battered metal cabinet and the black suitcase he'd found in the rubble.

The spaceman set the strobe light on a pile of debris where he could work with the light shining down. He opened a combination lock on the metal cabinet. Carefully he reached around inside until he found what he was looking for. Then his focus turned to the black suitcase.

Several times the spaceman tried to lift the suitcase, but it was too heavy. He then tried to drag it but there was no clear trail. The case made it only a foot or two before getting hung up in debris.

From his perch, Tate noticed digital numbers flashing on the side of the case, and a small red light blinking like the suitcase had a pulse. The spaceman fidgeted with the digital numbers, making them tick up and down until there was a loud click. With the click the light changed to green and the spaceman was able to open the lid.

Tate wanted to squirm and reposition himself to see over the man's shoulder. He was soaking wet with perspiration, hot from being inside the metal air duct. Still, he wanted to see what was inside the case. But in seconds the spaceman took what he wanted, stuffed something into a case of his own, and snapped the suitcase shut. Both cases lit up, each with a pulsing red light and with the same freaky rhythm that made them seem as if they were part of the same living organism.

Then the spaceman did something Tate didn't expect. He set aside the second case. Then he shoved the metal cabinet until it toppled on top of the first one. The cabinet's contents fell out, metal striking metal and glass shattering, burying the case.

Satisfied, the spaceman swatted a hand in front of his face shield, then grabbed his strobe light and left in the direction he had come.

Tate watched him maneuver his way down the tunnel until the light turned a corner and disappeared.

Tate waited. He wanted to make sure the man wasn't coming back. Just when he thought it was safe, he started to crawl out of the metal duct and heard another crash.

He jerked back inside and let his eyes search below

in the eerie green light of the night vision goggles. A large container had slipped from the overturned cabinet. It crashed and shattered.

Tate heard the hum before he noticed the contents. What appeared to be black specks scattered over the floor suddenly started coming to life, one by one flitting up, then suddenly gathering and moving together. They lifted up off the floor, a swarm of black. The humming grew louder as the swarm moved back and forth as if looking for the best escape route.

He ducked deeper into the air duct as the swarm moved past him. He recognized the buzz and caught a glimpse before it disappeared. And he wondered why in the world a swarm of mosquitoes had been kept locked up in a laboratory cabinet.

33

'It's been a while since I've had to dig up a body,' Dr Gunther told O'Dell.

Both were on their knees, carefully scooping. Ross and another guardsman took the plastic tub away when it got full, replacing it with a second one. The two men had the tedious chore of sifting through the mud for anything that might be considered evidence. O'Dell knew there was slim chance of that. No matter what had originally happened to these bodies – whether they were murdered or not – being caught up in the slide most likely had destroyed any trace evidence.

'I imagine you were surprised then when Mr Logan called you for this project,' O'Dell said.

She restrained herself from simply coming out and asking the woman why in the world she was here for such a supposedly sensitive mission. However, something in her tone must have tipped off Dr Gunther, because she shot O'Dell an irritated look.

'It wasn't Logan,' she said. 'I've never met the man. His boss and I worked together years ago.'

O'Dell nodded, satisfied. Of course it was something like that. It wasn't much different from Ben asking her. Old favors. Funny how they could feel an awful lot like payback.

'Your forensic background,' Dr Gunther began to ask, then she seemed to stop herself and reworded her thoughts. 'I understand you're an FBI agent. But you obviously have extensive experience in retrieving dead bodies.'

O'Dell hesitated, wondering if she should give the short, more appropriate answer. Somehow over the years, without a plan or strategy, she had become a leading expert in criminal behavior, specializing in dismemberment and ritualistic murders. Murders that often ended up being the work of serial killers. The doctor, however, was simply asking why she was a part of this mission.

'When you chase killers for a living, you find yourself examining their handiwork up close and personal whether you like it or not.'

'I don't understand why they think this body is not a victim of the slide.' She wiped a cloth over his face and shoulder, careful to clean off the mud but not rub hard enough to disturb or break the flesh. 'There's very little decomposition.'

'The mud would slow it down considerably.'

At that moment Dr Gunther grabbed for her flashlight.

'This is interesting.'

She flipped the switch and, instead of examining the shoulder more closely, the doctor pointed the light up higher, where something had caught her eye. Slowly she swept the beam over the portion of the man's head that was exposed. They only had a side view. The other half of his face was still buried in mud.

He'd shaved his hair down to the scalp. Dr Gunther's cleaning efforts now revealed circular marks, slight indentations that showed up in the harsh beam of light. The three circles were a bit shinier than the rest of his skin, as if some kind of greasy solution had been used that prevented the dirt from sticking.

O'Dell waited, expecting Dr Gunther to voice a theory, but the woman remained quiet. O'Dell could venture to guess the marks had been made by electrode pads. She wondered if his head had been shaved specifically for some kind of neurological test.

When Dr Gunther still hadn't said anything, O'Dell glanced at her. She could see the pinched furrow between the woman's eyes. Her thin lips were pursed tight. Without comment she moved the beam of light back to the shoulder and began wiping the dirt away. This time her fingers appeared more hesitant. Even as an image started to reveal itself, Dr Gunther slowed her movements.

Before the old woman had shifted her attention to the dead man's head, O'Dell noticed the corner of a tattoo starting to reveal itself on his shoulder. She suspected the yellow beak of an eagle. She could make out the top of letters curved above it and guessed it read: *US Airborne*.

Tattoos were often valuable in identifying a corpse. Ink pooled deep into the dermis, so even during decomposition if the epidermis had been shed, the tattoo actually showed up more brilliantly. But O'Dell expected this one might simply indicate that the victim had served in the military.

Dr Gunther stopped suddenly. Again she grabbed the flashlight with an urgency that warranted surprise. But again the woman remained silent and O'Dell was growing impatient. Was she not sharing her thoughts because O'Dell was an outsider? A federal agent?

'What is it?' she finally asked.

But now O'Dell saw what had grabbed the doctor's interest. Lower on the arm, close to the elbow, the skin bubbled up. Mean streaks of red-brown imprinted the areas in between.

'Burns?' O'Dell asked.

The doctor looked up at her and nodded. 'Maybe chemical burns,' she said.

O'Dell's eyes darted around the area outside the screened-in tent. If the chemicals were still present, would they have smelled them? And why in the world had they not been warned?

'Are you talking about chemicals leaked because of the landslide?'

'No, no. At least I don't believe so.' The woman shook her head. 'These would be serious chemicals administered to this individual to cause such a severe reaction. Most likely toxic.'

'Should we be in hazmat suits?'

But again Dr Gunther shook her head. She switched off the flashlight and struggled to her feet. She swatted at the dirt on the knees of her trousers before glancing back up at O'Dell. And when she did, O'Dell caught a glimpse of something beyond anger in her gray eyes. Something that resembled fear.

'What is it? What are you thinking?' O'Dell prodded.

The woman was packing up her equipment as she said, 'I think we need to have our young men here dig out this body as best they can and wrap him up. I'll want to take a better look at him after I can clean him up somewhere other than this hole in the ground.'

'But should we be concerned about touching him?'

She stopped and looked to be pondering this, then she shrugged and said, 'I have no idea. Perhaps you need to ask your Mr Logan.' And she started packing again.

'He's not *my* Mr Logan,' O'Dell spit out, reacting more than thinking. She wanted to tell Dr Gunther that she had never met or spoken to the man. But it wouldn't matter to the woman. Instead she asked, 'What about the body underwater?'

'Have them bag it up as well.'

'That's it?'

'This is not the scene of the crime,' the woman told her. 'What happened to these poor men didn't happen here.'

'Can you tell me, at least, where he might have gotten those burns?'

'I might have more for you after I've had a chance to examine him.' She waved her arms to indicate their makeshift surroundings. 'I cannot do that here.'

Before O'Dell could disagree, Dr Gunther was calling to Ross and explaining how she wanted him to proceed. She didn't even hesitate to check with O'Dell as she had earlier. Something had spooked the woman about the wounds, and O'Dell knew she wasn't going to get any answers right now.

Dr Gunther finished stashing her gear, her small hands moving quickly, dipping in and out of the pockets of her satchel. Without another word, she left on the same path they had used to come there – this time on the arm of a guardsman. O'Dell noticed the limp was more pronounced in her attempt to hurry away, as though she no longer had time or need to disguise the vulnerability.

As she watched the woman disappear into the fog, O'Dell could see the shape of a man coming up the incline. She caught a glimpse of the dog at his side and she felt an annoying flutter. But as he got closer she noticed the right sleeve of his jacket flapping in the breeze. It wasn't Ryder Creed.

34

'Is Ryder okay?' O'Dell asked Jason as she petted Bolo. 'I heard he got caught in a slide yesterday.'

'Oh, he got caught, all right. Completely buried. They thought they'd lost him.'

He must have seen her look of concern despite her best attempt to hide it. He quickly added, 'He looks like hell. May have broken a few ribs. Otherwise, I guess he's okay. He took Grace to look for an old woman who got lost in the storm.'

O'Dell thought of Dr Gunther again. Was this case simply too much for her? Was she in over her head?

'So you're stuck with Bolo and me.'

She glanced at him and noticed a defensive stance.

O'Dell had worked with Jason and Creed just a month ago to locate a crime scene in the backwoods of Alabama. She knew the young veteran was capable, though he was still learning. If Mr Logan wanted top-notch professionals he should have come to supervise himself. At this point, she'd take what she could get.

She stroked Bolo's lean, strong muscles. She had seen the dog in action before, too, and knew he could follow a scent even over water. And yet she caught herself glancing up the path, disappointed. It had nothing to do with having capable help. It had everything to do with the annoying uptick of her pulse just from the expectation of seeing Ryder Creed.

She was stingy with her emotions and more so with her heart. After her divorce she had promised herself no more romantic entanglements, because that was exactly how she viewed them: entanglements that strangled and sucked the life out of her. Even with Ben, there were more times when she was relieved they weren't 'together' than there were times when she longed for him.

But Ryder Creed was a dangerous distraction. He had kissed her twice – once catching her off guard; the second time with purpose and intention. But it wasn't just the physical attraction. There was a connection between them that she couldn't explain, one that unsettled her as much as it excited her. So far, she'd managed to stay clear, as if doing so would avoid the sparks that would most certainly lead to some sort of electric shock.

She introduced Jason to Ross, interrupting him as he continued to unearth the body under the tent. One of the guardsmen had accompanied Dr Gunther. The other two had left to make arrangements for the equipment they'd need.

The floodwater continued to gush and churn, carving an even wider path. It moved fast despite being muddy and dragging debris as it washed over rocks and chunks of concrete. There was no telling how long it might last or if this would now be a new channel of a river from farther up the mountain.

O'Dell watched, standing silently beside Jason and Bolo. She realized it was ridiculous to expect a dog to sniff out a body believed to be somewhere under the floodwater. Unless they were able to successfully divert the water, there was no way to recover anything that might be buried there.

'One of the first things I learned from Mr Creed is

never to send a dog into a dangerous situation,' Jason finally said, even as he noticed Bolo's nose held up high and working.

'Is it possible he's getting a scent? Or is it the body inside the tent?' O'Dell asked, although their backs were to the tent and Bolo looked to be sniffing the air over the water.

'From what I understand, all of this flowing in front of us could be carrying human scent.' He glanced at O'Dell before adding, 'You probably know that land-slides can rip apart a body, right?'

Actually, she didn't know that. Outside of hunting a killer during a hurricane, O'Dell had never worked a disaster site. This was supposed to be a favor to a friend. Just go check things out.

'It's tough on a dog,' Jason explained. 'Slides can unearth graveyards, too. Bolo's trained for both rescue and cadaver recovery. How long have these bodies been dead?'

'The one we started to dig up looks like less than a week. But that's my guess. You met the medical examiner leaving when you came up. She decided she didn't care to stay.'

She saw a hint of a smile as Jason said, 'I'm not

surprised. North Carolina's medical examiners' system has some challenges.'

'What makes you say that?'

'A buddy of mine died in a car wreck a few months ago. They said he lost control, slammed into a ditch culvert. Wasn't wearing a seat belt. Makes sense, right? Auto accident. No-brainer. The funeral director found four stab wounds in his back. One deep enough it punctured a lung.'

Those cases always made her stomach slide a bit. But they happened everywhere. 'Mistakes happen.'

'*Charlotte Observer* did a whole investigation. Found a lot more. Interviewed me, since I was one of the last ones to see him alive. His wife was arrested, though I never heard him say a single bad thing about her.'

'I'm not sure Dr Gunther is negligent.'

'Maybe not, but how long did you say the body in the tent's been dead?'

'I can only guess, but definitely less than a week.'

'But probably not from the slide, right?'

She didn't want to admit that just yet. 'I'm not sure.'

'So if they didn't die in the landslide, where did these bodies come from?'

She ran her fingers through her hair, slick with moisture from the fog. She couldn't tell for sure whether this man had been at the research facility just because the body of a murdered scientist had been found close by. Didn't Ross tell her earlier that objects could be moved up to a mile from where they were when the first slide happened?

And if this man was in the facility, she had no way to determine if he was also murdered. Besides, there was no way a killer could have predicted the landslide and hoped that these bodies would be treated as casualties. Now O'Dell wondered if the scientist could have been killed in an impulsive reaction to the disaster. Perhaps the murderer was taking advantage of the chaos. Attempting to protect something, or someone?

'That's what I'm here to find out,' she told Jason, but she was starting to realize that Benjamin Platt owed her an explanation.

35

O'Dell expected to leave Ben a message. She was surprised when he answered on the third ring.

'Maggie, are you okay? I just saw the newest weather forecast and was thinking about you.'

'Look, Ben, if you're holding back any information about these bodies, now would be a good time to tell me.'

She was up to her ankles in mud, and the damp fog had changed to a cold drizzle. If she wanted the latest weather report she wouldn't have been calling him. Yes, she was a bit impatient with him. Okay, maybe a little angry, too.

'I told you what I know. What's going on?'

'One body is literally stuck in the mud. The other is buried underneath what now looks like rapids. This is not a "go down and check it out" situation.' She let that sink in before she added, 'And I think you already knew that.'

Silence. Was he irritated about her accusation or feeling guilty that he'd sent her down without telling her what was going on?

'I'll see what I can find out,' he finally said. Before she could get irritated with that response, he added, 'Are you okay?' The tone was sincere and genuine, a concerned friend.

'I don't like to be left in the dark, Ben.' She took her anger down a notch, but she knew there was still an edge to her voice.

'Understood.'

'And why isn't Logan down here?'

'He isn't there with you?' This time he couldn't disguise his surprise.

'I haven't seen him and I'm at the site.'

Silence again. Enough this time that she pulled her phone away from her ear to see if she still had bars for reception. One. Maybe she'd lost him. She put the phone back in place and waited.

'Let me see what I can find out. I'm sure Logan must have gotten held up somewhere. I'll call you as soon as I know something.'

She almost pushed END when she heard him say, 'Maggie.'

She brought the phone back up and suddenly found herself holding her breath. 'Yes?'

'Be safe, okay?'

That was it? Why did she think it would be something else? Something like 'I love you'?

'Okay,' she answered, rolling her eyes for no one other than herself, thinking 'Okay' was as lame as 'Be safe.' What the hell was wrong with them? Were they both so gun-shy, so emotionally battered that neither of them could stand to bare their souls?

She pocketed the phone, jamming it deep, as if that would mean something. When she looked up she noticed that Jason and Bolo had wandered almost a hundred feet away to search the area alongside the floodwaters. Jason was staring at the ground. The big dog's tail was swishing back and forth in a rapid motion.

They found something!

O'Dell started walking toward them, dread filling her empty stomach. Ross noticed. He spun around to see what had her attention. Then he said something to his partner and left the tent. He trekked uphill, a diagonal line to O'Dell.

Jason's eyes darted up and found hers. He yanked at his jacket pocket, suddenly desperate to get Bolo's rope toy free. The dogs expected and needed to be rewarded. She'd seen Creed do it as soon as he knew it wasn't a false alert. From the look on Jason's face, this was definitely not a false alert. But even as she approached she still couldn't figure out what the object was.

Jason tossed the toy to Bolo and he caught it, prancing off, proud and pleased. O'Dell and Ross arrived at the same time. Both stopped within three feet of Jason and both stared at the ground.

There was a snarl of twigs and wet leaves. O'Dell anticipated another partially buried body. Something comparable to the one under the protection of the tent – face half stuck in the mud. But this was already unearthed except for the twigs and leaves.

The hand was severed just above the wrist and the fingers were still balled up in a fist. It almost looked like its owner had grabbed hold of something and had been wrenched away. Maybe washed away.

She glanced at Jason. The color had drained from his face but his eyes were intense and focused. She remembered his empty sleeve, and suddenly she felt a rush of heat crawl up her neck.

'Are you okay?' she asked him.

'I've seen worse,' he assured her, and stared down Ross when the guardsman noticed the connection.

She wouldn't insult him with any more attention. Instead she said, 'Are those teeth marks?' She squatted down for a better look. Both men joined her, though more slowly and apprehensively than O'Dell. Already she was yanking out her cell phone and taking several photos.

'Coyotes run in pretty much every county in North Carolina,' Ross said.

O'Dell slipped her phone back in her pocket and pulled out a fresh pair of latex gloves from another pocket of her windbreaker.

'That's probably what this is, right?' With a protected index finger she poked at the puncture marks on the back of the hand. They looked very much like impressions made by an animal's teeth.

'Would it rip it from the body like that?' Jason asked.

Dirt and dried blood prevented O'Dell from examining the dismembered area. All she could be sure of was that it hadn't been cut clean.

'You said earlier that landslides can tear a body apart,' she reminded Jason.

'It's just that it looks like the poor bastard was hanging on to something for dear life.'

She couldn't argue that point.

'Coyotes won't eat fresh meat,' Ross said.

'Excuse me?' O'Dell thought she might have heard him wrong.

'They'll usually leave it for days, maybe even a week, sort of let it ripen. I guess it's easier on their digestive systems. Probably why they left it.'

It confirmed what O'Dell already believed – that whatever had happened to these men must have occurred just before the landslide.

36

WASHINGTON, DC

'Mr Sadowski.' A young woman came out of the conference room and crossed the lobby to where Frankie and his daughter had taken up vigil.

She was the first person to pay any attention to them all afternoon. They'd been sitting waiting, taking a break only for a couple of sandwiches and mediocre coffee.

'So sorry, they won't be getting to you today.'

'What do you mean?' Susan asked. 'We've waited all day.'

'I know, I know. Some of the experts' testimony ran long. They'll probably be ready for you first thing tomorrow morning.'

The woman was the same clerk who had told Frankie he needed to be ready first thing that morning.

'Are you sure?' Susan was more annoyed than Frankie, and he hated that he'd brought her there to sit and waste her time. 'Because if it isn't going to be until afternoon—'

'No, no, I'm sure it'll be sometime in the morning.'

'But probably not first thing.'

As his daughter bickered with the clerk, Frankie noticed the senators and others leaving the chamber where the hearings had been.

'I'll be right back,' he told Susan as he wandered over closer.

He knew his own state senator was part of this committee. He was a volunteer for her re-election campaign. He'd met her briefly at a rally a few years ago in Pensacola, though he didn't expect her to recognize him.

When she came out of the chamber door, he called to her, 'Senator Delanor.'

Hat in hand, he approached her slowly. She smiled, but it was a tight, controlled effort to not keep walking. In this lobby she had to know he wouldn't be there unless he'd passed through security.

'I'm Frankie Sadowski,' he said, offering his hand. 'From Pensacola.'

She shook his hand, but her eyes were darting around as if she were looking for someone to rescue her, some excuse to pull her away.

'You responded to a letter of mine back in July,' he told her. 'You encouraged me to testify.'

He watched to see some recollection take place, but it never did. Now he was a bit embarrassed. Had the reply been written by one of her staff and placed with a stack of others simply for her signature?

'I'm glad to see you here,' she said. 'This committee certainly needs to hear stories like yours.'

'Senator Delanor,' someone called from behind Frankie, 'I have someone waiting for you.'

Frankie saw the relief on her face before she could hide it.

'If you'll excuse me.' She hesitated, as if trying to remember his name, then suddenly decided it wasn't necessary. 'I look forward to hearing from you tomorrow.'

He turned to watch her join the man who was waiting to deliver several folded messages and a tall cup of coffee. He was obviously one of her staff members.

She called him Carter. He had a headset over his neatly styled hair so he could talk on his phone without his hands, and from the way he chattered nonstop it looked like he was filling her in on a long list of things.

Frankie started to walk away when he noticed two men in dress blues who had just come out of the doors to the hearing room. One man was young, the other old, perhaps even older than Frankie, with wisps of white hair and stooped shoulders. They stopped to talk to another young man dressed in khakis and a leather bomber jacket. There was something so familiar about this man in the leather jacket despite the distance of fifty feet or more. Then the man looked over his shoulder. His eyes caught Frankie's before he turned away. He said something to the men and left.

Frankie stopped in his tracks and stared at the man, certain now, recognizing the clipped, confident gait. He felt the hair on the back of his neck stand up and a knot twist in his gut. It was the same man who had warned Frankie about testifying. And he was here with military men who had been a part of the hearings.

What in the world was going on?

37

Ellie waited until they were clearly out of earshot before she asked Carter, 'Did you recognize that man?'

'The old guy?'

She noticed he didn't turn to look at him again. Ellie did, however. She watched the tall, silver-haired gentleman take a seat beside the younger woman who had obviously accompanied him.

'He's testifying at the hearing.'

'I've got a long list of phone calls that you need to return. Where do you want me to start?'

They continued into her office, but she didn't glance through the papers he had handed her. It was after five PM. She couldn't think of anyone who couldn't wait, and Frankie San— No, not San, but Sadowski. She didn't even recognize the name.

'He said I replied to a letter of his, encouraging him to testify.'

Carter looked up at her and let out a sigh. 'We send out a ton of letters.'

'Form letters. It sounded like this was a personal reply.'

'And we send out a lot of those, too.'

He was off-loading a new stack of files and documents onto her desk, sorting as he piled.

'He said he was from Pensacola. My hometown. You'd think I'd remember that, at least.'

Carter was jotting on sticky notes and tacking them to several of the files he was leaving on her desk. She could tell he didn't care about Frankie Sadowski, but the man was testifying tomorrow. How many people had Sadowski told that she had encouraged him to come forward?

'Find a way to leak to the media that I encouraged one of my constituents affected by Project 112 to tell his story.'

Carter's head shot up. 'You're not serious?'

'Why not? Those people outside the Capitol are

asking that we finally listen to the veterans who were affected.'

'Listening and encouraging are two separate things. You don't even know what he has to say. What if he sounds like a crackpot?'

'Crackpot?' She smiled at him. It seemed like a strange word for someone his age to use.

'You know what I mean. This old guy probably doesn't have anything better to do with his time than promote conspiracy theories on the internet. What if he's a member of one of those radical groups?'

'He's here to testify. Senator Quincy wouldn't have allowed it if he was some radical crackpot. He said his staff vetted every witness, right?'

'I wouldn't know what Senator Quincy's staff does or doesn't do.'

She was getting tired of everyone in DC labeling people as radicals simply because they disagreed. There was something about Mr Sadowski that reminded her of Jimmy Stewart and the roles he played in the old classics like *Mr Smith Goes to Washington*. He presented himself to her as a gentleman and that was a rare quality these days, especially in this town.

'You're always talking about controlling the

message, Carter. So find a way to leak something positive. For God's sake, the man is from my hometown. At least make that connection before the media does or they'll spin it into something stupid.'

Finally he gave her a reluctant half grin. 'Let me see what I can do.'

'Oh, and Carter.' She stopped him as he was heading for the door. 'Find the letters.'

'Excuse me?'

'We keep copies of everything in this place.' She pointed to the boxes still stacked in her office: the copies of documents from the DoD. They were supposedly from as far back as the 1950s. 'I'd like to see Mr Sadowski's letter.'

'Who knows if the guy actually sent you anything.'

'We certainly have a copy of my reply. Find it.'

'It was probably a form letter.'

'Probably. Find it anyway.'

He frowned as he left. Ellie checked her wristwatch. Her fingers grazed the top of the pile he'd stacked neatly. Even the sticky notes poked out at different intervals so that she could read them with only a glance.

Then something struck her. Frankie Sadowski had

said he received her reply in July. How was that possible? She didn't even know about this hearing back then, or at the very least, it hadn't been on her radar. She didn't nag Quincy about being a part of it until about a month ago.

Ellie headed out of her office to catch Carter and get his take. She stopped. Then she took two steps back to hide herself against the pillar outside her office.

Carter was on the other side of the lobby talking to Senator Quincy. They were both looking toward the entrance where Mr Sadowski and his companion were talking to one of the clerks.

Carter whipped out his favorite notepad and started scribbling as Quincy seemed to be dictating. Then he clapped Ellie's chief of staff on the shoulder, pleased and satisfied. Carter was beaming and nodding. Both men set off in opposite directions.

By the time Quincy passed her office, Ellie was back inside, door closed. She stuffed her briefcase with everything she'd need. On her desk she spread open an innocuous file with a pen and pad beside it. She placed her coffee mug within reach so it looked like she hadn't left the building. Then she slipped out, heading for the back stairs.

38

Benjamin Platt hated that Maggie sounded like she didn't trust him. He knew her well enough to know that trust was a fragile commodity to her. That he had gained hers only to lose it in this way made him angry with himself. And it made him angry with Colonel Abraham Hess.

Hess had invited Platt to dinner. He knew the man was feeling pleased with how the congressional hearings had been going. He knew that Hess considered these hearings a mere excuse for Congress to cut the DoD's budget. They had reviewed Project 112 and Project SHAD twice before and done nothing.

Platt had watched his mentor deliver his testimony,

not only captivating his audience but controlling Senator Quincy and the rest of the committee. Now he wanted to celebrate and Platt was far from feeling any sense of victory. In fact, he had no appetite at all, but he wanted answers about North Carolina.

Earlier when Peter Logan met them after the hearing he seemed to have more questions than answers. He couldn't get ahold of his assistant, Isabel Klein, and although Logan made it sound like a simple communication problem because cell phone towers had been destroyed by the landslide, Platt could see it was yet another excuse. Frustrated, Platt mentioned that he hadn't had any problems getting through to Maggie O'Dell.

What disturbed Platt even more was that Hess and Logan didn't seem to be on the same page. Hess said something about a special team on-site and Logan looked surprised. He tried to hide it, but Platt saw the irritation. That's when Hess asked Platt to meet him for dinner and dismissed him with a nod of his head. As Platt left them he could hear Logan firing off more excuses. Platt glanced back in time to see Hess finally cut Logan short with a wave of his hand, and then he heard the colonel tell his deputy to 'get the hell down there'.

Now, several hours later, Platt found the colonel in their favorite corner booth at Old Ebbitt's. Hess was already enjoying what Platt knew would be a Scotch, neat. As Platt slid into the opposite side, Hess flagged the waiter, who came immediately.

'May I get you a drink, sir?'

'Coffee, black.'

Hess raised his eyebrows.

'Another Scotch for you, sir?'

Hess shook his head. As soon as the young man left, he said to Platt, 'What's wrong, Benjamin?'

'What's going on in North Carolina? Logan sounded like he had no information and yet it's been days since the landslide.'

'Logan.' He said the name like it left a bitter taste in his mouth. 'The man has potential. He was a good soldier. I met him when he was a platoon leader in Afghanistan. He was instrumental in testing some of our new products in the field.' He looked across the table at Platt. 'You know how important that's been?'

Platt didn't want Hess to get off the subject of North Carolina. He nodded, then asked, 'Instrumental enough that you made him a deputy of DARPA?'

Hess stared at him with narrow eyes, obviously not pleased with Platt questioning his judgment.

Before Hess could answer, Platt continued, 'There are dead bodies being recovered – one of them a scientist from your facility who may have been murdered. And Logan hasn't even been there.'

Hess held up a hand, stopping him just as he had Senator Quincy. 'Don't worry about it. I have a special recovery team there. They've already started to take care of things even without Logan.'

'So do you have any more information about the facility?'

'It appears it's buried. Gone. Completely shoved off its foundation and toppled somewhere under the mountain.'

Platt ran a hand over his face and held back his response as the waiter set a cup of coffee and a saucer in front of him.

'Don't look so troubled, Benjamin,' Hess said as he took a sip of his Scotch. 'Down there we can still control things. Up here is where the vultures will destroy us if we let them.'

By 'vultures' Platt knew the colonel meant political vultures. How could he look so content when an entire facility had been destroyed by a landslide and its staff members were gone, one possibly murdered?

'Have you been able to reach Dr Shaw?'

'No. Not yet.'

'By now you must know what was kept at the facility.'

'My team will take care of it.'

'Abraham, you asked me to send down an FBI agent. Is there a chance she might be exposed to something?'

'You know each facility takes all kinds of precautions. We have no reason to believe that anything has been breached.'

'What were they working on?'

Finally Platt saw a look of concern. Hess glanced around the noisy restaurant and scooted closer to the edge of his seat, placing his hands on his glass.

'In the 1950s we worked on a project to breed *Aedes aegypti* to use the mosquitoes as a carrier, a biological delivery system. The US Army actually did a small, limited trial, doing a release in Georgia and Florida. Probably too small to measure any level of effectiveness.

'But think about it for a minute. How perfect

would that be? If we could either breed insects that already carry certain diseases, like dengue fever or chikungunya, or perhaps infect insects with diseases or viruses, we could release them in areas without the enemy even knowing. Dr Shaw was fascinated by different delivery methods, especially organic carriers.'

'What exactly are you saying, Abraham? That she was working on using swarms of mosquitoes as a weapons delivery system?'

'Keep your voice down, Benjamin.'

'Do you know what viruses the facility had access to?'

'I'm working on getting—'

'No,' Platt interrupted, stunning the colonel. 'You *must* know by now.'

Platt waited out the silence, staring down the man he had respected and revered for almost two decades.

'You must not share this with anyone,' Hess finally said.

'You asked me to send someone I trusted, only so you could control the investigation and what information is released.'

'I assure you any dangerous pathogens are completely

safe. My team is in the process of recovering the lock-box that stores them.'

'How can you be certain it hasn't already ruptured from the pressure of the landslide? Everyone there could have already been exposed.'

'Because it emits a signal, and we're still getting that signal.'

Platt shook his head. As an army colonel and director of USAMRIID he knew the fine line they walked keeping civilians safe while trying to find new ways to help soldiers be more effective and keeping them safe, too. His life was filled with classified information. He worked in labs at Fort Detrick with viruses and pathogens that could wipe out a city if accidentally released. And he had, in fact, been at the helm of controlling an Ebola outbreak several years ago that could have killed hundreds if there had been a widespread panic.

'Twenty-four hours,' he told Hess. 'I'll give you twenty-four hours.'

'Are you threatening me, Benjamin?'

'I'm giving you a chance to do the right thing.'

39

HAYWOOD COUNTY, NORTH CAROLINA

By the time they made it back down the mountain, rain had replaced the drizzle. Ross dropped O'Dell, Jason, and Bolo at the high school. She had already checked the area for available lodging. The nearest hotel or motel was over fifty miles away and certainly not worth the drive with all the detours.

Ross had told them that one of the three community churches was housing and feeding the families whose homes had been destroyed. Since classes had to be canceled, cots had been set up in the school gymnasium for the rescue workers. They could use the locker rooms to store their gear and take a shower.

Hot breakfasts and dinner were being served in the cafeteria. Brown-bag lunches would be prepared and ready by eight AM.

'Just get your name on the list,' the guardsman had told them.

He pointed to the back of the long gymnasium. 'All three of you will need to go through Decon before you can enter the building.'

'Decon?'

'Sorry. Decontamination. All that mud we've been trudging through and digging up is considered contaminated. Landslides tend to produce a toxic cesspool. Most folks here have propane tanks for heating and septic tanks. We don't know how many have been breached. Not to mention all the insulation, asbestos, and other stuff. Basically they'll be hosing you off.' Then he shrugged and said, 'Not like we aren't already wet enough, huh?'

O'Dell noticed it was the guardsman's first attempt at humor. She studied his profile and realized he was much younger than she had initially thought. They were all exhausted.

On the drive down the mountain she had tried to get ahold of Dr Gunther, leaving two messages and a callback number each time. Ross had told her that the other guardsmen would be delivering the body they'd unearthed along with the hand to the temporary morgue, as per their instructions. She'd been hoping Dr Gunther would start her examination as soon as possible, but now doubted that would happen.

O'Dell, Jason, and Bolo followed the sidewalk around to the back of the long building. Other crews were pulling up along the curb, filing out and gathering gear. Sunset wasn't for another hour but the gray skies and rain would accelerate that.

'They served an excellent breakfast this morning,' Jason said, walking alongside her.

She glanced at him and saw that he was straining to maintain a casual tone. Then she noticed he was keeping Bolo tight on his other side, giving the dog a short leash with no alternative but to walk next to Jason, so close she imagined the dog was brushing against Jason's pant leg. And she could see the reason for the short leash. The line of hair that stood up on Bolo's back and pointed in the opposite direction – the line that defined him as a ridgeback – was now bristling with the rest of the dog's back and neck.

She remembered Creed saying that Bolo was

overprotective of him. That protection must extend to Jason. The dog eyed the other men climbing out of their trucks. His head pivoted to the sounds they made. He viewed them as a threat. This simple walk was far from his comfort zone. That was back up in the woods, along the floodwaters, where he could concentrate only on the scent he was asked to find.

'I'm parked in the lot just across the street,' O'Dell told him, getting a glimpse of it now. 'I need to grab my overnight bag or I won't have dry clothes.'

'Sure thing.' He nodded. 'We'll catch up to you at Decon.'

His tone was still even and casual, signaling that everything was fine. But she wondered if he realized his tight and strained posture was probably screaming at Bolo that everything was not fine. The dog was strong and muscular. Was Jason worried he wouldn't be able to control him with only one hand? Her own dog Jake – a huge black German shepherd – could knock her off her feet if he tugged suddenly.

She wanted to ask Jason if he'd be okay, but there wasn't any way to do that without contributing to Bolo's tension and making Jason even more self-conscious. Instead, she simply agreed she'd see them later and broke off in the other direction, trying hard not to look back.

O'Dell climbed inside her SUV to get out of the rain and immediately pulled out her cell phone. No messages from Ben. She tamped down her irritation. She didn't want to talk to him right now, anyway. Instead she called her boss, Assistant Director Kunze, and left him a message. Then she tapped another number in her phone's memory and waited.

Gwen had been disguising her depression for months now and the surgery had made that more difficult. O'Dell just needed to hear that her friend was okay. She never expected the cheerful and excited voice that answered.

'So have you seen him yet?' Her friend sounded like a teenager.

O'Dell couldn't help it. The exhaustion from the day caught up with her and she simply smiled.

40

Through the crowded Decon area, Creed was glad to see Dr Avelyn. Three large tents had been erected in what otherwise was a back parking lot behind the school's gymnasium. The line waiting to go through the process snaked around the corner of the building. Rescue workers had started calling it a day. And now they stood, wet and muddy, waiting their turn to be hosed down.

The rain was steady now with no signs of easing up, and nightfall would come soon. Creed felt what most of them were feeling – exhausted, hungry, dead tired, and yet reluctant to stop because they knew there might still be victims out there alive, buried under debris and mud, clinging to their last gasps. People like Mrs Hamlet, waiting out yet another night.

Creed had left Grace with the old woman while he found his way back up the hill. Before he left them he had entered their location in his handheld GPS's memory. He hadn't wanted to waste any time finding them again. When he reached Vance and Mrs Hamlet's daughter, he brought up the location and discovered a shortcut.

They were able to carry the woman to her anxious daughter and a waiting ambulance. And through it all, Grace had never left the old woman's side until they closed the medical van's doors. The little dog hadn't even complained about the pieces of glass buried between the pads of her feet.

Now Creed was eager to get Grace taken care of. There were only three search dogs waiting to be examined. He weaved his way through the rescue workers. When Dr Avelyn saw him, she waved and gestured for him to cut through.

Grace pranced among the booted workers, greeting them with a wagging tail. Some of them smiled and bent down to pet her. Others parted out of Creed's way when they saw Grace. By the time he reached Dr Avelyn's tented station, she was finishing her inspection of the last of the three dogs. When Grace recognized her, she could barely contain her excitement.

'Settle down,' Creed told her.

Dr Avelyn immediately contradicted his command. She squatted down, opened her arms, and called Grace to her. He unsnapped the leash and the dog flew on bruised and bleeding paws.

'I just checked through Jason and Bolo about fifteen minutes ago,' she told him.

'Good. I'm glad they're back. They okay?'

'Bolo's a little freaked by all the men.'

'I bet he was glad to see you, then.'

She smiled. 'I heard about your adventure today, Grace,' she told the little dog as she massaged her hands over Grace's body, feeling for signs of distress or wounds. She glanced up at Creed and gave him another smile. 'Sounds like you've had an interesting couple of days.'

'It's been crazy.'

'You look like hell,' she said. She pointed to the cut above his eye. 'You need to have that covered when you're working in the field.'

He reached up to finger it and her scold stopped him. 'Don't touch it!'

'I pulled some glass from her paws,' he said, wanting the attention back on Grace. 'But I think there's more.'

He dropped to his knees beside the vet, wanting to get a closer look for himself. Strobe lights hung from the frame of the tent, creating too many shadows. Dr Avelyn pulled on headgear and flipped on her own light. She grabbed a bottle of hydrogen peroxide and forceps, ready to get to work.

Creed lifted Grace up, cradling her back against his chest, his chin on the top of her head, making it easier for Dr Avelyn to get at her paws.

'This might sting, Grace.'

'She has a freakishly high tolerance for pain,' he told the vet, watching as she removed small fragments of glass and debris. Every time she dropped one on the stainless steel tray Creed wanted to wince.

'She's like her master.'

When Creed didn't respond, Dr Avelyn said, 'I heard you might have a few busted ribs. If you want, I brought the portable X-ray machine. We can take a look.'

'Medics hog-tied me with ACE bandage. Would you

do anything different if we found out the ribs were broken?'

'Not for a dog. I'm not sure for a person, but I'll check. An X-ray could show whether a rib's poking or threatening to poke something important. How's your breathing?'

'Okay, I guess.' He nuzzled the top of Grace's head. She was starting to get impatient with staying still. 'Almost done, girl.' Then to Dr Avelyn he said, 'My head hurts. Maybe I broke something up there.'

He smiled but she shot him a concerned look, one that made him regret mentioning it.

'They checked you for a concussion, right?'

'I guess. I don't know for sure. I don't really remember much. I was out for quite a while afterwards.'

'Ryder! That's like one of the top symptoms. Have you felt nauseated? How's your vision?'

'Vision's okay.'

'Do you remember what happened?'

'You mean being buried?'

She nodded. She was swabbing Grace's paws now.

'Not all of it.'

'Did anyone clear you today before you went back out?'

'Nope.'

'How do you feel right now? Any dizziness? Ringing in the ears?'

'Ringing off and on. No more dizziness.'

'No more? That means you had some?'

'A little. Right now the headache feels like someone's drumming a hammer into my head.'

'Some symptoms of a concussion can be delayed for hours. Even days. Sounds like you definitely had one. You might *still* have one.'

'Do you have something you can give me for the headache?'

'Yes.' She didn't hesitate in answering. She finished with Grace, taking one last look. 'No more work for you, Grace.' To Creed she said, 'She needs to rest for at least twenty-four hours.'

'Absolutely.'

'And so should you,' she told him. Then she looked up over Creed's shoulder at someone behind him and said, 'I hope you don't have any scorpions this time.'

Creed turned, surprised to find Maggie O'Dell.

41

'No scorpions,' O'Dell told Dr Avelyn.

The vet was referring to the last time the two had seen each other. O'Dell had fallen into a pit filled with scorpions. The thought of it usually made her shudder, but right now her focus was on Ryder Creed.

She hated that her heart seemed to skip a couple of beats as soon as his eyes met hers. Creed's clothes looked like he had rolled in the mud. His hair was slicked down. His face bruised and cut, jaw dark with stubble. But eyes bright and clear. The corner of his mouth lifted into a smile. Battered and dirty, the man still managed to look like the poster boy for *GQ* if they had an outdoorsman edition.

'What brings you down to this mess?' he asked.

'Official request.' And she left it at that. There was time later for business.

Both Dr Avelyn and Creed stood up. He still had Grace in his arms. When the little dog recognized O'Dell she started to squirm. He tucked her more securely under his arm and took a couple of steps closer for Grace's sake. Or at least, O'Dell thought it was for Grace's sake.

She offered the dog her hand to sniff and lick, then she petted Grace's head, careful so she didn't brush Creed's fingers.

Silly. Totally ridiculous. But she'd forgotten how powerful his presence was, and already she was annoyed that her pulse was racing and that she was avoiding his eyes.

'Did you and Grace find the lost woman?'

'Grace did. And we think Mrs Hamlet will be okay. She's dehydrated and worn out from being out in the elements for almost two days. Twisted her ankle. Otherwise she seemed okay.'

She felt his eyes run over the length of her. 'Looks like you've been out all day, too?' he said.

'Yeah, pretty much.'

She glanced down and realized her jeans were muddy at the knees and ankles, her boots caked, and her hair drenched like Creed's, despite her FBI ball cap. She had her overnight bag slung over her shoulder and even with her windbreaker zipped up she was starting to feel a chill.

'Jason told me about you getting caught in a slide yesterday. Are you okay?'

'You saw Jason?'

Before she could explain, a man coming out the side door of the gymnasium interrupted them.

'Dogman!' he called out to Creed. 'I've been waiting for you to get back.'

The man was shorter than Creed but lean and muscular. A bit older. White-blond hair, cut military short on the sides with a flap of bangs. He wore a leather bomber jacket, khaki pants, and expensive hiking boots that O'Dell immediately noticed didn't have a spot of mud on them.

'Peter Logan.' He stuck out his hand for hers, then crushed it in his.

'So you're Logan,' she said, returning the firm grip and watching his surprise. Actually, she didn't mind the crusher grip. She'd rather that than the soft, patronizing handshake that most men in authority extended to women colleagues. 'I have quite a few questions for you.'

He cocked his head at her and managed to keep his fake smile as he shot a look at Creed.

'I'm Agent Maggie O'Dell.'

Realization came over his face. 'Oh, so you're Ben's girlfriend.'

O'Dell felt the rush of heat travel up her neck.

42

Peter Logan was an asshole and Creed wasn't surprised to see that he hadn't changed in the seven years since he'd seen him last.

'You two know each other?' He looked from Creed to O'Dell and back to Creed, eyebrows raised like there was something inappropriate going on.

'We've worked a couple of cases,' Maggie told him.

Creed wasn't sure if he was irritated at Logan because he had embarrassed Maggie or because Logan knew more about the man who had an obvious hold on her heart.

Logan saw Grace. 'What's the deal, dogman? You bring the smallest dog you could possibly find to do a job for me? He doesn't look like he's even fifteen pounds soaking wet.'

Grace growled at him. Creed could feel the hair on the back of her neck rise up.

'Her name's Grace. And no, she's not working your project.'

'Yeah, I heard you didn't show up at the site.' Hands on his hips as if he still had a platoon to order around.

'Jason and Bolo did a great job,' Maggie said before Creed could answer.

Only then did Creed realize she was the FBI agent sent to supervise Logan's secret project.

'Yes, I heard you had a productive afternoon.' He wagged his head at Maggie in what Creed recognized as his familiar gesture of giving praise. That was about all anyone would get for pleasing him.

Grace was still rigid under Creed's arm, stiff-arming her paw against his arm. He could feel the slight vibration of a low, continuous growl. She was probably feeding off of Creed's animosity toward Logan.

'Until those floodwaters are reined in we won't be able to do much more,' Maggie said.

Logan's eyes darted around. Clearly he wasn't comfortable discussing it in the open, even though Creed could see no one paying attention to them. Even Dr Avelyn had gone over to the trailer set up for her and the others.

'We can talk about that later,' Logan told Maggie.

'Yes, that would be good if we could talk. I have some questions.'

'I'm sure you do.' He laughed like there was a private joke between them. 'You go get cleaned up. I'll see you in the morning.'

'Morning?' Maggie was visibly irritated. She glanced back at the Decon line, which had gotten considerably shorter. 'We should be finished in twenty to thirty minutes. Maybe we can talk over dinner. I heard they have a meal and a cot for us.'

Logan grinned and shook his head. 'I'm afraid I won't be staying here. I have other accommodations. But I'll see you both in the morning.'

To Creed he said, 'And I expect you up on the site tomorrow. Not one of your surrogates.' Then, as if he hadn't just registered a chewing out, he added, 'Good to work with you again, dogman.'

He reached out to slap Creed on the shoulder and Grace lunged for his hand, teeth bared, a growl deep in her throat.

Logan's eyes went wide before Creed settled her back against his chest.

'Good grief, dogman. Send that little bitch back home.'

'She saved an elderly woman today who probably would have died if Grace hadn't found her.'

Fake smile still planted on his face, but now with teeth gritted, Logan told Creed, 'Yeah, well, I'm not paying you to find elderly women.'

He headed toward the street where Creed could see headlights waiting for him.

Maggie watched him leave, then turned back to Creed and said, 'He's a real piece of work. Are you two friends?'

'Not even close. I owe him a favor and he's collecting it.'

43

O'Dell had the women's locker room to herself after a couple of female rescue workers left. It felt good to be clean again and in dry clothes. She wished she had thought to bring another pair of hiking boots. She scraped and wiped off the mud as best she could, then pulled them back on over a warm pair of fresh socks.

She was meeting Creed for the 7:30 dinner. The cafeteria staff had asked that the crews separate into two groups so they could accommodate all the workers and volunteers. She had been trying to get ahold of Dr Gunther. After leaving several more voice messages O'Dell gave up. But as she was stowing her gear and overnight case in a locker, her phone pinged.

At first she didn't recognize the phone number for the text that had just come through. But the message left no doubt who it was from:

AT RALPH'S. COME IN THE BACK DOOR.

She remembered that Ralph's was the meat locker they were using to store the body recovered from the government facility. She tapped a reply:

BE THERE IN 10.

She asked one of the volunteers for directions to Ralph's. The shortcut through the parking lot led her directly to the front door. Which was padlocked and had a sign warning to KEEP OUT. O'Dell made her way to the alley behind the building and found the back door. The heavy wood creaked as she shoved it open and darkness greeted her on the other side.

'Dr Gunther? It's Agent O'Dell.'

Suddenly a door down the hallway opened and light seeped out around the doorjamb.

'Are you alone?' the old woman asked.

'Yes, of course.'

'Then come on down here. I don't have all night.'

The room was set up with stainless steel work stations and multiple sinks. Three refrigerator doors lined one wall. O'Dell found Dr Gunther in baggy scrubs, teetering on a footstool that she had pushed up to one of the tables. The body on the table was the man with the shaved scalp. O'Dell noticed the hand they'd found on a stainless steel tray on one of the counters.

The old woman jutted her chin in the direction of a desk where there was a box of latex gloves, another with shoe covers, and still another with surgical masks. Over the back of the desk chair were a couple of scrubs tops. O'Dell pulled on the necessities and joined Dr Gunther.

'Sons of bitches padlocked the place. Don't know how they expected me to get in. I'll be registering a complaint with their boss.' Then she snorted through her face mask and added, 'Actually, I think they didn't want anybody inside.'

'So how did you get in?'

'Ralph gave me a key for the back door. You closed it, right?' She shot O'Dell a look.

O'Dell nodded.

'Why would they ask you to help recover the

bodies if they didn't want you to do the autopsies?'

'Maybe because they don't want anyone to find out what really happened to these men.'

If that were true, it hadn't stopped her. She'd already cleaned the body. Instruments crowded a tray beside the doctor. A tool that looked like hedge trimmers sat on the counter, and O'Dell knew it would be used to cut the rib cage. No Y incision had been made. No samples had been taken and cataloged. Empty vials waited to be filled and labeled.

Without the mud O'Dell could now clearly see the *US Airborne* tattoo with an eagle beneath it. What she thought had been burns farther down his arm now looked more like a large red bruise. Not a rash, but a bruise underneath the skin. Small white blisters like tapioca bubbled up around the edges. There were large red patches like this over most of his body. It reminded her of burns because in some places the skin had torn away. But this was different.

'What caused the skin to do this?' O'Dell knew it couldn't have happened postmortem.

'I've only seen something like this once before. Years ago. Back in the late sixties. My husband was stationed at Eglin Air Force Base outside Pensacola,

Florida. I was just a medical student at the time and he let me assist him. They were doing some kind of trials, spraying what they called tracer BG. It was supposed to be a harmless compound with fluorescent particles so they could track how the wind might affect an enemy attack with a biological weapon. We must have had two dozen airmen come in coughing up blood or bleeding from the ears. But there were blisters, too, and red patches almost like these.'

'Do you know what they actually sprayed?'

'Oh no, they never would tell us even while we were trying to treat those young men. They insisted the symptoms would go away. That what they used was completely safe. So safe they ended up conducting nine more tests. My husband was furious. It almost cost him his best friend.'

'Is it possible this facility was testing something similar?'

'I have no idea. But whatever this is, it's much more potent. Watch this.' Dr Gunther gently put an index finger on the bruise that covered his abdomen. She applied very little pressure and moved her finger an inch to the right. The skin fell away and peeled back with the motion of her finger.

She looked up at O'Dell over the top of her protective glasses. 'How in the world am I supposed to conduct an autopsy?'

'Could it have been some kind of allergic reaction or accidental exposure?'

'Possibly. It would have been extreme. There's more,' she said, and scooted over to hover above his face. With the same index finger and her thumb she pushed his lips up over his teeth, exposing his gums. The teeth were stained a rust color more prominent at the top, where the gums had peeled and bled.

The doctor waited for O'Dell's surprise, then dropped the lips back, again accidentally tearing one with the slightest movement.

'It's almost like the mud held him together.'

'He was hooked up to some kind of electrodes.' Dr Gunther pointed to the clean circles on both temples. 'And injected many times.' She moved his left arm for O'Dell to see all the puncture marks.

'It was a research facility,' O'Dell said, but her words sounded hollow even to her, with no passion to defend them. 'We already suspected that he didn't die in the landslide.'

'No, he certainly didn't,' she said definitively.

'Did this . . . whatever he was exposed to – was it the cause of his death?'

'No, I don't believe so.'

'How can you be so certain?'

'Help me sit him up.'

O'Dell stared at the woman, but she was already tugging at the man's right shoulder.

'Help me,' the woman instructed. 'Be careful not to touch his skin. I don't want to tear it.'

O'Dell moved around to the other side of the table and gripped his left shoulder. They raised him to a sitting position.

'Take a look at his back,' Dr Gunther insisted.

Still holding on to the body, O'Dell shifted so she could see whatever it was the woman wanted her to see. She found more bruising, but that wasn't what Dr Gunther was showing her. In the middle of his shoulder blade was a small black hole.

They eased him back onto the table.

'So he was shot, too.'

'Yes.'

'The first man they found – the scientist. Wasn't he shot in the head?'

The doctor glanced around the room. 'That's what

I was told, but he's not here. I checked all the refrigerators. There is no other body.'

'I thought Ross told us he was brought here.'

'Perhaps they have his body at the funeral home. That's where they're keeping the victims from the landslide.'

'Or they moved him already.'

'Well, there's just this gentleman here now. And the woman's hand.'

'You can tell the hand belonged to a woman?'

'I need to look more closely but it's small and has characteristics of a female. Also there's a gold ring with diamonds on the thumb.'

'Men sometimes wear rings on their thumbs.'

'Yes, but not many men wear red fingernail polish.'

44

Creed called Hannah to let her know everyone was safe.

'I didn't mean for Grace to go to work.'

'I know,' Creed said. He would have tried to keep it from her but Hannah always had a way of finding things out. 'She's okay.'

'She better be okay. I sent her with Jason so she wouldn't be moping around here missing you. Not to work.'

As he watched the Jack Russell terrier, he realized how much he liked having her here with him. She was curled up in a dog bed beside his cot. She had tried to keep one eye open, checking on him, but finally gave in to exhaustion. Now he could see her breathing heavy, fast asleep.

Bolo was sprawled on the floor at the foot of Creed's cot. One of the volunteers had set up two cots in the far corner of the gymnasium, making more room for Creed to be comfortable with the dogs and away from others so Bolo could relax. Still, the big dog lifted his head every time someone moved in one of the cots close by. He looked to see where the noise had come from, glanced over at Creed, then plopped his head down.

Jason and Dr Avelyn had found a place about five cots over. They had eaten at the first dinner, then fed both dogs while Creed cleaned up. If he stood up he could see them.

At 7:15 he waved at Jason to come over. They had agreed Jason would stay with the sleeping dogs while Creed met Maggie for dinner. But now as Creed made his way through the cafeteria, he couldn't find her. She seemed to have disappeared. Or maybe she changed her mind.

He hadn't been able to figure Maggie O'Dell out. Creed didn't usually have much trouble with women. Relationships were a different story, but most of the time women enjoyed his company.

He had worked with Maggie on two other cases in the last six months. One that ended in Blackwater River State Forest had almost gotten the two of them killed along with Bolo.

He knew there was chemistry between them. Could see she felt it as much as he did. But this guy, Ben – Logan had finally given him a name – had a hold on her. It was just as well. It looked like they'd be working together again, and Creed had only one rule about women – he never slept with women he worked with.

Still, he found himself watching the door.

Someone put a hand on his shoulder. Creed turned to find Oliver Vance, his tray piled with empty, dirty dishes.

'Thanks again for helping today.'

'Have you gotten any word on Mrs Hamlet?'

'Last I heard she was doing good. They're keeping her overnight at the hospital.' He waved at the spot he and his crew were vacating – the entire end of a table in the corner of the cafeteria. 'Get your dinner. Bring me a cup of coffee. I'll hold down a couple spots.'

Creed glanced at the door. Workers were coming in for the second dinner shift. But still no Maggie.

'Cream or sugar?' he asked Vance.

'Both. And grab me a piece of cherry pie if there's any left.'

'There's cherry pie?'

'Homemade.'

Creed was still grinning at the big man's enthusiasm when he headed for the line. That's when he saw Maggie come in the cafeteria door. She stopped and her eyes searched for him among the tables. She had her FBI windbreaker on but had definitely showered and changed from earlier, yet her hair was tousled and damp, her face flushed as if she had jogged there. When her eyes finally found him she smiled. He waited at the end of the line while she weaved around the tables and politely broke through the clusters of rescue workers, turning some heads as she passed by.

For a few minutes he didn't even notice the pounding in his own head.

45

Creed had hoped to have Maggie to himself despite the crowded cafeteria. Vance had ended up having a second piece of pie and a third cup of coffee, talking endlessly when Maggie asked if he had family affected by the landslide. He did not. He actually lived across the state, but that didn't stop him from bringing up photos on his cell phone of the wife and two girls he already missed terribly. By the time he got to the family dog pictures he realized he'd rambled. He clicked the phone off and tucked it into his shirt pocket.

'Your dogs are pretty damned amazing,' he told Creed, as if suddenly embarrassed and trying to stop hogging the attention. 'Jason told me they're all rescues that people dumped at the end of your property. Is that true?'

'Yeah, a lot of them are. I've gotten several from shelters. The breed oftentimes isn't as important as the dog's drive.'

'And the trainer,' Maggie offered.

'I've seen a lot of handlers get in the way, though.'

The big man was nodding and grinning. 'Ain't that the truth. One of my men worked with a FEMA handler and dog today. The dog alerted and they spent the next three hours digging up what they expected was a victim. Turned out it was a busted refrigerator with a whole lot of spoiled meat.'

'What was the trainer using for a reward?'

Vance shrugged.

'If they use food it might account for the dog alerting to the site. That's why it's best to use a toy.'

'Well, I sure wish I could have you back out with my crew tomorrow, but I know your boss and Agent O'Dell here are expecting you to work their site.'

'If they don't have the floodwater diverted, we won't be able to do a thing,' Maggie said.

'That must be where I saw the heavy equipment being trucked to. Funny, the feds will bust their asses to get anything necessary to recover a couple of dead guys, but I've been screaming for a couple more bulldozers and a few more dogs and all I hear are excuses.'

By the time they left Vance, the gymnasium lights had been dimmed. Creed had to strain to lead them through the rows of cots, most with already-sleeping occupants. Jason was stretched out on Creed's cot watching a football game on his phone. When he saw them he sat up and gathered his stuff in silence.

Grace's dog bed was between the two cots. She glanced up and wagged. Then she wiggled and started to get up when she saw Maggie, but Creed put his hand out for her to stay put. Maggie came around and patted her head as she sat on the cot that was saved for her.

Creed talked to Jason in whispers, making plans for the next day. He wanted him to stay with Grace. He also gave him a crumpled piece of paper from his daypack. On it was a name and phone number.

'This guy's supposed to have something for me. Would you mind calling him?'

'Yeah, I can do that.' But Jason still hesitated. 'You sure you don't want to stay and rest? I don't mind going back up with Bolo.'

'I appreciate that, but Logan made it clear he wants me on the site.'

Jason didn't press it. They said they'd see each other at breakfast and he left for his own cot.

Creed turned back around to find that Bolo had his head in Maggie's lap and Grace was up on Maggie's cot, her head already on the pillow.

'Grace—'

'I invited her up.' She hugged Bolo around the neck, then pointed him to his dog bed at the foot of the cots and he obeyed.

Maggie already had her boots off. She threw her windbreaker across the blanket, then peeled off her sweatshirt, leaving a T-shirt and her jeans. She snuggled back behind Grace.

Creed pulled off boots and shirt, leaving on his T-shirt. He was about to lie back when Maggie sat up, staring at him with concern.

'Are you still bleeding?' She pointed at the stain over his chest.

'I might have leaked a little.' After his shower he had wrapped a fresh ACE bandage around his ribs. In the process he'd opened a few cuts. He lifted up his T-shirt to check.

'You shouldn't have it wrapped that tightly.'

'The medic had it even tighter.'

'Must be old-school. It actually keeps you from breathing deeply. You could get pneumonia. Do you have more ACE bandages?'

He reached to the foot of his cot and pulled another roll out from the side pocket of his duffel. He wasn't looking forward to doing this again. It had been a challenge the first time.

Maggie held out her hand and he surrendered the roll.

'Take off your shirt,' she said. When he hesitated she added, 'We'll do it without too much pressure.'

He smiled at her and waited for her to realize what she had said. When she did, she rolled her eyes at him, but he noticed the slight blush.

He pulled off his shirt and started unwrapping the old bandage, but Maggie stopped him.

'Here, let me.'

For the next several minutes Creed didn't need to worry about his breathing because he was practically holding his breath. Every revolution to unwrap the old bandage and then wrap the new one required her hands to touch him, and she had to lean into him so close her hair brushed against his skin. She was avoiding his eyes but he couldn't take his off of her. By the time she was finished he was exhausted from trying so hard not to feel so much.

Her eyes were still examining her handiwork even as she lay back down. They were face-to-face except for about eighteen inches between their cots. That and a Jack Russell terrier who was already breathing heavy and fast asleep. Creed was pretty sure he wouldn't be able to sleep if he were in Grace's place, but he liked trying to imagine what it felt like to have Maggie's body against him.

'Thanks,' he told her.

'Thanks for saving me a cot.'

'You don't suppose Ben will be upset?'

She opened one eye and raised her eyebrow, waiting for an explanation.

'That we're sleeping together.'

She didn't answer. Closed both eyes again, but even in the dim light Creed could see her smile.

46

WASHINGTON, DC

Ellie had sneaked down the back steps and waited until she saw Carter leave the building. Then with the help of another staff member she had loaded the boxes into the trunk of her car. Now the contents of several of those boxes carpeted her living room floor.

'Mom, George is eating pizza in the game room.'

Ellie glanced up. Her daughter stood at the edge of the mess but didn't seem fazed by it, as if her mother always brought home copies of forty-year-old classified documents and scattered them around the house.

'I told him he could.'

Ellie dug out another set of file folders and started sifting through them.

Her daughter didn't budge. Ellie looked up at her again and waited.

'Are you okay?' she asked, scrunching up her nose at the mess as if seeing it for the first time.

'I'm fine, sweetie.' But still she waited.

She knew her kids missed their father. George Ramos was a liar and soon would be a convicted criminal, but the man had always been good to his children. The last year had been difficult for them. Sometimes Ellie wondered if the kids were waiting for signs that she might fall apart or leave them, too.

'Can I have pizza in my room?'

'Sure.'

'Really?' She stared at Ellie like it was a trick or a test.

'Would you bring me a piece before you go upstairs?'

The girl nodded, still eyeing her suspiciously as she left the room.

Ellie sat back, stretched her legs out in front of her, and arched her back. She'd need a dozen people to help sort through the mess and still not know what to look for. The DoD had overwhelmed them with so many documents – many of which seemed blatantly irrelevant – that she suspected that was their strategy. It was as if they were taunting the committee to try to find the needle in their haystack.

And what did it really matter? There had been a hearing years ago. That hearing had insisted a study be conducted. Hadn't those committee members gone over all these same documents? If there was damning evidence, wouldn't it have been found by now?

She tossed the files in her hand off to the side. She didn't even know what she was looking for. Did she really care or was she simply angry that Quincy might be keeping her in the dark? He was even using her chief of staff.

But why didn't they want her to know about Frank Sadowski? He was a veteran from her home state of Florida who was affected by Project 112. Of course she'd encourage him to testify. But in July she didn't even know about these congressional hearings. Was Sadowski the only reason that Senator Quincy had allowed her to be on the committee? Did he think he might somehow be able to control the veteran's testimony if Sadowski thought he had his own senator on his side? What kind of game was Quincy playing? And using her chief of staff to do it?

She wondered if Quincy had ever intended to treat her like a full-fledged member of this committee. But how could she complain? She had used being the token woman as a trump card to get on the committee. And her reason for wanting on? She needed to lift her profile for re-election. How lame was that? How selfish was that?

Ellie raked her fingers through her long hair and leaned against the sofa.

Dear God, she was as bad as the rest of them.

Games, compromises, quid pro quo – everything came with a price. From the very beginning she should not have put up with any of their sexist actions and degrading comments. Her first month in the Senate she was stunned when one of the most senior members had told her that she had the 'prettiest bottom' for a senator. Okay, so at least he hadn't pinched it, but his remark certainly set the stage for what the others thought was appropriate.

She thought it would get old and go away. Sort of like a fraternity initiation ritual. But just last week another senior senator had asked her if it was tough being without her Latin husband, insinuating that she must be accustomed to sex and lots of it. In so many words he went on to offer his services. She had laughed like it was the funniest joke she had ever heard because she had no clue how else to respond.

Isn't that what the men did – tell each other rude, crude jokes and then roll with laughter?

She pulled out another stack of files and stopped. This was ridiculous. A waste of time. She started to shove them back into the box when a manila envelope fell to the floor. Even before she picked it up she could tell it was old. The metal clasp indented the fold and rust encircled it. The envelope felt brittle between her fingers. There was something thicker than paper inside.

Ellie glanced at the outside of the box. All these files were copies of original documents. Was it possible someone had mistakenly dropped an original?

She tried to carefully and slowly bend the metal clasp. One side broke off in her fingers and she felt a slight panic. She set the piece of metal aside and caught herself actually thinking she might be able to glue it back on.

Stupid and silly! Just open the damned envelope.

She slid the contents out onto her coffee table. And then she stopped, her hand in midair holding the now empty envelope. The black-and-white photographs were eight-by-tens, the kind a professional photographer would take. The dates were stamped in scalloped white edges: 1953, 1958, 1962, 1965.

Ellie held each one up. They were nothing like she expected. So much talk about ships and bases being sprayed, about sailors and soldiers being exposed to biological weapons.

But these were not photos of sailors or ships. These photographs were of schoolchildren.

47

Ellie dug back into the box and found the file folder she thought the envelope had fallen out of. Unlike the others, this one was not labeled.

In all, there were five photographs. The children were lined up and smiled for the camera as a man in a suit waved a strange wand with some kind of light beam. Ellie didn't recognize it as any kind of magic trick.

In one photo he held the wand over their feet. In another, they were facing away from the camera while he waved the light beam across their little backs.

There was no explanation in the envelope. Only the date stamped on each. She pulled out yellowed newspaper articles from the folder. They were from the *Chicago Tribune*, *The New York Times*, and the Minneapolis *Star Tribune*. Two were from 1994. One was dated 2012. All had disturbing headlines:

MINNEAPOLIS CALLED TOXIC TEST SITE IN '53
ACCUSATIONS RAISED, DATA DEMANDED
ARMY SPRAYED ST LOUIS WITH TOXIC AEROSOL

'You haven't touched your pizza.' Ellie's daughter startled her. She was standing over her and Ellie closed the folder and plopped it on top of the photographs.

'I will. I just got carried away.'

'What are you doing, anyway?'

Usually her daughter wouldn't notice unless it somehow involved her. Such was the mind of a twelve-year-old.

'I have some homework.'

'Seriously?'

'Seriously.'

She walked away shaking her head.

Ellie opened the folder again and pulled out one of the articles to read. In 1953 the army sprayed clouds of what they believed was a nontoxic material – zinc cadmium sulfide – in an effort to test how chemicals would disperse during biological warfare. Multiple cities were used as test sites, as were multiple areas within each city. In Minneapolis the material was sprayed sixty-one times in four parts of the city from generators in the rear of trucks or from rooftops.

One of the sites sprayed in Minneapolis was a public elementary school. Students were tested at various times with 'special lights' to determine if the chemicals – zinc sulfide is a fluorescent phosphor – showed residual traces on their shoes, clothing, or bodies. And if it showed up, how long it stayed.

Ellie stopped. Took a deep breath. She was feeling a bit sick to her stomach and now the pepperoni on the pizza didn't help matters.

The articles talked about demands for full disclosure from the army. Zinc cadmium sulfide was now believed to be toxic and could possibly cause cancer and some birth defects. Yet a committee of the National Research Council in 1997 determined that the amounts used in these studies were not harmful.

However, they admitted their research was 'sparse' and relied on incomplete information supplied by the army and Fort Detrick about the 'quantities dispersed' and the 'exact composition of the fluorescent particles' used.

They did admit that more than a hundred biological warfare simulation tests such as these were conducted by the army in urban and rural areas between 1952 and 1969 without the public's knowledge. Some used zinc cadmium sulfide. Others used *Bacillus globigii* or *Serratia marcescens* – both common bacillus found in water, food, and sewage.

Ellie placed the articles back in the folder. Carefully she slid the photographs into the envelope and noticed that there was another photograph, stuck to the inside. She pried it loose and pulled it out.

This one was stamped 1968. Another group of schoolchildren, but this time posing with three men who were all dressed in uniforms. They stood behind the children, smiling for the camera. She glanced at the photograph, then stared at the men, stunned to recognize two of them.

No, it wasn't possible.

She held it up to the light, then flipped it over to find a label on the back. She read the caption identifying the men, and now she was certain. The man in the middle was a young Colonel Abraham Hess. To his left was an army doctor named Dr Samuel Gunther. And the man standing on Colonel Hess's right was Ellie's father.

DAY 3

48

HAYWOOD COUNTY, NORTH CAROLINA

Creed had awakened in the middle of the night to the battering sound of rain on the gymnasium roof, so he wasn't surprised to find water running in the streets the next morning. By now he expected to trudge through mud. He didn't, however, expect the cold.

Overnight the temperature had fallen. The chill in the air hit him in the face as soon as he stepped out the door. Both he and Maggie looked at each other and headed back inside to pull on extra layers.

Peter Logan and Ross picked up Creed, Maggie, and Bolo in a Land Rover. Mud covered every inch of the vehicle; the windows were splattered, making visibility difficult. The bumpy trek up the mountain and the two strange men in the front seat made Bolo nervous. Creed let the dog sit on the leather seat between him and Maggie, despite Logan's disapproving look.

Thankfully, the rain had stopped. The fog had not returned, either, but the blue-gray clouds still looked swollen and ready to erupt without warning.

The Land Rover could go only so far. Then the foursome pulled on daypacks and followed Ross to the digging site.

Logan was subdued this morning. There were no wisecracks, no slaps on the back or inappropriate comments. Gone, too, was the leather jacket. He was dressed this time like he expected to get dirty. Creed wondered if Logan's boss was getting impatient.

Why had it taken two days for Logan to feel enough urgency to come to the site? Even his surrogate, Isabel Klein, seemed to have disappeared. Neither of them had been concerned about finding survivors – possible staff members caught inside the facility during the first major slide. No one had explained if the bodies they were searching for today were employees. Creed remembered Vance telling him that the rescue crews hadn't been given any information on the facility at all.

So many secrets. Everything classified. He knew that was the way Logan liked it. Creed could understand that DARPA might have safety and national security reasons for keeping things quiet. He and his dogs were hired to do a job. He asked only the questions that would help them do it. His number-one priority was the safety of his dogs.

Whether they searched for drugs or cadavers he had learned it was better if he didn't know the details. He couldn't afford to be caught up in any emotional turmoil that may have already affected the law enforcement officers he was working with. A trainer knowing and expecting too much could lead his dog to too many false alerts. You started to look for telltale signs and anticipate what your dog should be looking for rather than letting the dog's nose lead the way.

In his attempt to maintain his professional distance, it occurred to Creed as they tromped through the sludge that he didn't even know what role Maggie was playing in all of this. All he knew was that her so-called boyfriend, Ben, knew Logan well enough that he had arranged for her to be there. He didn't care how she had ended up there, he just knew it felt good to wake up and see her lying so close to him.

Maggie had worked with Ross yesterday and the two of them took turns filling in what they had found. Ross explained that his crew had worked through the night to create a barrier uphill to divert the flow of water. To Creed that seemed like a huge undertaking just for them to be able to recover a couple of bodies when there were still possible survivors from the landslide in other areas.

From this level those barriers couldn't be seen. Nor could the equipment used to create and hold them. Creed listened for engines but there was only the faint smell of diesel. What was left behind concerned Creed.

Deep gashes in the earth veined out. On the bed of silt between those gashes were chunks of concrete – some as large as boulders – along with frayed cable lines knotted around branches, splintered two-by-fours, and scraps of metal with sharp, ragged edges.

Studying the area from the ledge he noticed thousands of pieces of glass embedded in the muck. He had sprayed Bolo's pads with a protective coating that Dr Avelyn had given him to help prevent the absorption of toxins, but Creed couldn't put out of his mind the cuts on poor Grace's paws. Putting any sort of boot or cover on a dog could do more harm than good, tripping him up. He needed to keep a close watch and not allow Bolo to be down in this sludge for long periods of time.

Ross left them and headed farther uphill after whispering with Logan. At one point Creed thought he heard Logan say something to Ross, reminding the young guardsman that he was still in charge. An odd thing, Creed thought, for the deputy director of DARPA to say.

Then Maggie took her turn with Logan. Creed could hear her questioning him, continuing on when she wasn't satisfied with his answers. Creed tried to ignore them and prepare.

He set his GPS and slid a separate unit into the mesh pocket on Bolo's vest. Already he could smell the big dog's anticipation. Creed called it 'sweaty head smell', although dogs didn't sweat like people. The cooler weather would be better for Bolo, but it wouldn't necessarily help with scent. It would slow the decomposition rate.

And just because they had drained the field didn't mean that they took all the smells with it. Even Creed could detect mildew mixed with something caustic. The mud and silt would have already absorbed and mixed in a brew that most likely included human decomposition.

Maggie left her discussion with Logan and was already on her cell phone. Logan made his way to Creed's side. He noticed Creed glance in Maggie's direction. He shrugged and said, 'Women – they're usually a pain in the ass.'

'Then why did you invite her here?'

'I didn't. My boss wanted someone official with forensic experience, someone from the FBI that he probably thought would be on our side. I doubt that he expected Benjamin Platt to send some woman he's screwing.'

Creed felt the heat rush to his head. The throbbing had never left. The anger would only make it worse.

'I've worked with her before, Logan.' He steadied his tone because Bolo's eyes were on him, shooting nervous glances toward Logan. If the dog believed Logan was any kind of threat to Creed, he'd drop Logan in seconds without warning. 'She has plenty of forensic experience.'

'Yeah? Well, I don't need someone questioning me and making me look bad with my boss.'

'So what's going on, Logan? Why are these bodies so important?'

Instead of telling him it wasn't his business, Logan stared at him. Creed couldn't help thinking the arrogant son of a bitch actually looked like he wanted to tell him. Logan's eyes darted uphill, then back over his shoulder at Maggie.

'DARPA has research facilities all across the country,' he told Creed, keeping his voice low. 'They operate with a lot of independence. That's the way the head guys like it. Something goes wrong, the head guys can't be held accountable if they didn't know what the hell was going on, right?'

'Are you saying you don't even know what this facility was working on?'

'We have a general idea.'

'You haven't located the director yet?'

Creed watched Logan's entire face stiffen before he said, 'Yesterday your dog found all that might be left of her.'

Jason had told Creed last night about the hand they'd recovered.

'How do you already know it's hers?'

'I've only met Dr Shaw a couple of times but I

recognized her signature red nail polish. She wore a diamond ring on her thumb. Of course, we'll still run fingerprints.'

'The rest of her body is probably buried here somewhere,' Creed told him.

'All I know is that my boss has his panties all in a twist. Congressional hearings are going on this week – right now. That's why Ben Platt couldn't be here. The Senate's looking for scapegoats for something that happened over fifty years ago.'

'What does that have to do with this?'

'Are you kidding me? Please don't tell me that you're still that naïve, dogman. This slide couldn't have happened at a worse time. And I'm the new guy. I haven't been on the job a year, but it's my ass that's on the line.'

'But you just said you can't be held accountable for something you don't know.'

'You missed the part about me saying it's the *head guys* who can't be accountable.'

'So what is this, Logan? Because if you have me involved in another cover-up, I'm not sticking around.'

'*Another* cover-up?' Maggie asked, standing less than four feet behind them.

49

WASHINGTON, DC

'They're ready for your testimony, Mr Sadowski.'

Frankie hadn't gotten any sleep last night. Too many strange sounds outside his hotel room door. That, and his concern that he wasn't sure he could trust anyone. He regretted bringing Susan with him.

The strobe lights blinded him. If the clerk hadn't guided him to his seat he might not have been able to find his way. Already he was perspiring and his pulse raced.

Senator Quincy asked him some basic questions. Then he went into a lecture about Project 112 and Project SHAD. He kept saying that he wanted Frankie and the others to understand what these projects were according to the Department of Defense.

'These series of tests were conducted between 1962 and 1974 by the Department of Defense. During these projects, the Department of Defense has admitted a number of weapons containing chemical and biological agents were tested. It is believed that some of these chemical and biological agents included VX nerve gas, Sarin nerve gas, and E. coli.'

The senator was reading from what was obviously an extensive document. Frankie could see him flipping pages.

'The purpose of these tests, according to the Department of Defense, was to identify the United States' vulnerabilities to attacks with chemical and biological warfare agents. They had hoped to use these tests and their results to develop procedures to respond to such attacks. They sought to find out how chemical and biological agents behaved under different climatic, environmental, and other conditions.

'During a variety of these tests, a chemical or simulant of a chemical was sprayed from military jets. In the case of Project SHAD, the chemical was sprayed over a ship. Sailors were trained how to decontaminate a ship after a test and how to conduct air samplings.

'In some cases the chemicals were sprayed over a particular area and drift tests were conducted. One such test' – Senator Quincy pushed his glasses up before continuing – 'was Project SHAD's Shady Grove. Tests took place at Eglin Air Force Base in Florida outside Pensacola. It's my understanding that this is one of the tests that you believe you were exposed to, Mr Sadowski, allegedly without your consent or knowledge of what the test involved. Is that correct, Mr Sadowski?'

'It wasn't just without my consent or knowledge of what the test involved. I simply didn't even know I was part of any test at the time. We were never told.'

'What did you think you were taking air samples for if it wasn't a test?'

'I never took air samples. But I was stationed at the base when Shady Grove took place.'

'How do you know that if you didn't even know what Shady Grove was at the time?'

Frankie wiped at his forehead. He had expected

this to be tough but he hadn't expect it to be an interrogation.

'I only know about Shady Grove now, after reading about it.'

The room buzzed as if he'd been caught misspeaking. But it was the truth. Frankie and his friends only learned recently about the tests and what they were called.

'Senator Quincy.' It was Senator Delanor who spoke now. 'We know the facts of these tests. None of the dates are in question. We also know Mr Sadowski's service record.'

Frankie thought Senator Delanor looked tired. Even the carefully applied makeup couldn't hide the swelling under her eyes.

She continued, 'We gave Dr Hess plenty of uninterrupted time to speak yesterday. Surely we can afford the same courtesy to Mr Sadowski. Can we please hear his story? He's been waiting a long time to share it with us. And I, for one, am very interested in hearing it.'

'Very well,' Senator Quincy said.

Frankie hesitated, but then he told them. He talked about what he remembered of the jet flying overhead.

Of the problem he'd had breathing almost immediately. He told them about the reunion and all the ailments, the surgeries, the cancers, and about Gus. And before he finished he decided to tell them about his own cancer.

50

HAYWOOD COUNTY, NORTH CAROLINA

O'Dell looked at Creed, but she could tell from the pained look in his eyes that he wouldn't or couldn't tell her. She looked at Logan.

'This has nothing to do with you,' Logan told her. 'Can we please get to work? Note that I'm using "please", and I'm not a man who uses that word.'

Logan stomped off, yanking his cell phone from a jacket pocket.

When she looked at Creed he was tightening straps on Bolo's vest and finishing his preparations. He didn't glance up when he said, 'It's not mine to tell.'

'Right. It's classified.' She was getting tired of the

secrecy. Ben hadn't had anything to tell her, either.

'I didn't say it was classified.' He snapped the leash on and stood. 'Why are you here?'

The question surprised her. Maybe even more so because she didn't have a clear answer.

'I'm beginning to wonder that myself.'

He stared at her, waiting for a better explanation. When he realized he wouldn't get one, he turned away. The gesture felt like he had slammed a door in her face.

She had talked to Assistant Director Kunze before they left the gymnasium, filling him in on what Dr Gunther had discovered and what she had said. Then she waited for his response and instructions. In the past her boss had no qualms about sending her into dangerous situations, once even sending her literally into a hurricane. But that morning he had sounded concerned.

She was used to politics coloring his judgment. He tended to be swayed easily by certain administration officials and several senators, Senator Ellie Delanor being one of them. Usually he was willing to protect those in powerful positions, so she was surprised when AD Kunze said, 'I don't like this. Those congressional hearings are going on right now.'

That's what she was thinking, too, but neither of them would say it out loud over a phone. Someone wanted to control the investigation of these murders. Was Ben a part of that or was he being used, too?

Kunze told her to watch her back. Said he'd ask some questions of his own and let her know what he found out.

In the meantime she wasn't sure whom she could trust. She told Logan about the gunshot wound that she and Dr Gunther had discovered last night. Mostly she wanted to watch his response and hopefully learn something from it. He seemed more upset about them breaking into the temporary morgue than he was about the condition of the body.

'Protecting those bodies is my responsibility. You two had no business being there without me.'

'How did you intend for Dr Gunther to do her job if you didn't give her access to the victims?'

'She should have waited until someone with authority could be there with her.'

'I was there with her,' O'Dell had told him.

He didn't say a word, but the look he gave her told her what she and Kunze suspected. Ben had asked her to go down and take a look because they needed someone discreet whom they could trust. But what they really wanted was someone who would keep all of this quiet, at least until the hearings were finished.

Seems the only ones down here she could trust were Ryder Creed and his dogs.

O'Dell noticed that Bolo's nose was already working as soon as Creed led the big dog off the ledge and onto what looked like an empty riverbed. An empty riverbed that had been cut and carved out by the violent rush of floodwaters. It was still slick with patches of water. Creed was keeping the leash short and tight, letting Bolo lead him while trying to guide the dog around the debris. She imagined the dog would leap and rush if left on his own.

They had been at it for less than twenty minutes when a boom came from uphill. O'Dell felt the vibration under her feet. It sounded like an explosion. She looked for smoke, trying to see beyond the trees. Creed was hurrying her way, yelling something she couldn't hear. He'd dropped Bolo's leash and was gesturing for the dog to run.

She turned to find Logan and saw him farther up in the riverbed. His back was to her, phone still pressed to the side of his face.

'Run!' She heard Creed now. She thought he was yelling at Bolo but now he meant her, too. His face twisted in panic. He was slipping on the silt, back-tracking. Bolo had fallen and Creed was pulling the big dog up. They were still in the middle of the riverbed.

O'Dell ran toward them even as Creed waved her in the other direction. But she dug her feet into a patch of grass on the ledge, trying to decide the best way to help them. If Creed could carry Bolo to the ledge, she could pull them up over the wet, slick riverbank.

A second boom. Closer.

This time she realized what had happened. It wasn't an explosion. The barriers uphill had given way. A roar followed, and she could already see the wall of water coming down on them.

51

At first Creed thought it was another slide. He dropped Bolo's leash and ordered the dog to run. But silt made it impossible. The dog's legs twisted over each other and he stumbled. Creed stopped, wishing he could scoop the dog up under his arm.

'Settle, boy,' he told him as he lifted all eighty-five pounds into his arms.

Maggie was waiting for them at the ledge even though he had yelled for her to run. He still had five feet to go when the water hit. It knocked Bolo out of his arms and upended Creed. He tried to keep his feet together. Tried to stay on his back as the gushing water swept him up. But not far. The wave slammed him into one of the concrete boulders and Creed grabbed on.

'Bolo!' he yelled, but the thunderous roar filled his ears.

Creed climbed on top of the boulder, finding an edge and grabbing tight. It was like watching rapids rumble by. He searched for Bolo. Panic clawed at him when he saw no sign of the dog. Then he looked for Maggie and couldn't see her.

A knot of branches punched into him, almost toppling him over the concrete. He kicked and sent it rolling on. Waves splashed over him and more debris threatened to shove him off. When the roar settled down he pulled himself higher, stopping when the pain stabbed in his chest.

'Creed!'

Upstream he finally saw Maggie. She was on her feet and keeping to the ledge. She had something over her shoulder. He wiped the water off his face to see better and his hand came back streaked with blood. He searched over the riverbank downstream.

Still no sign of Bolo and nausea kicked in his gut.

He should have held on. He imagined the dog's crumpled body battered against one of the concrete rocks and he felt his hands slip. He wanted to let go and join him.

'Creed!'

Maggie was parallel to him now, ten feet away on the bank. So close and yet too far to stretch out and touch him.

She had rope coiled around her shoulder and she was unwinding it. In seconds she had one end tied around a tree trunk.

Creed laid his cheek against the cold rock. His arms ached. The water was slowing but was still too fast for him to stand and hold his balance. He closed his eyes, suddenly sick to his stomach. He'd never lost a dog. Hannah said it would eventually happen and he'd never be ready for it and she was right. His feet had slid into the cold water, weighing him down, allowing the current to pull at him. And still he hugged the concrete and kept his eyes closed.

'Creed! I need you to catch this.'

He wanted her to go away. Leave him. At least for a while.

'I'll get to you next, Bolo. Just hang on.'

Creed's eyes flew open. What did she just say? He stretched up on exhausted elbows. Maggie was looking at him, holding the knotted end of the rope, ready to toss it to him. When she saw the question on his face she pointed upstream. He had only looked downstream.

There in the middle of the rushing water was Bolo, standing with all four big paws clinging to the flat top of another concrete boulder.

52

Once he had the rope, Creed tried to make his way through the water. He attempted to stand and twice the water knocked him off his feet. If he hadn't clung to the rope he would have been riding downstream, his body pummeled against the debris like an arcade pinball.

It seemed to take forever to get to the edge of the water. He could hear Maggie encouraging him in between telling Bolo what a good boy he was and to stay put for just a little bit longer.

Every time Creed heard her say something to the big dog he wanted to smile.

Finally he felt Maggie grabbing the collar of his

jacket. She pulled as his feet found traction in the slimy mud of the bank. He rolled onto his side, trying to catch his breath. Trying to tamp down the pain in his chest.

He felt Maggie's fingers on his face and opened his eyes. She was kneeling beside him, caressing his cheek, her hand palming his chin, her thumb running over his lips.

'I was afraid I lost you,' she said in almost a whisper. And then, as if an alarm went off, she pulled him up to a sitting position. 'I need you to help me get Bolo. Do you think you can do that?'

She started to help him get to his feet, but he waved her off. His knees were wobbly. When he stood up straight he winced against the pain in his chest. He waited for it to recede. It didn't. Maggie's hand was on his arm again.

'Maybe you can just tell me what to do,' she said.

She gathered up the rope, but Creed was looking at the ground for sturdy branches. He glanced up at Bolo. He could finally see him without any obstructions. The dog noticed and started to wag.

'Just stay, Bolo. Don't move,' he told him in a calm voice.

The dog tucked his tail again, adjusted his feet, and eased his body down. Creed had trained his disaster dogs to navigate floodwaters and climb atop rubble exactly like the concrete boulder. He knew the dog would be okay. He had no idea how he was going to get him from there to here. Maggie must have sensed his doubt. She was back in front of him.

'I can get him,' she said. 'But you need to tell me how to do that.'

'You can't carry him. He's eighty-five pounds.'

She glanced back as if reassessing. Her eyes came back to his. 'You barely made it out of the water. You won't be able to carry him, either. It's going to be harder if I have to pull you both out.'

'Where's Logan?' He didn't care before, but now that the man might actually be able to help, he looked for him.

'Knocked his head. He's out cold. I pulled him under the tent when I went searching for the rope.'

Creed was slow to respond.

'Ryder! You're gonna need to let me do this.'

He knew she was right. He could barely hear over the banging in his head and in his chest. Still, he didn't like it.

'Can Bolo swim?'

'He's a great swimmer, but the water's too fast.'

'I can tie the rope around my waist. I can hold on to him. Let him dog-paddle while I guide him.'

'The water's muddy. There's debris you can't even see.'

'He's not going to be able to stand there much longer. You've got to let me at least try.'

She grabbed his arm. Waited for his eyes. He could see that what she was about to ask of him was something she knew was precious and rare.

'Ryder, you're going to need to trust me.'

53

'Okay, you're right,' Creed finally said. 'You need to take off your clothes.'

'Excuse me?'

He thought he saw a flush go over her face. The tough FBI agent always seemed a bit shy and vulnerable about taking off her clothes.

'They'll waterlog you. Seriously, taking off your clothes will cut down the drag. Keep your shoes on. You don't want to cut up your feet and maybe they'll give you some extra traction.'

He started looking again at the ground for a sturdy branch to use as a pole. It might help keep her balance. If nothing else, she could use it to probe for debris. When he glanced over she was peeling off her last layer, leaving on her sports bra. She unzipped her jeans, then stopped and looked back out at the water. She caught him watching and zipped the jeans up.

'I'm not having some sewer rat bite me.'

He nodded. Tried not to smile.

He helped her wrap and tie the rope around her waist. They tied the other end to another tree trunk. He took hold of the middle. He'd try to dole out what she needed as she needed it and also pull her in. He handed her the tree branch.

'Keep it on the upstream side of your body. It'll be easier to hold on to and it'll stay in place. Otherwise it's of no use to you. The current's going to push and pull. If it knocks you down, keep your feet out in front of you. You want your feet hitting those rocks instead of your head.'

She was nodding and taking it all in.

'Do you remember some of those deep gouges?'

Another nod.

'If you step into one of those, don't panic. The deepest the water's gonna be is chest-high.' He had no idea if that was true, but as fast as the water was still running, he didn't think she'd ever touch bottom in those crevices.

He pointed at a spot on the riverbank. 'It's going to be easier if you wade against the flow at a forty-five-degree angle. I know that sounds strange but you're gonna need to trust me on that.'

He helped her down into the water and could feel her shiver.

'Whoa! That's cold! Hold on, Bolo, I'm coming.'

She did better than Creed expected. She didn't fight the current. Instead she worked her way slowly, sometimes walking, sometimes floating. Once she capsized and Creed reeled her in so she wouldn't be swept downstream. She waved her thanks and started again, holding the branch to steady herself.

By the time she reached Bolo he was wagging, excited and ready to join her in the water. Then she did something that Creed did not expect, that they had not discussed. She took the dangling leash and weaved it around her waist, knotting it tight. If she lost her grip on the big dog he'd still be attached to her. But he could also yank her down the stream with him.

Creed fisted the rope in his hands, wrapping it around his wrists. He checked the knot on the other end that circled the tree trunk. It was still secure. The mud was slick underneath his shoes. It wouldn't take much of a jerk to knock him off his feet. He bent his knees and squatted when he felt the current suck at Maggie. She had Bolo in the water now.

It looked like it was taking considerable effort for her to convince Bolo to go slow. He had to be exhausted and yet what pent-up energy was left made him want to swim like the dickens and get to his owner. But Maggie held him alongside her.

The branch, her balance pole, had been swept away when she helped Bolo off the rock. She couldn't keep her feet on the bottom and finally gave up. Instead she dog-paddled with Bolo, letting Creed reel them in.

She used her other hand to push off the debris, anticipating it even when Creed couldn't see it. She was maneuvering around the obstacles she had already encountered and noted on her way to get to Bolo.

When he finally had them at the riverbank, he gestured for her to hold on a minute. He kept the rope taut as he moved to the tree, adjusting the slack and retying it so it would hold Maggie in place at the ledge while he helped them up.

She untangled the dog's leash from her waist. Bolo clawed up the muddy bank while Creed pulled and

Maggie pushed. On land the big dog slobbered Creed's face with kisses.

'Hold on, buddy. We need to get Maggie up.'

And Bolo joined Creed at the ledge. He went down on his belly, paws over the edge, as if he was ready to help. Creed gave him a section of the rope and the dog took it in his teeth. As he pulled Maggie up, Bolo pulled, too. Creed wrapped his arms around her and fell to the ground.

Finally safe, he tried to catch his breath. Maggie's weight was crushing his chest but he didn't care. He still held her tight against him. His lips found her cheek, then her ear. His voice was hoarse when he said, 'You did it!'

She pulled up, careful to put her hands on the ground instead of pushing against his chest. She was smiling and breathing hard, pleased with herself, but he also saw relief. Incredible relief.

Bolo was ready to play. He head-butted Maggie, knocking her off Creed and into the mud. She grabbed his big wet body and pulled him in for a hug.

Creed tried to pull himself to his knees, and that's when the pain stopped him. He lay back down, this time facedown in the mud, and he closed his eyes.

54

WASHINGTON, DC

Ellie had tried to listen carefully to Frank Sadowski's testimony. She jotted notes to stay focused, and yet her mind kept returning to those photographs of schoolchildren. She couldn't shake the image of her father smiling as he posed with them.

She loved and respected her father more than anyone else in her life. Her ex-husband had said many times how difficult it was to compete with the man who had died a hero to his daughter when she was only twenty-two years old. She had worshipped her father. Now she had to shove down all the conflicting emotions battling inside her. She needed to deal with the facts – all of them – even those facts that countless government officials and elected representatives had conveniently swept away over and over again for the past fifty years.

Sometime between last night and today's testimony, Ellie had come to the conclusion that Senator Quincy had always planned for her to be on this committee. She remembered that it was Carter, her chief of staff, who set the bait, making her want to be a part of these hearings by making it sound like a smart PR move. It was Carter who had suggested she cast herself as a sympathetic listener to the many veteran constituents who'd be deciding her re-election.

There were still things she didn't understand, but she was convinced that Carter and Quincy had played her. And why? Maybe because they believed she could be easily manipulated. Of course she'd agree and be on Senator Quincy's side. As for Carter – being Quincy's chief of staff would certainly bring him more power, more prestige, and even more money. In this city, only one of those goals was enough reason for betrayal.

Now Ellie understood that Quincy had no intention of doing anything about the veterans, like Frank Sadowski, who'd been physically and emotionally affected by Project 112. It was all a show for Quincy to make himself look good, to wield his authority – or look like he was. At the end of the hearings he would do nothing more than any of the other committees that had had their chance in the years before. At the end of the day, Senator John Quincy would pretend he had done everything he could, then deliver absolutely nothing at all.

They were taking a short break after Mr Sadowski's testimony. A chance for everyone to stretch his or her legs. An opportunity for the media to get their sound bites out for the next news cycle. Ellie knew when they reconvened, Quincy would most likely be wrapping things up.

She saw Amelia Gonzalez come in a side door, her arms filled and her eyes darting around as if looking for permission to enter. Ellie waved at her assistant and watched her small frame politely weave through the crowd. The girl had listened to every word Ellie had told her, taking notes to make sure she got all the instructions. And here she was, the stack of envelopes in her arms, the task complete and just in time. Gonzalez would become an excellent chief of staff as soon as Ellie fired Carter.

She helped her distribute the envelopes, one at each committee member's place. Ellie took her seat and the shuffle of the room followed suit. In minutes Quincy was restoring order.

'We've heard from all our witnesses,' he said. 'If there's no objection, we'll conclude these proceedings.' He didn't even look around the room and was ready to dismiss them for the day when Ellie spoke.

'With your permission, Mr Chairman, I believe each of us reserves the right to recall any of those witnesses if we wish to have some clarification. Is that correct?'

She used her most polite tone and he shot a bemused look around the room, one that said without any words that, sure, they could make time for the only woman on the committee.

'Yes, of course, that's correct,' he told her. 'I'm sure our clerk won't mind asking Mr Sadowski to return.'

'Oh, I have no more questions for Mr Sadowski.'

Quincy looked confused now, but Ellie didn't hesitate.

'I'd like to recall Dr Abraham Hess.'

55

They had to wait almost five minutes for the room to settle down and for the clerk to find Colonel Hess. During that time Quincy glared at Ellie while she instructed the committee members to wait before opening the envelopes she had left at each of their places.

Colonel Hess shuffled in with Colonel Platt beside him. The two men had been inseparable during the last several days. She had seen the same admiration in Benjamin Platt's eyes that Ellie once felt for the colonel. As she watched the others in the room and the way they revered this man, she suddenly felt butterflies in her stomach.

What in the world was she doing?

Hess settled into his chair and adjusted the microphone to accommodate his slouching. Then he looked up at her and waited. They were all waiting.

'Dr Hess,' she began with the same polite tone she had addressed Quincy, 'you were kind enough to tell us the history and the importance of Project 112 and Project SHAD. As you pointed out, the 1950s and '60s were a tumultuous time. It's difficult to understand the level of threat when many of us here were children or, in some cases, weren't even born yet.'

Hess nodded and she noticed that everyone seemed to ease back for what they now believed would be a boring summary and public pat on the back for Dr Hess.

'I think what none of us realized was that these tests – like those that were simulated for Project 112 – weren't the only ones going on across the country.'

She paused and let that sink in. She hoped to see Dr Hess look surprised or at the very least maybe just a little rattled. He remained unmoved, his gaze unwavering. Perhaps he tilted his head a fraction as he waited her out.

'What exactly are you saying, Senator Delanor?' It

was Quincy who appeared anxious. This wasn't what he had expected.

'There were other tests,' she said casually. 'Minneapolis, Saint Louis, Detroit.' She waved a hand at the envelopes. 'Go ahead and take a look. The evidence was documented many years ago. It just hasn't been brought to the attention of this committee. Or, to my knowledge, to any of the committees that have investigated Project 112 or Project SHAD.'

'Those tests have nothing to do with either,' Dr Hess said in a calm voice. 'If you've read the reports, you certainly know that.' The professorial tone was back.

'I beg to differ, Dr Hess. There are similarities. The army sprayed clouds of what they believed was a nontoxic material.' She pretended to refer to her notes but the details were still fresh in her memory. 'I believe it was zinc cadmium sulfide. Does that sound correct, Dr Hess?'

'I don't have the benefit of having those details in front of me, so I'll have to take your word for it.'

'Between 1952 and 1969 multiple cities were used as test sites, as were multiple areas within each city. The "nontoxic" material was sprayed from generators in the rear of trucks or in some cases from rooftops. At least one of those sites in Minneapolis was a public elementary school.' She paused and looked up at Hess. 'Does this sound familiar now?'

He shifted slightly in his chair.

'Zinc sulfide is a fluorescent phosphor, chosen so scientists could actually test the students at various times with "special lights". Residual traces would illuminate on the children's shoes or clothing or even on their bodies. The test was used to see if it showed up, and then how long it stayed.'

Now when Ellie glanced up and around the room she saw that she had everyone's attention. There were no looks of boredom.

'What I'm wondering, Dr Hess, is who determined the quantities that would be dispersed?'

'Excuse me?'

'The zinc sulfide. The army and Fort Detrick conducted these tests, but who was it who decided the composition of the fluorescent particles or how much was a safe level to spray?'

'As with any of these matters, there is a group who makes those decisions.'

'A group?' This time she smiled before she said,

'Are you telling me the army did things back then by a democratic vote?'

There was a nervous laugh that spread across the room but it didn't last, and now Hess couldn't hide his irritation.

'Let me be more specific.' Ellie told him. 'Who determined how much zinc cadmium sulfide was safe to spray on elementary-school children?'

He stared her down. Good Lord, her father would be so angry right now. But she continued, 'It was you, wasn't it, Dr Hess?'

'I was the scientist in charge of that particular area.' There were a few whispers, and as if Hess wanted to extinguish them, he added, 'Along with your father.'

She paused and allowed the room to whisper. Hess meant for the comment to connect her to this atrocity and discount her, but Ellie hoped for just the opposite. If she insisted on bringing this to light in spite of her father's involvement, perhaps it would make her case even stronger.

'Zinc cadmium sulfide is now believed to be toxic. Studies show that it's toxic enough to cause birth defects and even cancer. Isn't that correct?'

'At the time it was said to be a safe, nontoxic

material. Because of its phosphor principles it was easily traced. No one was known to be harmed.'

'And how would they have known, Dr Hess, if their cancer or their child's birth defect was actually caused by your "nontoxic" material? How could they know when you didn't even tell them that they were exposed?'

Silence, but his glare answered for him.

'How many other tests like this were conducted, Dr Hess?'

'I'm unaware of the number.' This time he shrugged like it made no difference.

'The army admits that more than a hundred similar tests were conducted in multiple cities across the country on unsuspecting citizens.'

Now the room seemed to come alive as people shifted in their chairs, cameras clicked, and committee members flipped through the copies of photographs and information from inside the envelopes.

'You have no right to judge.' Dr Hess's voice boomed over the room, a teacher scolding his students into silence. 'It was a dangerous time. We faced an enemy like no other. The Russians were already far more advanced and had stockpiles of biological and chemical weapons that could level any one of our cities in a matter of hours. The Russians didn't hesitate to use those weapons on their own people.'

'Apparently you and my father and the United States Army didn't hesitate to use them on our own people, either.'

'The sacrifice of a few to save millions.' He shook his head as he said it, like she would never understand.

'Schoolchildren, Dr Hess?' She held up the photo of him with her father and the row of smiling elementary-school students for everyone, especially the cameras, to see. 'If you'd do it to schoolchildren without the public knowing, without their parents' consent, why would we not believe that you'd do it to sailors and soldiers without their consent? Without their knowledge?'

The room went silent again.

'We need to give veterans like Frank Sadowski and all the others the medical benefits and care that they've been asking for. That they deserve. Even if it's fifty years late.'

56

HAYWOOD COUNTY, NORTH CAROLINA

The smell of mud and mildew was replaced with antiseptics that stung Creed's nostrils. It already hurt to breathe. He saw needles in his arm and tubes trailing from his body. And all he could think about was his dog.

He craned his neck. Tried to sit up and was met with pain. Lay back down on sterile pillows and white sheets stained with his blood. Machines gurgled and whirred somewhere beside him. His vision wouldn't focus, breaking everything into pieces with halos of bright light around the edges. Still, he strained to lift his head enough to see over the bedrails. He needed to see if his dog was okay. If Rufus was safe.

Never leave their side. No matter what.

Not like Brodie. He should have gone with her.

Something startled him and Creed sat up. But he wasn't in a hospital. He was back in his cot. Back in the high school gymnasium. Grace stirred beside him and looked up at him, ears perched forward. Concern in her eyes. On the floor in between his cot and what had been Maggie's cot last night was Bolo, stretched out on the floor, fast asleep.

He realized the antiseptic smell came from his own body. He was shirtless beneath the blanket. Fresh bandages wrapped around his chest. But these weren't tight. Instead Creed could see that they were used only to keep a thin ice pack the length and width of his chest pressed against him.

He fingered his face and felt stitches now where the butterfly bandage had been. He looked around the open space. Almost all the cots were empty. No one was milling around. And through the small windows near the roofline he could see clouds rolling by. So it wasn't nighttime. But that was all he knew.

His body felt numb but he could breathe again despite the stabbing in his chest. The pressure in his head threatened to explode. He tried to think. Tried to remember. He stroked Grace but she still stared at him. He let his fingers run over her paws and she didn't flinch.

'You okay?' he asked. 'Is my girl okay?'

Her body wiggled against him. Ears went back and she relaxed.

'I'm okay, too,' he told her.

'You had us all worried.' He heard a voice behind him.

Dr Avelyn came around and sat on Maggie's cot where he could see her and she could observe him.

Suddenly he remembered the rush of water that had knocked him off his feet, that had separated him from Bolo. Creed had been battered against the rocks and debris, and so had the dog. He jerked up and his eyes darted around to where Bolo was lying.

'Whoa!' Dr Avelyn grabbed his arm. 'He's fine. A few minor scrapes. He's exhausted.'

Creed watched the big dog until he was satisfied. Then he asked Dr Avelyn, 'You the one who patched me up?'

'I wrapped some ice packs against your ribs. Not tightly. Maggie's right. The medic probably shouldn't have ACE'd you so tight like that on the first day.

Compression wraps used to be recommended for broken ribs. But they just make it harder for you to breathe and double your risk for pneumonia.'

'Do I have pneumonia?'

'Not yet. And hopefully not on my watch.'

He nodded. 'So is this what you'd do with a dog with broken ribs?'

'No, I'd wrap his chest tight.'

He raised an eyebrow at her and asked, 'Then how did you—'

'Did you know that Maggie was premed before going into forensics?'

He smiled and felt light-headed but otherwise no major pain. He looked back at Dr Avelyn. 'You gave me something?'

'If you're in a lot of pain you won't breathe as deeply as you need to. Don't worry, it's nothing that will incapacitate you.'

'Thanks.'

And he didn't worry. Dr Avelyn was one of the few people he trusted explicitly with his dogs. It would be silly not to extend that trust to include himself.

Which reminded him. 'Is Maggie okay?'

'Some scrapes and bruises, but yes, she's fine.'

'Any idea where she is?'

'That I can't help you with.' She stood back up. 'I need to get to my post.' She glanced at her wristwatch. 'The crews will be coming in for the night. I'll check on you at dinner.'

'Do you know where Jason is?'

'Said something about an assignment you gave him this morning.'

Morning had been a long time ago, but Creed pretended to know when he had no idea. Maybe she was right about a concussion.

'Promise me you'll stay put and get some rest?'

He nodded.

'No really.'

'I'm not leaving Grace and Bolo.'

That satisfied her and he watched her leave. What he failed to mention was that he could take both dogs along with him.

57

'You need to tell me what's going on,' O'Dell told Peter Logan.

When he hesitated, she added, 'I pulled your sorry ass from being washed downstream.'

She was exhausted and tired of arguing with the man. It had been a battle tracking down Ross and the other guardsmen, then getting both Creed and Logan down off the mountain and back to safety. Dr Avelyn had assured her that Creed would be fine but that he desperately needed to rest. Logan, despite having been knocked down and knocked out, appeared to be back to his normal, arrogant self.

'Ross's team thinks they found part of the facility.

It's buried farther up from where we were digging. They think they have a secure opening to get down into it.'

'Are there more victims trapped inside?'

He shook his head and she saw an exasperated look that he held back behind a smile.

'Now I understand that it was never about that,' he said, watching her, and she knew he was still trying to decide whether or not he should trust her.

At first introduction she had thought he was a bureaucrat, a political bully accustomed to everyone following his orders and giving in to his demands. In the last several hours she had caught glimpses of a man unsure of himself, on the verge of desperation.

She'd seen it before in the eyes of men who realized they'd been used or betrayed. What they did about it could often be the dangerous part. And she wondered what Peter Logan was capable of doing to survive if he had actually been hung out to dry by those powers above him.

They were sitting in the front seat of his Land Rover – the only place he insisted was safe from being overheard. Every once in a while he cranked the engine and blasted hot air. O'Dell had showered and changed into clean, dry clothes but she wasn't sure she'd ever remove the chill from her body. It was as if the ice-cold floodwaters had gotten inside her veins.

'Ben told me that USAMRIID and DARPA were working together on something,' O'Dell said. 'Is that what this is about?'

He seemed surprised and almost relieved.

'But he didn't tell you what it was?'

'No. He said it was classified.'

'And you were still willing to come down here?'

'I work for the FBI, Logan. The murder of these men is a federal investigation. I know how to work around classified issues. I don't, however, like having things kept from me, especially when they almost get me killed.' She let that sink in, then added, 'At some point my help to you is worthless unless I know more details.'

'Fair enough. I hear you.' And still he hesitated. 'At first I was told that we needed to find any survivors and recover whatever bodies there were. It wasn't until this afternoon that I realized that wasn't the only mission.'

'Bodies that had been murdered,' she reminded him.

The first man, supposedly a scientist, had been shot

in the head. O'Dell had never seen his body. The other man had been shot in the back. Logan still hadn't given her an explanation for who the victims were. Maybe he was getting ready to tell her who he suspected had murdered them.

'And a woman's severed hand,' she added.

'Dr Clare Shaw.' He nodded. 'She was the director of the facility. Dr Richard Carrington was the man they found first. I have no idea who the other man is or the one that's still buried out there. We believe someone murdered them all right before the landslide.'

'And you honestly have no idea who it was?'

'No. But I think I know what the killer may have been after.'

O'Dell stayed quiet and waited.

'Many of our facilities are researching new drugs and vaccines, new procedures to help our military. Back when I was a platoon leader I had my guys testing stuff like go pills and blast briefs.'

'Pills and briefs?' She wasn't sure what any of this had to do with anything.

'We called them "go pills".'

He'd misunderstood her reaction. She wasn't asking what they were. She tried to be patient.

'I'm not sure what they had in them. They'd keep us awake on long missions. No hangovers or aftereffects. Blast briefs are underwear with Kevlar. My point is, there's always something that's being developed and studied. I was always willing to try stuff out. It was for our safety, right?'

'The man lying in the temporary morgue certainly didn't look like anyone had his safety in mind when they experimented on him.'

'Experimented? What are you talking about? I thought you said he was shot in the back?'

'That's probably what killed him, but his entire body looks like one big red bruise, like he was exposed to something.' She watched his face. 'Wait a minute, you didn't know that?'

'Ross's men said they delivered a mud-covered body.'

'But you knew enough about the hand to believe it's Dr Shaw's?'

'That's a no-brainer. They told me they had seen red nail polish. And there was the ring.' He waved his hand in front of himself like none of that was important and she was derailing his train of thought.

'But you see, the bodies are incidentals.'

'You're not concerned that one of your facilities

might have been using people as human guinea pigs?'

'If there were experiments, they were done in a professional manner with volunteers who were aware of the risks. It's no different than the private sector, like pharmaceutical companies paying people for their studies. These facilities do amazing research. That's what you need to be focused on.'

She did understand that. It was what Ben and his colleagues did at USAMRIID. But the man on the stainless steel table in Ralph's Meat Locker had been exposed to something extraordinary. And she couldn't imagine him volunteering for something so severe.

'In order to do this kind of research,' Logan was still explaining, 'they sometimes have samples – dangerous samples – on hand.'

He stopped and looked at her, checking to see if she knew what he was getting at. She stared back, waiting.

He took a deep breath and went on. 'The samples are often stored in what you might call a lockbox. It's a portable, self-sufficient biocontainment unit that keeps them climate-controlled and at a temperature that keeps them from being hazardous.'

'Biocontainment? What kinds of samples are you talking about?'

'Anthrax, dengue fever, a variety of man-made viruses.'

'Ebola?'

'Possibly.'

Now she understood his sudden change to desperation.

Once upon a time O'Dell had spent a week in isolation after being exposed to Ebola. Fort Detrick called their isolation unit the Slammer. It had been one of the most frightening experiences of her life. Any one of the Level 3 or Level 4 pathogens would be deadly. That someone may have killed the facility's scientists in order to get their hands on those samples sent a new chill through her.

58

Creed had his boots tied and was working on getting a T-shirt over his head when he noticed Grace's head go up. Then suddenly Bolo was getting to his feet, too. He turned to find Jason making his way down the side of the gymnasium with a small brown dog trotting at his side. Her floppy ears were pinned back and her head jerked from side to side, nervous about the new surroundings.

Her right leg was wrapped in a bandage and the back of her neck had been shaved to accommodate the sutures that now poked out. He couldn't help thinking that the dog looked like him – beat-up, stitched up, but not broken.

'Hey, Grace, Bolo.' Jason stopped and addressed them from about ten feet away.

Both dogs glanced up at Creed as if asking permission to go check out the new dog. He put his hand up and kept them in their places.

'When you told me the guy had something for you, you could have maybe told me it was a dog.'

'I guess he didn't find any family?'

'Grandparents, but they aren't able to have a dog where they live. He said they sounded really relieved to know she had someplace to go.'

Creed reminded Grace and Bolo to stay, then he went around the cot and got down on one knee. He held out a hand for the dog, keeping it low so it wouldn't be over her head. When she didn't approach, Jason brought her closer. Creed waited for her to sniff his hand before he attempted to pet her.

'The guy said you found her in a vehicle buried underground?'

'Bolo found her. She was the only one alive inside.'

'No wonder she's skittish. What do you suppose she is?'

'Hannah will know. I'm guessing she has some golden in her.'

'She's small for a golden.'

'Do we know her name?' Creed asked.

'Dog tag says Molly.'

Her ears perked up.

'Hey, Molly.'

She wagged her tail but kept it down.

'New recruit?' he heard Maggie say from behind him.

'One of the survivors from the landslide,' Jason told her.

When Creed had woken up and didn't see her, he was almost afraid she had gone back to DC. He was glad to see she hadn't. Immediately he noticed the bruise on her jaw. He stopped himself from reaching out to touch it.

'How are you feeling?' she asked him.

'A little bit like I ran into a big concrete block.'

She smiled and he could feel her eyes running over his body, as if to see for herself how he was doing.

'Are you up for a short stroll? Just to talk for a few minutes?'

She looked to Jason before Creed did.

'I can handle this,' Jason told them. Already he had Molly at the side of Creed's cot, letting her exchange sniffs with Grace and Bolo.

'Grace.' Creed waited for the dog's attention, then pointed at her. 'Be nice.'

Creed asked if they could go outside. Maggie still had her jacket on and he grabbed his, wincing as he put it on. Maggie noticed but thankfully didn't try to help.

The air was crisp but not as damp. Different shades of purple stained the clouds where the sun had gone down. When Creed looked up he could see patches of sky through the thinning layers. Even some stars.

He took guarded breaths, trying to breathe more deeply, remembering what Dr Avelyn had said about pneumonia. The pain meds made it easier but he could already feel them wearing off.

'I didn't get a chance to thank you for saving me and Bolo.'

'As I remember, both of you saved me once.'

She walked alongside him. They kept to the sidewalk across the street from the high school to avoid the rescue crews starting to come in. He let Maggie lead them away from the noisy engines and boisterous exchanges. The rest of the town's streets remained fairly quiet.

'I need you to tell me about Peter Logan,' she said, and Creed found himself disappointed. He wasn't sure what he had hoped she wanted to talk about, but it certainly wasn't Logan.

59

'You seem to have some sort of loyalty to Logan,' Maggie said. 'And yet there's an animosity between the two of you.'

'Yeah, that's true. I don't like him.'

'And the loyalty?'

'It's not loyalty. I owed the man a favor. He's collecting it.'

When Creed noticed Maggie shivering he pointed to the neon light of a small diner. They settled into a corner booth. The place smelled like greasy fried food, and despite how good the free meals had been at the school cafeteria, both Creed and Maggie ordered cheeseburgers and fries.

'How do you know each other?'

'If you want to know about Peter Logan, why not ask your friend Ben?'

She looked away, out the window, and Creed wanted to kick himself.

'Look,' Creed said, 'I didn't mean that the way it sounded. It's just that before this week I hadn't seen or heard from Logan for about seven years. I don't know much about him at all. It sounds like Ben works with him. He must have a helluva better understanding of him than I do.'

'I'm here because Ben asked me to check on a couple of victims who may have been murdered. The facility was federally run by DARPA. So the murders will be a federal investigation. My boss approved me to come down here.'

To Creed it seemed as if Maggie was going through this explanation for herself as much as for him. Like she needed the reminder of why she was even involved.

Their waitress, who had introduced herself as Rita, interrupted them with their Cokes, served in tall glasses made of red plastic.

Outside Creed noticed the clouds were feathery wisps, allowing an almost full moon to finally shine.

'We were in Afghanistan together,' Creed said as he watched streetlights flick on and more neon fill store windows. 'My K9 unit was assigned to Logan's platoon. He was the platoon leader.'

'So you were comrades.'

'No. That's not the way it is. K9s move from one platoon to another for weeks at a time. For that reason we're the outsiders. Also we're the first out, first to die. They know not to get attached to us. But they have to depend on us to get them through a field. What we do – it's always a little bit like magic to them. They're not sure whether we'll end up saving them or getting them all killed.'

'That's why Logan calls you dogman. I didn't know you were in the military.'

'I signed up to escape. After Brodie was taken, life just kind of crumbled.'

'How old were you at the time?'

He glanced at her. They'd never talked about this, but he figured she knew that his sister's disappearance had been the reason for starting his business. Even Jason had found out that much by doing a simple internet search. Maggie was FBI. She had access to much more.

But she couldn't know – no one knew – how agonizing those searches in the beginning had been. Hell, who was he fooling – many of them were still agonizing. Because each time he found the unidentified cadaver or remains of a young woman, he found himself wondering if it could be Brodie.

'I was fourteen. Brodie was eleven. My mom was obsessed with searching. She'd get a tip about a little girl fitting Brodie's description and she'd drop everything and go. One week it'd be LA. Then Houston. Portland, Chicago. It was crazy. After a while she went a little crazy. And yet it was my dad who ended up shooting himself.' He shook his head at the irony.

Rita interrupted again, setting down platters with burgers, fries, and enough garnishes to make a salad. She thumped down a bottle of ketchup and a jar of mustard, asked if they needed anything else, and off she went, leaving a new and awkward silence.

Despite the circumstances, Creed's mouth watered as he smothered the fries in ketchup.

In between bites Maggie asked him, 'How did you choose to be a K9 handler?'

'Brodie and I always had dogs growing up. As far

back as I can remember I guess I always preferred their company. Present company excluded.'

'You're just saying that because you're gonna want whatever fries you think I won't be able to eat.'

'Oh, I've seen you eat before. I'm pretty sure there won't be leftovers.'

They enjoyed their meals and Maggie didn't ask any other questions. It was Creed who brought up the subject again. Maybe he felt like he owed her for saving Bolo. For saving him, too. Besides, it didn't matter anymore.

'When I was with Logan's unit I knew he was selling stuff on the black market.'

She looked surprised.

'He always had free samples, whether it was pills or designer running shoes, sunglasses or protein bars. He was giving his guys stuff. I think some of it was experimental. But he was selling some of it, too. There was this Afghan kid named Jabar. Logan had him coming in and out of the camp so often that everybody knew him. So he never got stopped. Never got checked.'

Creed pushed his plate aside and stared out the window again. The memory was fresh because of the recent nightmares. Seven years and he could still see that kid's crooked smile.

'One day Jabar came into camp and he was acting strange. Erratic. He was arguing with Logan about something. My dog started alerting. We were in the middle of camp. It wasn't like we were out anywhere that IEDs could be. It didn't occur to me that it was Jabar he was alerting to until I saw the kid reach under his jacket.'

'My God. He had explosives?'

Creed nodded. 'I woke up in a military hospital. Later I found out that Logan was being hailed as a hero for saving his platoon from a suicide bomber. No one even questioned that maybe he was the one who put all of them in jeopardy in the first place.'

'Wait a minute. You said you owed Logan a favor. This sounds more like he owes you for keeping silent.'

'Yeah, it does, doesn't it? I landed on my dog when the bomb went off. Thankfully he wasn't hurt. I loved that dog. Before the explosion I was even going to sign up for another tour of duty so we wouldn't be separated.' He saw the look on Maggie's face. She knew where he was going.

'But dogs are considered the military's.'

'Equipment. That's how they were categorized. At least back then. Rufus was reassigned to a new handler. I tried everything I could think of to bring him home. For four years he was my rock, my stability, my life. Nobody would listen. Nobody except Logan.'

'Rufus is the chocolate Lab that sleeps beside your bed.'

Creed nodded, impressed that she remembered from her brief visit about a month ago.

'Logan made it happen. He got me my dog back.'

60

They were headed back to the high school gymnasium. O'Dell felt a bit numb with exhaustion. She knew it had been tough for Creed to share what he had. They were a lot alike in that respect – both slow to trust and stubborn about keeping their personal lives personal.

They walked side by side along the narrow sidewalk and she hated that each time their arms brushed she felt a spark of electricity. Suddenly she was keenly aware that later that night they'd be lying in their cots watching each other, less than two feet separating their bodies. Those broad shoulders, six-pack abs – and she imagined what he'd feel like beneath her touch. The scrape of his bristled jaw against her skin.

Later she'd realize the irony that she had been thinking about sparks when she saw the first flames. She wasn't totally familiar with the layout of the town, but she knew immediately that they were coming from Ralph's.

Creed pulled out his cell phone and was punching in numbers. She left him behind. Took the shortcut through the alley. The front door would still be padlocked. She'd take a chance that the back door might be open. She was half sick to find that it was. She didn't get far. A body lay just inside the door, and in the darkness O'Dell tripped over it. Her hands came down in a puddle of what she suspected was blood, still warm and sticky.

She heard a gurgle. *Maybe not dead.*

The door opened and Creed stood against it. In the light that seeped in from the back alley, O'Dell could now see Dr Gunther's crumpled body. Her throat was slashed.

'We need to pull her out,' Creed yelled.

Already smoke billowed at them from deep inside.

O'Dell helped Creed lift the old woman, and she was sickened by the rag-doll feel of her body. He carried her to the back parking lot and laid her down on the concrete. In seconds he was on his knees, his hands trying to staunch the bleeding. But O'Dell could see the gap was too wide.

She could hear shouts and calls from the street on the other side of the building. Sirens filled the night air. So loud. So close.

The old woman was gone and yet Creed kept his hands pressed into the wound. O'Dell knelt on the opposite side and searched for a pulse. She didn't know what else to do. She was worthless to the dying. She never had a clue what to do or say. Only after they were dead did she know what her job was.

Volunteer firefighters made their way into the building. The sound of water rushed from a nearby hydrant. The heat was enough that she was drenched in sweat on a night that had made her shiver earlier.

O'Dell imagined everything inside would be lost to the flames. Everything including the body and the severed hand. Every piece of evidence of what may have happened at the government facility that once sat up on the mountain.

And O'Dell couldn't help thinking it was no

coincidence that this should happen only hours after she had told Peter Logan about the strange bruising and rash that covered the dead man inside. The man whose body was now being incinerated.

61

'You think Logan started the fire?' Creed asked Maggie and watched her face in the flickering light of the blaze that engulfed Ralph's Meat Locker.

Her eyes had been wild with adrenaline just moments ago when they pulled the woman from the building. Now he worried as she stared, almost hypnotized by the dancing flames.

Rescue crews who had been coming in from a day of working the landslide had joined the firefighters. They were hosing down the neighboring buildings, hoping to keep the fire from spreading. A second explosion inside the brick structure prevented them from entering.

Creed felt the spray of cold water raining down even as the heat from the flames felt like it would scorch his skin. He and Maggie stood in the back alley, guarding the old woman's body, now covered by a tarp.

Earlier, one of the medics had taken over, shoving Creed aside. But he knew it was too late. The blood had been warm on his hands but there was no sign of life. No fluttering eyelids. No beat of a pulse under his fingers. Not a single gasp of breath.

Maggie had told him the old woman was Dr Gunther, the medical examiner. And then she went silent. Now she stood, arms crossed over her chest, looking angry and annoyed that the firefighters had asked them to keep back and stay with the body. Maybe it wasn't anger as much as frustration. That's what he was feeling – frustrated that there wasn't anything more he could do.

But then out of the silence, Maggie said, 'Logan did this.'

It was almost as if she was telling herself. She didn't even seem to have heard his question.

Just when Creed was about to ask again, she said, 'You don't think he's capable of doing something like this?'

'If he thought it might save his own skin, I think he might be capable of doing just about anything. But why would he do this? Especially after being such a pain in the ass about recovering those bodies?'

Now Maggie's eyes darted around. Was she looking for Logan? Or was she worried they'd be overheard? No one was paying attention to the two of them. People were rushing by, once even bumping a hose over the tarp, not noticing as Creed pulled it up and readjusted it.

'The body we dug up yesterday had a strange bruising all over it. At first Dr Gunther thought it looked like chemical burns.'

'There's a lot of weird stuff that leaked into the mud.'

She shook her head, moved closer to him, and turned so that she was facing him. 'They weren't postmortem.'

'She was sure about that?'

'The skin had bubbled up in places. We discounted burns. It almost looked like a rash, except that it was deeper. More like a bruise. And in some areas the skin practically fell away with the slightest touch.'

'Fell away? Not from decomp?'

'He wasn't dead long enough for that kind of decomposition.'

He realized that she had quieted her tone. Anything less and she'd be whispering.

'What did she think it was from?'

'She hadn't been able to make that determination. I'm guessing that's what brought her back here tonight.'

'Why come at night? Wasn't she hired to process the bodies we recovered?'

'Someone padlocked the front door. Ralph gave her a key to the back door. Otherwise she wouldn't have had access until Logan allowed it.'

'So Logan didn't really want anyone examining the bodies?'

'I guess not. But here's the weird part. I told him about the condition of the body, and he seemed surprised. He knew about the bullet hole in the back, but he pretended not to know about the strange bruising.'

'So you think this is how he prevents anyone else from knowing?'

She was biting her lower lip when she nodded this time.

'Only one problem,' she said. 'He knows that I know.'

62

Creed hadn't noticed in the last twenty-four hours whether or not Maggie was carrying a weapon. Now as she sat on her cot and peeled off her sweatshirt he saw the shoulder holster snug against her side, just under her left breast. There was an unsettling nervous energy about her. Even the dogs sensed it.

All the way back she had been obsessed with her cell phone, leaving messages, then checking every five minutes. She had it beside her. Creed sat down opposite her on his cot, so close their knees brushed.

'Maggie, what's going on?'

'I'm trying to find out.' Her eyes were on the phone,

waiting. 'Logan told me recovering the bodies was only part of their mission. He said the facility had samples of Level 3 and Level 4 pathogens.'

'Why would they have those?'

'They're a research facility.' She shrugged. 'It's actually not that unusual. Unfortunate, but not unusual. If they were trying to come up with a vaccine or antidote, they'd need samples of the real stuff.'

'Wait a minute. What are we talking about? You mean like anthrax?'

'Anthrax. Possibly the bird flu. Maybe Ebola.'

Creed took a deep breath and winced. He was hanging on to the final threads of the pain medicine Dr Avelyn had given him.

'He said the samples are stored in a lockbox. He thinks someone was trying to steal it. That they murdered Dr Shaw and Dr Carrington and these other men and hoped it would be covered up by the landslide.'

'Why didn't you tell me about this?' he asked.

'I am telling you.'

'When did you find out?'

'Just before I came to get you.'

'But you're only telling me now?'

'Logan told me in confidence. The bastard,' she mumbled. 'Now I don't even know if it's true.'

'Wouldn't Ben know about all this?'

She rubbed her hands over her face, wiping at the exhaustion.

When she didn't answer he realized it was one of the phone calls she was waiting for.

Creed let it go and asked instead, 'Do you think this dead man – the one with the strange bruising – do you think he might have been exposed to one of those deadly samples?'

Her eyes looked up at him and he could see that she had already thought about this.

Creed said the obvious: 'If he was, isn't there a chance that you and Dr Gunther were exposed?'

'We had gloves and masks on. We didn't come in contact with any of his bodily fluids.'

'Are you sure?'

His eyes held hers until he saw the realization strike her. She grabbed his hand.

'I know what you're thinking. Your hands were drenched in her blood. I can't say for certain that we weren't exposed, but I do know that she was careful. She hadn't even cut him or taken any blood.'

Her phone rang, startling both of them.

She grabbed it, looked at the screen, and answered without a greeting.

'Thanks for calling me back. Have you heard from Logan?' Her face remained unchanged as she listened. 'He told me earlier that you found where the facility is buried. I need you to take me there.'

63

At midnight O'Dell finally got a call from Ben.

'You sounded upset. Are you okay?'

'No, I'm not okay. You need to tell me what the hell is going on.'

She was talking in a forced whisper so she wouldn't wake those in the cots around her. She saw Creed stir but she knew Dr Avelyn had given him another dose of pain meds. She hurried to find an exit.

Clear skies, but the air was crisp and still held the smell of the smoldering fire blocks away.

'Maggie, all I know is that the second body you dug up was shot in the back. And that Dr Shaw is now believed to be one of the victims.'

'You had to know that this facility had Level 3 and Level 4 pathogens.'

She waited out his silence.

'Is that what Logan told you?'

'It would have been nice if *you* had told me.'

'We suspected it,' he said. 'But I swear to you, Maggie, I didn't know when I asked you to go down.'

'I can't believe you let me dig around in the mud knowing what could have been mixed in the debris.'

'The lockboxes they use wouldn't have been broken open.'

'Did you know that landslides can be so strong and violent that they can literally rip a body apart?'

'No, I didn't know that. But I understand that may have happened to Dr Shaw.'

'If they can rip buildings to shreds and dismember bodies, why wouldn't a landslide be able to breach your lockbox?'

'It hasn't been breached. I understand they're still getting a signal from it.'

'I can't believe that I had to hear about this from Logan. When did you think you were going to tell me, Ben?'

He was quiet again. She hated that calm he could

manage in the middle of any storm. He had performed surgeries in Iraq and Afghanistan with mortars firing around him. He had treated patients with Marburg in Sierra Leone. He had treated Maggie and her former boss after the two of them had been exposed to Ebola. And always he maintained that disciplined calm that could be as reassuring as it was annoying. Right now, O'Dell found it completely annoying.

'I examined the body of the dead man last night with Dr Gunther, the medical examiner. His skin looked like it had been exposed to something, Ben. Something extreme.'

'What did the ME think it was?'

'She wasn't sure. But she thought she'd seen something like it before.'

'What do you mean?'

'In the 1960s, when the US Army sprayed some experimental simulant over Eglin Air Force Base. She told me airmen were spitting up blood and bleeding from their ears. She thought the blisters and rash on the man we dug up looked similar.'

'How could she know this so many years later?'

'It obviously made a hell of an impression on her when she saw it the first time.'

'If they can ship the body up here, I'll take a look at it myself.'

'Not gonna happen.'

'I'll talk to Logan about it.'

'Someone set the place on fire tonight. Everything went up in flames.'

He was quiet again, then said, 'I didn't know. Maggie, I didn't know.'

She stopped herself from sharing her suspicions about Logan. Then realized it was because she no longer trusted Ben. She had been waiting all evening to talk to him about all this, hoping he had answers or at least a better explanation for why he had kept such vital information from her.

'Look, Maggie, maybe I can talk to this Dr Gunther. If she can explain what she observed, I might be able to help narrow down what happened to this man.'

At that moment she realized that even Ben was being kept out of the loop.

'Unfortunately she can't do that, Ben. She's dead. The same person who started the fire cut Dr Gunther's throat.'

More silence.

Then he said, 'I'm coming down there first thing in the morning.'

It didn't matter. O'Dell didn't bother to tell him she would already be gone by the time he arrived.

64

Dr Avelyn had given Creed another dose of pain meds to help him sleep, but they weren't working. Instead he dozed in and out of consciousness. Twice he noticed Maggie's cot was empty except for Grace curled up on the pillow. Around midnight he'd crawled out of his bed, fighting the exhaustion but needing to make sure she was okay.

'Which way did Maggie go?' he asked Grace.

She looked over her shoulder toward the back exit. Sure enough, Creed saw her pacing up and down the sidewalk with her cell phone pressed to the side of her face.

He went back to his bed and pulled the covers up,

waiting for her to return. He must have dozed off again. When he opened his eyes she was curled next to Grace, but in the dim light of the gymnasium he could see her watching him. He pulled himself up on one elbow to meet her eyes.

'Why is this so important to you?' he asked.

She seemed to be thinking about it.

'A few years ago my boss and I were exposed to Ebola.' She pulled herself up on one elbow, too, and Grace tucked herself even closer.

'Grace goes home with me, no matter what,' Creed said, and he saw Maggie smile at the little dog. 'Go on. How did you get exposed?'

'A note led us to a house where we thought there might be a hostage being held. The note was actually delivered to the Behavioral Science Unit – not an easy feat to accomplish. Assistant Director Cunningham took it seriously enough that he insisted on being part of the response team.'

She swatted at a strand of hair and stared over Creed's shoulder like she was searching for the rest of the story.

'When we got there this little girl answered the door and let us in. We were still thinking hostage situation.

The girl was dressed in soiled clothes. Her hair was tangled. Dirty dishes were everywhere. It looked like she had been abandoned and was living on her own. But that was only partly correct. Her mother was in one of the bedrooms. Very sick. At the time we didn't realize that she was already crashing with Ebola.'

'So you were both exposed?'

She nodded.

'And the little girl?'

'She survived. Her mother, of course, did not. Cunningham and I were immediately put in Fort Detrick's Slammer. That's what they call their isolation unit. Dr Benjamin Platt took care of us.'

Creed didn't think he flinched but she looked at him as if he had and added, 'It's not what you think. It wasn't a case of patient falling in love with the doctor who saved her. I had to trust him with my life. I suppose there's a bond that naturally develops. It's not necessarily a bad thing. We became friends. And ultimately, he did save my life.'

'What about Cunningham?'

Her eyes left his, strayed back over his shoulder again to the shadows.

'He didn't make it.'

Creed could feel the emotion in that brief sentence. Maybe it was simply survivor's guilt. He knew that all too well, but he suspected Cunningham held meaning in her life. He didn't ask.

'Bottom line,' she said, 'I know how dangerous these samples are. It's not just a matter of recovering them so that they don't fall into the wrong hands. They're still receiving a signal from the box. But if it's not found, who knows what could happen?'

'Why not leave it to the experts to retrieve it?'

'The experts already screwed it up, didn't they? I talked to Ross and now he says that he doesn't even know where Logan is. I'm afraid Logan is more determined to burn and bury this mess out of existence than he is with doing the right thing.'

Creed groaned.

'What?'

'Why do I keep surrounding myself with women who always want to do the right thing?'

She smiled. Creed reached out his hand across the space between them and over Bolo's head. Maggie hesitated for only a second or two before she took his hand and squeezed it.

He held tight as he told her, 'You do realize that

the same man who saved you was willing to send you down here to possibly be exposed to something equally dangerous?'

This time she didn't look away. She didn't respond, and she didn't pull her hand away from his.

DAY 4

65

EARLY MORNING

WASHINGTON, DC

When Colonel Hess opened the front door he scowled at Benjamin Platt.

'This had better be as urgent as is the hour.'

Hess was dressed in trousers, a collared shirt, cardigan sweater, and fine leather shoes. Even after being awoken in the middle of the night the man needed to look in control. Platt, on the other hand, had thrown on blue jeans and a sweatshirt. In his hurry, he'd forgotten socks and a jacket.

'The situation in North Carolina is more urgent than we thought,' he told the colonel.

'Have there been more landslides?'

'No. But there's been a fire. The building they were using for a temporary morgue was destroyed.'

His bushy gray eyebrows rose. 'And the bodies?'

'As far as anyone knows, they were destroyed.'

Hess nodded and Platt stared at him. He didn't seem fazed by the news.

'Has Logan checked in?' Platt asked. 'Has he told you anything about this?'

'Logan.' He made a noise as he waved his hand, indicating he'd had it with Logan.

'I sent someone down there,' Platt said, 'who might now be in danger. Someone I care very deeply about. And I sent her there because you asked me to choose someone I trusted implicitly. You told me that facility might – and you emphasized *might* – contain Level 4 samples. You never told me about the experiments.'

'Calm down, Benjamin.'

'Look, I respect you, Abe. You've been a tremendous mentor to me—'

'One you repay by waking me in the middle of the night with your suspicions.'

'I just need to know what the hell's happening down

there. This isn't about us protecting the world anymore, Abraham. We have a responsibility. This facility isn't even a part of Fort Detrick. It's DARPA. It's your responsibility.'

'Exactly. You're correct. I was wrong in asking for your help. However, I have everything under control. I have a team down—'

'Under control? Wait a minute.' And it only just occurred to Platt. 'You mean under *your* control. Your special team isn't just searching for the lockbox. They're cleaning up to make sure no one ever knows about any of this.'

'You don't know what you're talking about, Benjamin.'

'That fire destroyed evidence.'

This time Hess stared at him as if mention of the fire had finally struck a nerve.

'You're not the only one, Benjamin, who has lost someone. I sent someone there, too. Someone who I once trusted many years ago. She was married to one of my dearest friends. I thought I could still trust her.' He shook his head like it didn't matter. Then added, 'We all make sacrifices.'

'I have no idea what you're talking about.'

'Your friend is a bit of a rebel, isn't she? Just like my so-called trusted friend.'

'I suppose you could call Maggie a rebel. What does that—'

'You failed to mention that. Rebels have a tendency to meddle more than help.'

'She does what she believes is the right thing.'

'The right thing? The right thing? We're faced today with a new threat that makes the Cold War look like child's play. That's what no one understands. Your friend has no idea what the right thing is in this case. She can't possibly know. I suggest you go home and get some sleep, Benjamin. You need to trust me to take care of this.'

'And what if Logan is the rebel?'

Hess stopped and stared at him as if he hadn't given it any thought until Platt said it.

'What if Logan is destroying evidence? What if he has other intentions?'

Hess shook his head. 'I'll take care of everything. You go home. Get some sleep.'

'I'm going down there first thing in the morning.'

'There's no need.' And now Hess had his arthritic hand on Platt's back and was guiding him toward the door. 'By morning everything will be taken care of.'

Platt couldn't help thinking that the colonel made it sound like he already knew what was going to happen.

66

HAYWOOD COUNTY, NORTH CAROLINA

At sunrise the sky was still clear, but Creed had checked the weather forecast and knew it would be short-lived. Maggie had argued about him coming with them up to the site where the facility was buried. She had argued harder when he told her he'd bring Grace in case the viruses could be sniffed out or the electronic ping was too faint to be registering. Perhaps Grace would be able to hear it.

She told him that she suspected they'd need to trek on foot for a good portion of the way. That he and Grace would only slow them down.

'If that happens you can leave us behind.'

She rolled her eyes at him, then she said, 'I would never leave Grace behind.'

He was glad to see she had her sense of humor because the Maggie O'Dell he had witnessed throughout the night made him still concerned about her motives. He had heard the sincerity when she explained about needing to do the right thing, but he also knew she was angry with Logan. He suspected she was even angrier with Ben. From his own experience, anger could be a destructive force.

This morning he, at least, felt clearheaded. The throbbing had eased. His chest ached but he could breathe more deeply. He examined Grace's pads, pleased with how they looked.

Jason arrived bleary-eyed, bringing Molly with him. They settled in with Bolo.

'Maybe Bolo and me should be going with you.'

He watched Creed prepare his pack with the gear he and Grace would need. Creed was taking along a mesh carrier that he planned on using with Grace. It fit over his head and shoulder and swung down by his side. She weighed only fifteen pounds so it wasn't any different from carrying his backpack. He had used the carrier before, placing Grace inside so she could ride against him but be comfortable and have access to enough air to still do her job.

He looked around to make sure Maggie was out of earshot when he sat down next to Jason and said, 'If we're not back by nightfall, give this to Vance.'

Jason stared at the tracking device, then asked, 'You already think you're gonna need to be rescued, don't you?'

'Just a precaution.'

Truth was, he didn't have a good feeling about this. What Jason didn't know was that Creed would be tucking the companion to the GPS tracking device into Grace's vest so at least she would be found.

He saw that Maggie was ready to go and he clapped Jason on the back.

'One other favor,' Creed told him. 'Call Hannah. Tell her what's going on. But wait until I have a head start.'

Jason smiled at the last part. 'I'll call Hannah, but you have to do one thing for me.'

Creed agreed before he realized the kid had something serious in mind. Jason left for the locker room and when he came back he was carrying the one item he wanted Creed to take along. That's when he knew

Jason also thought this trip up the mountain was a bad idea.

The three of them climbed into Ross's SUV. Grace barely got settled before she started to stare at Creed. She was alerting.

How could she already be alerting?

Creed glanced around the vehicle. Maggie sat up front with Ross. He and Grace were in the back. Creed turned his body so he could get a good look at what was in the very back of the SUV. It was possible that the vehicle had carried equipment or there was residue from a previous cargo, but he couldn't see anything suspicious. Other than Maggie and Creed's gear in the back, there was only one other backpack. Presumably it belonged to the young guardsman.

Ross was dressed in crisp camouflage fatigues. Creed had noticed that his boots were spit-and-polish clean. Maybe his weapon was tucked away somewhere, but Creed doubted that would set Grace off. Once he caught the dog's eyes wandering to the back of Ross's head. Then she immediately looked to Creed again.

Ross told them that he had good news. The trip

up to the facility would take less time because of the clear skies. He had a helicopter waiting for them just outside the city limits.

Grace appeared to have settled down. That actually made Creed feel better. Perhaps whatever she was alerting to had been residue in the SUV. He was relieved they wouldn't have to trudge through the mud. Plus they could get this over with more quickly. Although helicopters reminded Creed too much of Afghanistan, Grace loved the adventure and the roller-coaster ride. Perhaps that would make her relax.

However, Creed took one look at Maggie's face and knew she did not agree that the helicopter was good news.

67

A *helicopter!* O'Dell's jaw clenched and her stomach took a nosedive.

She hated flying, and doing it in a helicopter was a special hell of its own. She put on sunglasses and stared out the window. She'd been hoping to see blue sky for days.

Careful what you wish for.

She asked again about Logan, and again Ross told her his team hadn't heard from the man since the day before. The young guardsman seemed on edge this morning, but then so was O'Dell. She hadn't been able to relax the knot in her chest. Last night she had the nagging urge to crawl into Ryder's cot. Even now as she thought about it, she scolded herself and repeated in her head, *Careful what you wish for.*

She considered talking Ross out of the helicopter. She hadn't paid any attention to the forecast, but what if the clear skies didn't last? Did they have another mode of transportation available to come back down the mountain?

But she stopped herself. More than anything, she wanted this over and done with. There wasn't much time to waste. She reminded herself about Dr Gunther. Whoever set that fire last night – whether it was Logan or someone else – had meant to destroy what was inside. She had to be next. She knew that.

She didn't think she could wait for Kunze. She did tell her boss that they needed to find Peter Logan. It wasn't a coincidence that he'd suddenly disappeared.

All night she kept watch, flinching and rising at any sound that seemed out of place. She didn't think Logan would risk burning down a gymnasium and taking with it dozens of rescue workers and volunteers. But she'd seen desperate men do desperate things.

It was best that she beat him back up the mountain. She needed to recover the deadly samples before someone mad enough to kill an old woman and incinerate evidence got there. She couldn't depend on Ben. He had called several times since they talked last night. She silenced her phone and ignored his messages.

O'Dell knew what she needed to do. She only wished she could have talked Creed into staying behind.

68

The wreckage up there was more severe. Creed was glad he'd brought the mesh carrier for Grace. No way he was allowing her to step foot onto that mess.

To Creed it looked like the remnants of a bombed-out village in Afghanistan. Only rubble left. Stubs of trees stripped of their branches. Pieces of rooflines sticking up out of the ground. An eerie reminder that they were walking on top of the buried building. He imagined hallways still intact underneath. Maybe more bodies trapped down there.

The smell of diesel and propane was dangerously strong and he searched for greasy puddles even as he followed Ross and Maggie.

The pilot had stayed with the helicopter. So far no one else was there to meet them. And Ross didn't look like he expected anyone else.

'It's not much farther,' he told Maggie. He glanced back at Grace then asked, 'What exactly can the dog find?'

'A number of things. But she hasn't been trained with any of the viruses we're looking for.'

If Creed hadn't known better, he'd have thought Ross looked pleased with that information instead of concerned about Grace's limitations.

Grace, however, was unsettled again. She had wiggled into the carrier willingly but then stared at him again and fidgeted. Now traveling securely at his side, she pawed at him every once in a while. When he looked down, her nose was twitching, her breathing rapid. She obviously had found a scent she was working.

Multitask dogs were exceptional, even phenomenal. But sometimes they could get confused. The smallest miscue or misunderstanding of what their owner expected could result in a false alert. Creed used different commands and a variety of harnesses and vests for each task. If he didn't make it clear what he expected the dog to search for, there could be confusion.

But Grace didn't get confused.

Still, a dog might smell something that they recognized as a scent they'd been trained to search for. When they smelled it – even though they hadn't been asked to find that particular scent at that particular time – they might alert to it. The landslide had smeared the mountain with enough scent to drive a dog crazy. Was she smelling human decomposition?

Earlier Creed suspected she was alerting to something inside the SUV. Now she was alerting again, staring up at him. The only common denominator was Ross.

He eyed the guardsman's backpack. Creed watched the fit and swing of his jacket. Did guardsmen always carry weapons?

He looked down at Grace. Her nose was twitching again. She pushed her shoulders out of the carrier to get a better sniff.

'Looks like Grace is onto something,' Maggie said.

And this time when Ross glanced back Creed saw that the man didn't look pleased.

Creed patted his jacket pocket and stopped. 'I must

have dropped her special collar when I was getting out of the helicopter,' he said while trying to catch Maggie's eye.

'Collar?' Ross asked.

'Yeah, no wonder she's so unsettled. Without it, she's not really sure what she's supposed to be searching for. Maggie, would you mind running back and getting it? I'm a little slow after getting banged up the last couple of days.'

But he could see she didn't understand. She knew Creed used vests and collars to let Grace know which scent he wanted her to find. He wanted to alert Maggie that something was wrong, but more than anything, he wanted Maggie away from there.

'Sure, I can do that,' she said.

'It won't be necessary,' Ross told her. And in seconds he had a revolver pointed at Creed's chest. 'Agent O'Dell, you'll need to give me your service weapon.'

69

The hole in the ground reminded O'Dell of the entrance to a storm cellar. Deep, dark, and narrow, with a wooden ladder providing the only steps down. In the beam of her flashlight she could see fragments of what used to be an office or a laboratory. Shattered glass cupboards, light fixtures swinging from wires in the ceiling, walls partially caved in.

She couldn't believe that she had let Ross's uniform fool her. She had been convinced that Peter Logan was the problem. It never occurred to her to suspect the men who had worked beside her to recover the bodies in the mud.

Ben had called them a cleanup team that Colonel

Hess had sent down to help. But now she understood why the colonel had used the term 'cleanup.' She and Kunze were right. Hess and maybe others at the DoD didn't want anyone to know about this mess, especially not while they were battling Congress to keep their other secrets under wraps.

'So your job was never recovery,' she said as she handed over her Glock. 'You were here to cover up all this mess. Is there even a lockbox?'

'My men found it this morning. It's already being transported down the mountain and into the trunk of my SUV. Before nightfall I'll have it in a safe place.'

'I understand why you need to get rid of me,' O'Dell said. 'I saw the results of the experiments that were going on here. Is that why you murdered Dr Shaw and the others?'

Ross frowned at her. 'I didn't kill them. And I don't know anything about experiments. I arrived after the landslide. Who knows what happened here? My team was hired to recover the bodies and lockbox.'

'And make sure no one knows about any of it.' She glanced back at Grace and Creed and a knot tightened in her stomach. 'They didn't even see the bodies. Let them go.'

'I didn't suggest they come.'

The knot moved up into her throat and threatened to choke her. *My God, he was right.*

That's when Maggie saw something else down in the hole. A flap of blond hair, bloodied by a gunshot wound at the temple. Peter Logan.

70

When Ross pulled out the gun, Creed had seen something else almost tumble out of his pocket. It looked an awful lot like a detonator.

And suddenly Creed understood what Grace had been alerting to. There were explosives down below. Ross must have helped set them. He still had residue on his hands or clothes. Creed kept his hand inside Grace's carrier, petting her, reassuring her as best he could.

'Why bring us all the way out here just to kill us?' Maggie asked.

She was trying to remain calm, but Creed had already caught a glimpse of panic in her eyes.

That Ross had the gun pointed at him instead of Maggie was good. It could give her a chance to fight even if it was only seconds after he fired at Creed.

'The place is ready to blow up,' Ross told her. 'Accidents happen. There's an awful lot of spilled fuel, ruptured propane lines. It's a shame that you two were poking around up here when it happened.'

'So you started the fire last night.'

He shrugged.

'And you killed Dr Gunther. That was no accident.'

'Collateral damage.'

He said it with no emotion, like a dozen other soldiers Creed knew. It was drilled into them. But this wasn't war. And then something occurred to Creed.

'The floodwaters yesterday. That wasn't an accident, either, was it?' he asked the man.

'Would have certainly made it a lot easier if you'd both died then.'

'By "both" you mean me and Logan,' Maggie said.

The stoic look on Ross's face told Creed that Logan was already part of the collateral damage.

'So who exactly do you work for?' Creed asked.

'More importantly,' Maggie added, 'who do you kill for, Ross?'

When he said nothing, Maggie added, 'It's Colonel Abraham Hess, isn't it?'

Creed knew if Ross couldn't force them down into the hole he'd have no problem shooting them and dropping their bodies down. He'd probably even shoot Grace. And that made Creed angry.

'I'm letting Grace go,' he told Ross as he started to bend down, making sure to put his body between the dog and the gun.

'No, don't move. Stop right now or I'll wound you and make you watch me shoot the dog.'

Creed stopped but stayed hunched over the carrier, protecting Grace as best he could. He kept his hand in the carrier. He glanced at Maggie and caught a glimpse of her eyes again. He expected to see regret. If not for him, then for Grace. That's not what he saw. Instead he saw anger and fight. And while Ross was paying attention to Creed crouching down on the ground, he wasn't paying as much attention to Maggie.

Sometimes when Creed did a search and rescue it took them to strange and dangerous places. He usually came prepared, not necessarily to protect himself but always with the thought of protecting his dogs. There were plenty of things in the wilderness that could harm them. And although he never wore a gun, he armed himself with whatever might be needed to fight off coyotes or even bears.

With his hand hidden inside the carrier he found the canister of pepper spray safely stowed in the back pocket. His fingers wrapped around it even with Grace fidgeting.

'Get back up on your feet. Now.'

Creed slid the carrier off his shoulder and rested it on the ground with Grace still in it. He'd need to shoot the spray up into Ross's face without getting any of it on Grace. As he started to rise he heard the gunshot.

It knocked Creed off his feet. The bullet had hit him in the chest. Pain exploded inside him. Sucked the air out of his lungs. Creed fell on top of Grace. All he could think about was protecting her with his body. Just like seven years ago when he protected Rufus.

He saw starbursts behind his eyes. He didn't even hear the second gunshot.

71

O'Dell lunged for her own weapon on the ground. She expected Ross to turn his gun on her. Instead, he shot Creed in the chest.

No, she didn't want to believe what she saw.

Seconds ticked by. Her fingers grabbed the handle. She heard Creed gasp. She heard the thud as he dropped to the ground. She was rolling onto her back while her finger desperately searched for the trigger. Ross turned the gun on her.

Too late. She'd never make it.

She heard the second gunshot and knew it wasn't from her gun. Before she could fire she saw the blossom of blood on the side of Ross's head. She watched, stunned, as his gun slipped from his fingers. He fell to his knees, eyes already dead before he hit the ground.

O'Dell struggled to her feet.

A man stood about ten feet away with a rifle now slung down and pointing at the ground. He wasn't one of Ross's team. He wore what looked like medical scrubs, dirty and torn. His feet were wrapped in bandages.

Carefully, O'Dell made her way to Creed while watching the man.

'You folks okay?' he asked.

'I don't know,' she answered.

She wanted to find out and yet she couldn't bear to see how badly Creed was hurt. If she couldn't save him.

Or if he was already dead.

She knelt next to him. Grace squirmed out of the carrier and circled around and around. She was sniffing at her owner. O'Dell looked for blood. He had taken a direct hit to his chest.

Grace was licking his face.

'I'm so sorry, Grace,' she told the little dog.

Then Grace started to wag.

O'Dell heard a groan. Suddenly she saw movement.

Creed was flat on his back. Eyes open now, looking up at her.

'How in the world—'

'Jason,' he said through gritted teeth as he tried to raise himself up.

'Just stay put for a minute.' She put her hand against his chest and that's when she felt it under his jacket. 'Jason gave you a bulletproof vest?'

'Supposed to be the newest, lightest—' He was gasping for breath. 'His buddy Tony. He's a paranoid bastard.'

She put a finger to his lips. 'Please, just stay still.' And even as she was telling him this, she meant it for her own heart, because it was galloping in her chest. 'It stopped the bullet, but we need to be careful about your ribs. We need to make sure they don't puncture a lung.'

'You shoot him?' he asked. 'Is he dead?'

She wiped the hair off his forehead. 'He's dead, but I didn't shoot him.'

She looked up and the man in the raggedy clothes had ventured closer, slowly.

'Is he okay?' he asked.

Creed craned his neck to take a look at the man.

'These guys have been up here since yesterday. I knew they were up to no good. They were planting IEDs down in the tunnels.' He held up the rifle. 'They forgot this.'

'Who are you?' O'Dell finally asked.

'My name's Daniel Tate.'

'But how did you—'

Before O'Dell could ask, Tate interrupted. 'Not right, him threatening to shoot that dog.'

He bent down and offered Grace his dirty fingers to sniff.

'Just wasn't right, at all.'

72

It took some convincing to get the helicopter pilot to leave without Ross. O'Dell had to show him her badge. But he was a local contractor and not part of Ross's team. He ended up more concerned about the weather and getting them back safely. In the distance they had already heard the beginning rumbles of thunder.

O'Dell had found the detonator in the guardsman's pocket when she searched for the SUV keys. Creed told her that Grace had been alerting ever since they got into Ross's vehicle.

'I just couldn't figure out what it was.'

She told him about Peter Logan and they realized

that up near the hole, Grace was probably alerting to the body. The poor little dog had too many scents to tell them about.

Daniel Tate she delivered to Vance. After listening to his story she realized Colonel Hess hadn't counted on a survivor. Someone who had been used in the facility's experiments. He kept talking about a spaceman opening a special suitcase and she wondered how many drugs were still in his system. How much of what he told them was real and how much were hallucinations?

She delivered Creed and Grace safely back to their cot in the gymnasium. By then he didn't have any fight left in him to argue with her. She knew he was in tremendous pain. She only hoped his injuries weren't severe. All she could concentrate on was that he was alive. For several minutes on the mountain she thought she had lost him a second time.

She left him with Dr Avelyn and Jason.

'What are you going to do?' he wanted to know.

'I'll be back,' she promised. 'I just need to check and see if Ross was telling the truth about the lockbox.'

The rain had started again when O'Dell headed back out. She was on her way to the SUV when she stopped in the middle of the street. She could hardly believe her eyes. Benjamin Platt was talking to a rescue crew on the sidewalk. He glanced up. Did a double take when he saw her. He said something to the crew and they looked back at her, too.

'God, I am so glad you're safe.'

He hugged her so tight he practically crushed her to his chest. And only then did she realize how much her body ached from the water rescue yesterday. *Was that only yesterday?*

'I left you a bunch of messages.'

'I was a little busy.'

'Have you heard from Logan yet?'

'Logan's dead.'

'What?'

She told him what had happened, giving him as much detail as she could and ignoring the alarm on his face. She was still angry with him.

'My God, I'm so sorry, Maggie,' he said when she was finished. And almost a little too quickly – ever the scientist and soldier – he added, 'I got here as soon as I could. I brought down a team with a hazmat van in case we find the samples.'

She was surprised at how disappointed she was

that he sounded like the cold government official, the director of USAMRIID, instead of like her boyfriend. He was more concerned with deadly samples in a lockbox than he was about her. Of course, the samples were more important. And it was silly, but she was surprised how much more she needed the boyfriend than the director right now.

'I might be able to tell you exactly where those samples are.'

She ignored his look of astonishment and led him to the muddy black SUV in the far corner of the parking lot. She raised the lift gate. Then she removed the rubber mat from inside to reveal the trapdoor for the spare tire. When she lifted the hatch, she was almost as surprised as Ben. What looked like a harmless black metal suitcase was exactly where Ross had said it would be.

73

Creed had listened to Dr Avelyn lecture him about resting. This time she insisted on a chest X-ray. No perforations. A couple of ribs were definitely fractured. She no longer questioned whether or not he had a concussion. About the only thing she had told him that he was happy about was that she didn't want him to travel for a few days. Although Hannah wanted him back home where she could fuss over him.

How could he leave now when he knew Benjamin Platt was there?

Creed glanced at the three dogs in the corner next to his table in the cafeteria. Jason had insisted that Creed sit while he waited on him.

The dogs had eaten and were lounging next to each other. Molly already fit in, though it broke Creed's heart when she looked up at everyone walking by, still looking for her owners. He reached down and petted her.

When he looked back up Maggie had come in the cafeteria door. He took small pleasure in the fact that she was alone. But he hated already wondering whether or not she'd be in the cot next to him tonight or if she'd be with Ben Platt.

She saw him from across the room, and as she walked over her eyes never left his. Even as she sat down, choosing the chair across from him. She scooted close so she could plant elbows on the table. The whole time, she didn't say a word as her eyes held his. So much emotion between the two of them. In less than forty-eight hours she had saved him twice.

Finally she glanced away, using the dogs as an excuse and smiling when Grace pranced over to her.

'Jake and Harvey would instantly fall in love with you,' she told the little dog while scratching behind her ears. Maggie's eyes darted back to Creed's.

'You still can't have her,' he said, and Maggie laughed.

Then she said something Creed never expected.

'Jake and Harvey would fall in love with you, too.'

Before Creed had a chance to say anything, Oliver Vance was making his way directly to their table.

'I'm glad you're both here,' Vance said. 'My crew pulled a vehicle out of a flooded ravine yesterday.'

When Jason and Creed came to the cafeteria they had passed by the whiteboard Vance kept in the gymnasium. The tally for missing persons had gone down to three. But the death toll had risen to seventeen. He was afraid Vance was getting ready to raise that number again.

'How many passengers?' Creed asked.

'Only one, but I recognized the victim.' He looked at Creed. 'It was Isabel Klein.' He let the name sink in. 'That government woman who brought you here.'

'Klein?' Maggie asked.

'She was Peter Logan's assistant,' Creed said. 'I haven't seen her since that day. What happened? Did she slide off the road?'

Vance shook his head. 'Not unless she was rushing herself to a hospital.'

'What do you mean?' Maggie asked.

'She was shot in the back.'

'Could it have been Ross?' Creed asked Maggie.

'It's possible.'

'There's more,' Vance said. 'Her left hand was severed at the wrist. So far the rescue crew hasn't found the hand anywhere inside the vehicle.'

Creed looked at Maggie and her face paled.

'The one Jason and Bolo found in the field,' she said. 'It was a left hand. Dr Gunther said it was a woman's. But Logan insisted it was the director of the facility's. He seemed certain it was Dr Shaw's.'

'Why would someone kill this woman, take her hand, and plant it at the flood site?' Vance was shaking his head. 'This sounds like something from Daniel Tate's messed-up mind. That man is telling some wild tales.'

'There was a diamond ring on the thumb,' Maggie said. Creed could see the alarm building in her eyes. 'Logan was sure the ring belonged to Dr Shaw.' She looked at Vance. 'This may sound like a ridiculous question. Did you happen to notice if Isabel Klein's fingernails were painted? A bright red?'

He thought about that and again shook his head. 'I looked at her hand pretty good. There was no fingernail polish.'

'Why would Ross take Isabel's hand and try to make it look like it was Dr Shaw's?' Creed asked.

'I don't think Ross did it,' Maggie said.

Creed stared at her, and finally the realization hit him.

'Dr Clare Shaw's still alive.'

74

Platt had wanted to take more time and make sure Maggie was okay. He knew she was still very angry with him. He deserved that. When all of this was over he'd find a way to make it up to her. She was safe. That was the important thing.

He'd spent almost an hour moving and securing the lockbox in the mobile lab. Another thirty minutes to gear up in the special hazmat suit he'd brought. Already he was perspiring and fogging up his face shield. He could barely see without wiping a glove across it every few minutes.

The mobile lab was cramped and a far cry from what he was used to. The USAMRIID laboratories at Fort Detrick were state of the art, furnished with some of the best equipment and technology in the world. They'd come a long way from those archaic methods that they had talked about in the last several days during the congressional hearing. Much could be learned from history. What Platt hated to admit was that some things had not changed. There were still threats, just as Hess had said. And there were still too many secrets kept in the name of national security.

But as messy as this situation had been, it could have been worse. Much worse. Hess had dodged yet another bullet.

Now Platt just needed to make sure nothing had ruptured inside this lockbox. And if it had, that nothing had leaked out.

He tapped the numbers of the combination, having memorized them from his conversation with Hess. The digital display remained unchanged. He thought he had gotten the numbers wrong when the light that had been pulsing red suddenly blinked to green and the lock snapped open.

With careful fingers, Platt eased the heavy lid up. He felt the cold rush up. Even after all these hours, the inside remained icecold. That was a good sign. No rupture. The tension started to leave his shoulders.

He could see the sealed vials standing in their slots, side by side. Unharmed. Unbroken.

Suddenly he noticed an empty slot. Then another. And another. No spills, no glass fragments. There was no way for the vials to have fallen from their slots. No way except to have been removed.

Three empty slots. Three missing vials. Three deadly viruses, gone.

75

MEMPHIS, TENNESSEE

Dr Clare Shaw exchanged the SUV for a sedan. She pulled out a credit card, but before she handed it across the desk to the rental car agent she checked the name on the card to see who she was pretending to be that day. Over the last year she had accumulated a stash of credit cards and photo IDs. Along with other important items like cell phones and extra cash.

She could remember the exact day she realized she would need an escape plan. It was the day she succeeded in replicating H5N1. If she could duplicate avian flu, what else was she capable of doing? But despite the so-called independence DARPA claimed to give her and the facility, her superiors had suggested new security measures, new checks and balances in the near future. They would never embrace her brilliance and allow her to continue. Even Richard had begun questioning her research procedures, complaining that some of her experiments were extreme.

Poor gutless Richard. Killing him was one of the easier parts of her plan. It pained her more to sacrifice the men who had been her current guinea pigs. And that government woman.

For all her planning, she'd never expected an actual landslide. The weeklong rains and the massive flooding were enough for her to put her plan into action. The landslide took her by surprise. She had almost lost the lockbox in the ruins. But the chaos that followed had provided her necessary cover.

Now, in the glass that separated the small office from the garage of cars, she checked out her reflection. She had cut her long hair but kept the bangs and decided she would enjoy being a redhead. The rental car agent seemed to approve.

He gave her back her card along with the keys to the sedan.

'Do you need any help with your bags?' he asked.

'No, I've got them.'

She picked them up, making it look effortless. She had already risked too much, paid too high a price. She couldn't afford to make some stupid mistake now. She certainly wasn't going to let anyone else handle the small gray case, despite how heavy the miniature lockbox might be.

Author's Note

As I write this I'm reading reports from the National Disaster Search Dog Foundation. In the last twenty-four hours, a Himalayan earthquake – a massive 7.8 – has claimed an estimated 2,500 lives. Aftershocks continue to trigger avalanches and landslides that have already buried entire villages. Search teams – dogs and handlers – from across the United States are being deployed to assist in rescue and recovery. I can't imagine all the things they will encounter. I pray they'll be safe and I will be anxious to hear their stories when they return, because real life is so much stranger than any fiction I can write.

Many of you who read my books already know

I'm a news junkie. I watch the newscasts about the Nepal earthquake or read about the bird flu and, unlike most other people, I'm taking notes as I watch or read. I'm also a history buff, so it's not unusual for me to include real details – present and past – in my novels. I wanted to mention a few of those real details in *Silent Creed*.

The tests that Senator Ellie Delanor stumbles upon actually did happen, including at least one that used schoolchildren at Clinton Elementary School in Minneapolis in 1953. From 1952 through 1969, the Army dropped thousands of pounds of zinc cadmium sulfide in nearly three hundred secret experiments conducted in such places as Fort Wayne, Indiana (1964–66); St Louis, Missouri (1953, 1963–65); San Francisco, California (1964–68); Corpus Christi, Texas (1962); and Oceanside, California (1967). The Army has insisted that the levels used in these tests were harmless. But various studies now suspect that cadmium in humans is a carcinogen that causes kidney damage and that can contribute to liver disorders, nervous system problems, and perhaps reproductive health problems.

Project 112 and SHAD were also series of actual

tests conducted by the Department of Defense from 1962 through 1973, during the height of the Cold War. The individual tests were code-named – Autumn Gold, Flower Drum, Night Train, and Shady Grove were just a few. Sailors and soldiers had no clue that they had been exposed, or if they did know, they believed the aerosols were harmless simulants. In some cases VX nerve gas, Sarin nerve gas, and a variety of bacteria including E.coli were used as part of the biological and chemical tests.

It wasn't until 2002 that some of the facts about Project 112 were made public. Why did it take so long? The DoD claimed that too much of the information needed to be kept classified. In the meantime, veterans experiencing illnesses related to their exposure were denied VA benefits and medical help. After all, how could they be sick from something that didn't happen?

I have a deep admiration and respect for the men and women – and the dogs – who have served and continue to serve our country. They sacrifice much and risk their lives. They deserve to have their country take care of them. Which brings me to another hard fact that is touched on in *Silent Creed*.

Robby's Law (H.R.5314) made it possible for military dogs to be adopted instead of euthanized when they are retired. Can you even imagine that that was acceptable for these four-legged heroes? That after they saved so many lives, their final reward of retirement meant death? Robby's Law also allows for the dogs' former handlers to be first in line to adopt them.

But here's the catch – the military still does not guarantee transport of these dogs back to the United States. Right now the military says it's too expensive and requires resources they simply don't have, so oftentimes the cost for transport falls to the adopter. Currently there is a push for legislation in Congress that would change this and require that the military bring these dogs home first, then retire them and, when possible, reunite them with their handlers or offer them up to the long list of others who would gladly adopt them.

It's amazing to me that we need legislation to do what should naturally be the right and just thing for these four-legged heroes. Yes, real life is stranger than fiction.

Acknowledgements

As with each of my novels, I have a whole lot of people to thank and acknowledge.

Thanks go to:

My friends and family who put up with my long absences and still manage to love me and keep me grounded: Patricia Kava, Marlene Haney, Sandy Rockwood, Amee Rief, Patti and Martin Bremmer, Patricia Sierra, Sharon Kator, Maricela and Jose Barajas, Patti El-Kachouti, Diane Prohaska, Annie Belatti, Nancy Tworek, Cari Conine, Lisa Munk, Luann Causey, Patti Carlin, and Dr Elvira Rios.

My fellow authors and friends who make this business a bit less crazy: Sharon Car, Erica Spindler, and J.T. Ellison.

The experts who I know I can call or email with the strangest questions and the oddest requests: Leigh Ann Retelsdorf, Melissa Connor, Gary Plank, and John Beck.

Ray Kunze, once again, for lending his name to Maggie O'Dell's boss. And to set the record straight – the real Ray Kunze is a nice guy who would never send Maggie on wild goose chases.

My pack depends on some amazing veterinarians, and now they've become friends as well as invaluable resources for writing this series. Special thanks to: Dr Enita Larson and her crew at Tender Care Animal Hospital, and Dr Tonya McIlnay and the team at Veterinary Eye Specialist of Nebraska.

Once again, an extra thank-you to Dr Larson for allowing me to name my fictional veterinarian after her children, Avelyn Faye and Ayden Parker. We'll continue to see Dr Avelyn Parker in each of the Creed novels.

Thanks to my publicist, Megan Beatie at Megan Beatie Communications, for finding new and creative ways to get my books in front of readers.

My publishing teams: Sara Minnich, Ivan Held, and Christine Ball at Putnam. And at Little Brown/

Sphere: David Shelley, Catherine Burke, and Jade Chandler.

My agent, Scott Miller, and his colleague, Claire Roberts, at Trident Media Group.

Thanks also to the booksellers, book bloggers, and librarians for mentioning and recommending my novels.

A big thank you to all of my VIR Club members, Facebook friends, and faithful readers. With so many wonderful novels available, I'm honored that you continue to choose mine. Without you, I wouldn't have the opportunity to tell my twisted tales.